The Vicar

and

The Village

Jayne Lind

Copyright ©Jayne Lind 2011

All rights reserved. No part of this publication may be reproduced, stored in a retrieval system, or transmitted in any form or by any means—electronic, mechanical, photocopying, recording, or otherwise, without the prior written permission of the copyright owner.

This book is a work of fiction. Names, characters, places, and incidents are products of the author's imagination or are used fictitiously. Any resemblance of actual events or locales or persons, living or dead, is entirely coincidental.

ISBN 1466278846
EAN 9781466278844

Dedicated to MEC

Other books by Jayne Lind

Talk With Us, Lord
Powerdigm
Are You Running on Empty?
In The Days of Noah
The President's Wife is on Prozac

Prologue

The vicar of the Church of The Redemption, sometimes mocked by skeptics in the village as 'beyond redemption' had taken early retirement and under rather odd circumstances left before his replacement was hired. The congregations of the Church of England had been retiring as well, but even with the declining numbers, there weren't enough clergy to go round. So in desperation the church relented, and although many did not approve, made the sensible decision to let women do the work.

The village of Cambersham needed a new vicar and the bishop chose the Reverend Annie O'Donnell. Not only was she a woman—she was Irish.

"Irish!" exclaimed Christopher Martin. "Do you hear that? She's Irish! Not only are they putting this woman here, but she's Irish! "He was speaking to his wife, Miriam, who had developed the ability years before of nodding and muttering when he was talking, making him think she was listening to every word. She was thrilled to have a woman vicar. Maybe she would listen to people when they came to her with their troubles, she was thinking, all the while not listening to her husband.

"I don't know what the PCC was thinking about! I should of stayed on, I shouldn't of quit the council, then maybe I could of done something. It's a disgrace. Makes one want to go and become a Catholic."

"Most of the Catholic priests are Irish," his wife pointed out, in a whimsical tone.

"But at least they're men!" her husband responded, still worked up.

Meanwhile, a variation of this conversation was repeated in many houses of the village of Cambersham. There was a general buzz—the village seemed to be waking up a bit. Over at the Duke of Wellington Pub, there was no other topic of conversation other than the football scores, of course. The men, when away from the women, their own woman in particular, were intrigued. What would she look like? Was she old? And grey? And maybe even fat? The Vicar of Dibley had had its effect. Would she be dowdy or wear makeup and earrings?

The commuters, the younger population who went to work in London every day, who lived in the village for the beauty of the countryside and the peace and quiet, didn't enter into these debates. They thought nothing of a new female vicar; it was normal as far as they were concerned. They sometimes went to church, sometimes did not. The children were sent, of course. The church and God didn't really interfere with their lives, whose main purpose was to make as much money as one possibly could, so that someday, one could retire.

Meanwhile, what about this new vicar? How did she feel about this new posting of hers?

She was terrified.

Chapter One

Annie O'Donnell was a petite redhead, with pale green eyes and burnished, fiercely rosy cheeks, the kind seen often in Wales and Ireland, cheeks that look as if their owner had just come indoors from the cold. Her eyes were bright with mischief and not many things frightened her. She was brought up with two older brothers who treated her as an equal and with whom when they were young, she got into trouble on a daily basis. Her father was a vicar in Belfast and it was from him that the three children inherited their lively sense of humor.

She had been sent to Cambridge for her theology training because her father thought it would be good for her to be out of Northern Ireland, out of the Troubles. Her intelligence shone at Cambridge; she thrived under the intellectual atmosphere. She had a missionary's heart and wanted to go out to save the world. Instead, she was sent to Cambersham. She looked on this assignment as a training ground, a temporary job that would mould her into someone who would then be given grander things to do. She had served two years as a curate in a church in Cambridge and enjoyed the lively congregation made up of students and professionals. She grew up in the large city of Belfast and had never experienced life in a village.

Armed with a laptop computer, her clothes, and some of her books, she arrived one very cold, very damp morning to an empty vicarage with no one to greet her. The front door was unlocked. She stepped into the small hall with a mixture of emotions as her only companion. A staircase rose on her right. She walked past it, straight on into the living room where she saw a fireplace, three small sofas placed haphazardly around the room, a few very old, very doubtful looking tables, and an empty bookcase. A large mirror hung over the mantle, in which she saw the look of dismay on her face. The house felt very large and very empty. The heat was on, so at least it wasn't cold. She toured the rest of the rooms before she took her things out of the car. There were four bedrooms and a bathroom upstairs. The kitchen, at the back of the house, was spacious and looked out on what she thought was probably a lovely garden in summer. A wonderful house if one had a family. Not that she wanted a family. She didn't want to get married anytime in the near future. She hadn't met anyone she felt strongly enough to marry anyway, but this large, empty house made her feel terribly alone. She would have liked a friendly greeting.

By the time she had brought all her things inside, the doorbell rang. She opened the door to a rather large woman with a smile to match.

"Hello, I'm Joy," she boomed. "I'm one of your churchwardens. Welcome to Cambersham!"

Annie smiled and stood out of the way for her to pass, "Oh, come in, come in," she urged, relieved to see a human being.

Joy stepped in and with no pause for breath, began talking. "I apologize for not being here to meet you, I got held up on the phone with an elderly aunt of mine, she has arthritis which she wants me to share with her on every possible occasion and as she never lets me get a word in edgewise. I couldn't tell her I had to end the conversation, not that it's a conversation at all you see, it's just her telling me in great detail about every single joint that hurts as if I haven't heard it before and yet she phones me almost every day."

Annie just smiled and invited her to sit down.

Joy shook her head as she made her way familiarly to the kitchen. "I think we should find the kettle and see if there's any tea here before we sit down, don't you?" Not waiting for Annie to answer, she began opening cupboards and slamming them shut.

Annie obediently followed her, admitting to herself that even though she had a lot to do, it certainly would be nice to have a cup of tea.

"I turned on the heat for you this morning—oh, here's some tea—no telling how old it is, but it will have to do. I was going to bake you some biscuits, but I didn't get round to it; you must come to my house for supper tonight—I know you won't have had time to shop."

Annie smiled at this gregarious woman. She sensed she had a good heart and though she might become annoying in the future with her non-stop patter, it felt good for now to have someone to talk to. When the tea was ready, they each sat on one of the sofas in the living room.

"Now, tell me all about yourself. Everyone in the village is anxious to meet you," Joy said, beaming her sizeable smile at her over her teacup.

Annie smiled back and shrugged her shoulders. "Well, I'm just an ordinary person. You know this is my first church after being a curate. And," she sighed, 'I don't know, it just feels like I'm going to rattle around in this big house."

"Yes, I know, but it belongs to the church, you see, so there wasn't anything to be done about it, but this village is perfectly safe, you know. You don't need to be frightened to stay here alone."

"Oh, no," Annie hastened to reassure her. "I'm not. It's not that. And I'm sure that after my books are unpacked and I put some photographs around I'll feel more at home. It's just that I've never lived alone. My best friend from theology college, Emily, shared a flat with me in Cambridge."

They talked for half an hour and Joy stayed on for a while after that, showing Annie where things were, teaching her about the heat, the boiler, etc. The house had been thoroughly cleaned by women from the church and had the bare necessities in terms of furniture. "There's money for you to buy furniture in the discretionary fund, you know," Joy assured her. "So you decide what you need and I can help you shop if you like. Not a lot of money, mind you," she rolled her eyes, "you'll find that people in this parish aren't very generous when it comes to giving—they expect a vicar to subsist on air, I sometimes think. One man, who is quite well off, gives a pound a week!" She laughed, "Regularly!"

Annie knew her salary was quite small, but thought that probably was because she was single and had no family. However, being a vicar's daughter, she knew one certainly didn't go into it for the money. She declined Joy's offer for a meal, saying she really wasn't hungry. She had some fruit she had bought on the way and thought that would do.

As Joy left, she patted Annie on the shoulder. "You're going to be just fine, now don't you worry. And if you need anything, just phone. I won't bother you unless you phone me. I understand the importance of your privacy, but I warn you that everyone in the village doesn't understand that. So I'll wait till I hear from you, all right?"

Annie nodded gratefully and shut the door to once again greet the silence. She built a fire in the fireplace, moved one of the sofas over in front of the fire, and sat down with her computer on her lap.

Hi Emily: This is my first day in the vicarage. There are FOUR bedrooms and it seems very lonely. The only visitor I've had is one of the church wardens, a loquacious lady who made me a cup of tea and stayed on to help a bit. She says the village is curious about me—you know what that means—it's code for 'does she have two heads?' This house is enormous! And it creaks—it's almost a hundred years old. It would be a wonderful house for a noisy family, but I'm feeling very alone. Please write often. By the way—how are *you*? Love, Annie

By bedtime, she was exhausted, worn out emotionally, she told herself, as she drifted off to sleep. She slept soundly and woke at six o'clock to darkness and a cold house. Padding downstairs to the kitchen to turn up the heat and put the kettle on, she went into the living room and once again started a fire in the fireplace. Then with her cup of tea and her Bible, she sat down for her morning reading and prayers. She found it difficult to concentrate, however. She was feeling very alone in this large house, as large as the one she grew up in. That made her think of her father and she knew he would be up as he, like her, was an early riser. She rang the number in his study.

"Rev. O'Donnell, here," her father answered in his Irish brogue, much broader than Annie's.

"Rev. O'Donnell here as well," Annie laughed.

"Annie! Are you all right? It's right early for you to be calling."

"Oh, Dad, I know, but I knew you would be up and in your study. It's just that...I'm here all alone in this big house and I guess I need some moral support."

"Oh, sure, my darlin," he said in a sympathetic voice. "Sure, now—I knew you were moving in yesterday. Tell me all about the house."

She did, in great detail. Then, "But I'm wondering why on earth I'm here! I didn't get a welcome yesterday from the village or the council or anyone except this lady Joy. Is that normal?"

"No, it isn't normal. Nothing about that posting was normal. The council should have interviewed you early on—you should have been invited to the village before the retiring vicar left so that he could show you around and orient you. And there certainly should have been a welcoming group. I confess, I've been worried about this strange sequence of events all along, but I didn't say anything because I hoped it would straighten out of itself. And maybe it will, darlin."

"Oh, I hope so. I'm feeling pretty bereft at the moment. I haven't been able to concentrate on my morning Bible reading, so I thought of you."

"Well, you know the answer, don't you?"

"Pray?"

"Yes."

Annie rang off, feeling better because she had connected with another human being, the one whom she loved more than anyone in the world. Pray, he had reminded her. Her prayers were fairly unorthodox. She didn't plead or petition, she simply talked to God as if he were there with her. Only now, she didn't really feel his presence. *"Oh, Lord—why am I here?! Why didn't you send me off to an undeveloped country where I would know why I was suffering? In a mud hut or something? No one is going to feel sorry for me in this nice house—furnished and warm. I feel like you've thrown me to the lions....but no, I really don't. I'm sorry. I shouldn't have said that. I'm a people person, Lord—you know that! You know me! I've always loved the hustle and bustle of a city, of Cambridge, which was a small city, I know, but there was lots going on and here I am in a village! Oh, Lord, Lord, where are you in this?"*

The Lord didn't answer.

Giving up, she took a hot shower, dressed in jeans and a warm pullover and began unpacking her suitcases. The boxes with the rest of her belongings were supposed to arrive today.

Meanwhile, the village was waking up to the news that the new vicar had arrived. The telegraph system, which had been in place in Cambersham since time began, had been perfected over the years to the point that if it could have been packaged and advertised, it would have brought a revolution to the communications world. By the time the delivery truck arrived with all of Annie's worldly goods, fifteen boxes to be exact, Horace arrived as well.

When Annie opened the door, he immediately stepped inside without an invitation. She had to quickly jump out of the way or he would have bumped up against her. He was a tiny man, about five foot two, with extremely bowed legs and a head that looked as if it had problems squeezing through the birth canal. This egg-shaped head had a fringe of dark grey hair around the ears and back with a few carefully arranged long hairs over the top. If he were an actor, he would be typecast as a villain. He didn't smile—he leered. His lips were permanently wet and his irregular, brownish teeth protruded without his permission.

"I've come to welcome you to the village," he said,

beaming at her with moist eyes. "You'll get used to the fact that I never knock, I just open the door and stand in the hall yelling 'hallo' and if you don't answer, I'll wander on into the kitchen and make myself a cup of tea!" he announced with pride in his voice.

Up to this point Annie hadn't uttered a word. The image which came into her mind was of a snake. Finally, she mustered a nervous smile. "And why do you do that?" she asked. By this time, he had wandered into the sitting room and made himself comfortable on one of the sofas. She still didn't know who he was.

"Oh, it's just that I feel so at home here, you see. Yes, I've been in this village most of my life and I've seen vicars come and go, but I'm always here." He looked around inquisitively, inspecting the room as well as the stacked up boxes.

"And your name?"

For the first time, he looked a bit embarrassed. "Oh, I thought you knew—Horace, Horace Wiley. I'm one of the elders."

Annie's heart sank. Maybe this was one of the reasons the previous vicar left in such a hurry. She was horrified to think of someone opening her door and coming on in. "Well, how do you do. I'm Annie O'Donnell," she said, extending her hand.

Horace made a move as if he was going to embrace her, but she quickly stepped back. "We don't shake hands here, you'll find, we hug each other and give a kiss of peace in this village," he beamed. "And I know who you are, so I thought you would know who I am."

Annie failed to see the logic in his last statement. "Um, is there something I can do for you?" she asked.

He looked surprised. "Oh, no, I just came to get acquainted and to get you acquainted with all the goings on at the church, who is who, and all that."

Annie had for a moment felt intimidated by this quirky little man, but her Irish temper, which had been percolating below, at last came to the surface. "Well, this isn't very good timing, I'm afraid. I need to get myself unpacked."

He didn't respond, but got up and began idly reading the labels on the boxes.

She tried again. "I don't technically go to work until next Monday, you see."

He sat down again. "Would you like me to fix us a cup of tea? I know where everything is," he offered hopefully. "I have this hour free and I planned to spend it getting to know all about you."

Annie didn't know what to do; she had never come up against anyone like this. She wasn't afraid of him, probably because he was tiny, about her same weight and height. He was like an immovable force; she hadn't been able to penetrate his rude resolve. *Not very charitable of me. I'm always judging people on my first impression, shouldn't do that, Annie.* At that moment, the phone rang. Excusing herself and relieved for the break in the confrontation, yet at the same time loath to leave this nosey man alone with her belongings, she rushed to answer the phone in the kitchen.

"Good morning," Joy's booming voice greeted her. "I know I told you I would wait for you to phone me, but I wondered if you needed rescuing. I happened to see Horace walking toward your house."

"Yes," she lowered her voice, "yes, of course."

Joy laughed. "I should have warned you about him. I'll be right there."

Annie went softly back down the hall to the sitting room. Sure enough, Horace was just lifting up a lid of an open box. He jumped as she entered the room. "Who was that?" he asked.

Annie shook her head. This man was unbelievable. Not answering him, she opened the box he had been fingering and began to draw out books.

"I don't read much myself—don't have the time, you know. I spend my time helping people. You'll find I'm the village good samaritan, always helping the old folks out, visiting them—they get pretty lonely living alone and all. There's some folks who read all about Christianity, who think they're experts but it's better to get out and help people, I always say, instead of keeping your nose in a book."

Annie straightened up and looked him full in the face. The way he licked his lips incessantly, yes, he was like a snake, she thought. With speckled green eyes to match. "Are you married?" she asked, wondering how his poor wife put up with him.

"Oh, yes, I thought you knew. Yes, my wife will be round later, she's most anxious to meet you."

Just then the doorbell rang. "I'll get it!" Horace had sprung to the door on his bandy legs before she could move. He was quick as a snake as well, she thought. It was Joy.

"Come in, come in," Horace said graciously.

Joy brushed past him. "It's time for us to go, dear," she said rolling her eyes and shrugging backwards toward Horace. "Remember, that appointment we have?"

Annie sighed with relief and smiled, "Oh, yes, all right."

Horace looked stunned. "Where you going?" he asked.

But Joy was shooing him out the door ahead of her and signaling to Annie as she put on her coat to lock the door. Before she knew it they were in Joy's car and had driven away.

"Thank you. What an unpleasant man!"

"Yes, he's the village pest, goes around to people's houses all day long, gossiping and bothering them. By the way, I told you to lock the door because Horace would have gone back in. I know you have a lot of work to do, but we'll just drive around for half an hour and then I'll bring you back. I'll show you some local scenery," she said cheerily.

"Do you do this often? Rescue people from him?"

"Oh, no, it's just that you're new and you're the vicar and I should have warned you about him. I should have known he would be at your doorstep first thing this morning. You'll have to learn how to get rid of him yourself from now on," she laughed. "Let's drive over to the next town and I'll show you how to find the supermarket."

Annie looked out the window with interest at the beautiful, rolling hills as they drove ten miles to the nearest town. Sheep were grazing attentively and the fields of crops were a complete mystery to her. "I'll have to learn what's grown here, I'm so ignorant of farming life," she mused.

"They grow quite a bit of sugar beets and carrots around here, some wheat and barley, and of course, you can see all the sheep. In the spring, it's lovely to see the tiny lambs, but not everyone here is a farmer, you know. Lots of people work in London, which is why it seems so quiet during the week and there are lots of retired folk, like me."

As Joy chattered away Annie was experiencing mixed emotions, not many of them positive as yet. *What am I in for?* When she was home again, she turned on her laptop to see if anyone had emailed her. Thankfully, Emily had.

Dear Annie: I feel so sorry for you!!!!! I wish I were there to help you out, give you a little bit of company. I'm feeling somewhat secure here in my posting in the States. There isn't any prejudice against women clergy in the Episcopal Church, thank goodness. So I've been warmly welcomed and provided for. My one bedroom flat is entirely adequate--there is a large bedroom and so my computer is in one corner and there are plenty of bookshelves as well. I wonder what God is up to with you? How are you doing with him—are you in sync or are you feeling abandoned… Write often, daily if it would help. I can be your sounding board and as always, your good, good friend. Lots of love, Emily

Emily was American. She had come to Cambridge for a post-graduate degree in theology and from the first meeting, she and Annie had clicked. Emily was the one who was lonely in those days, away from her family and friends. Annie, who had been in Cambridge for three years by then, swiftly incorporated

Emily into her circle and after the first year, they became flat mates. It was invaluable to have a non-judgmental friend to whom they each could sound off, sharing their doubts about God when they arose. It always seemed that one of them was in a doubting phase when the other one wasn't, which was good. One lifted the other up.

Dear Em: Thanks for understanding. Yes, I will write often, maybe more than once a day some days. It's this big house and not having any friends and being scared witless about being an actual vicar—in charge and all that. Oh, Em, what is God up to indeed! Yes I'm talking to him, but not often enough, obviously. I'm sure things will be better once I've started work. But the whole process has been skewed. I should have been interviewed by the church council and I should have been briefed by the departing vicar. It seems as though everything has gone wrong!! Sure miss you, Em. Write me a long email telling me all about your church, the people, etc. And one of these days, I may even phone you, need to hear your voice, my good friend. Much love, Annie

Chapter Two

That afternoon, still not having finished sorting out her boxes or arranged her things in some semblance of order, she walked over to look at the church. Joy had left her the key, informing her that people in the village didn't lock their doors in the daytime, but the church had to be locked because of a spate of vandalism in the past.

Annie thought about the historical reason for the Norman towers as she approached the church. When William the Conqueror, king of Normandy, invaded the British Isles in 1066, he established churches every ten miles with high, square towers in order to secure his defenses. These Norman towers can be distinguished from earlier Anglo-Saxon towers, which are round. The result of all this history is that every tiny village has a church and now with church attendance in Britain at an all time low, many of these churches were being made redundant.

The walls of The Church of Redemption were made of rough primitive stone with Gothic windows. A small church porch guarded the front door, provided for people to gather their umbrellas before plunging out into the elements. Gravestones surrounded the church, some very old by the looks of them. Annie was curious about them, but more curious about the interior of the church. She opened the door tentatively, but expectantly, and took in a quick breath of surprise as she stepped inside the cold building. It was beautiful. Whereas the outside had been plain and drab, the stained glass windows muted from the outside, inside there was serenity and beauty. The old, rough wooden pews were intricately carved. A worn, light blue carpet on the centre aisle led to the altar, beyond which shone brilliant stained glass scenes of the Last Supper.

She walked slowly to the altar and stood there admiring the windows. Jesus was depicted larger than the apostles who were seated with him. What really arrested her attention was the look on his face. He seemed to be looking right at her and he was smiling. Annie smiled back. And sank to her knees at the altar, never taking her eyes off him. She talked to him silently, in her heart. *"Help me, Lord, help me to help you here in this church, in this village. Help me to not feel so very alone—help me to cope."*

Annie didn't bow her head when she prayed. She always held her face up to heaven and there were times when she could feel God's anointing upon her, when she felt as if her face glowed. This was one of those times. "It will be all right," she heard the Lord say. "It will be all right." She never heard his voice. It was always a thought, a strong thought, as she had often heard it described. And there was never a doubt it was the Lord rather than just her own thoughts. It was always something she wouldn't have said, either in terms of the way it was stated or in content. She smiled once again at the depiction of Jesus. As she rose from her knees, she felt better. *It was going to be all right, wasn't it?* She looked around the church for awhile, acquainting herself with all its little nooks and reading the church bulletin, which was something she was going to have to cope with since there was no secretary and no backup support at all. Good thing I have computer skills, she told herself.

As she left the church, a man was getting out of his car parked on the street in front of the church. He walked quickly up to her and with a wide smile on his face, said, "Hello, Rev. O'Donnell, I'm Matthew Young. He extended his hand. "I'm on the council. I've been out of town and couldn't be here to meet you properly. I've just been to your house and hoped I would catch you here."

Annie looked at him appreciatively. He was extraordinarily tall and extraordinarily good looking, with very dark hair and very blue eyes and very white teeth, making his smile inviting.

"Very pleased to meet you, Matthew," she said, shaking his hand. "Only I'm Annie, please. Would you like to come over for a cup of tea?" she asked, hopefully.

"Oh, yes, I would like a chat with you. I feel so badly about how everything went wrong surrounding your arrival. It really wasn't anyone's fault, you know, just a series of circumstances." He left his car where it was and walked the short distance to the vicarage with her. He adjusted his stride to a slower pace for Annie's short legs.

After they were settled in her sitting room with a cup of tea, he again apologized. "I work in London, as many of the villagers do, and this week, I had a seminar up north so I wasn't here the day you arrived. When I got home, there was a very long message on my answer machine from Joy, filling me in on how things had gone. I'm really terribly sorry, Annie, it shouldn't have been this way."

"What do you do in London?" she asked.

"I teach. At LSE—London School of Economics." He smiled.

What a refreshing smile, she thought. It reminded her of a breeze that changed the way you felt about the weather on a hot day. "Teach?" Annie asked.

"Political science. A never changing subject." He smiled again.

"What happened to the retiring vicar?" she asked. "Why did he leave so suddenly?"

"Well, I'm sure you will hear the story eventually, I'm sure Horace would have told you if you had given him half a chance," he laughed. "Joy told me about her rescue as well. He had a problem with depression. No one but his wife knew about it for a long time, but he became more and more withdrawn and less and less active in the church. Finally, the council confronted him with the fact that he needed to get help. He was told he needed to take a sabbatical and go for professional help and the next thing we knew—he was gone. He just packed up and left.

Didn't say anything to anyone. So we haven't had a vicar for almost a year now and when your name was put forward, I, for one was delighted. By the way, I need to warn you that there are those who do not approve of a female vicar."

Annie shrugged, "Oh, I'm well aware of that, and it doesn't surprise me." She liked this man. Matthew seemed more like the people she was used to in Cambridge; he was articulate, well dressed, and spoke to her as an equal. And being terribly good looking didn't hurt did it? "I hope no one in the village is upset about my being from Northern Ireland."

Matthew shrugged. "Well, I'm not up on the latest village gossip. I try to stay out of it, but there may be some opposition. There are plenty of people, I'm afraid, who think of Northern Ireland as Irish, rather than British. Your accent is very faint, by the way."

Annie laughed, "Cambridge squeezed the last bit out of me, I'm afraid, but when I'm back, when I'm home, it comes out again."

"So tell me about yourself. I'm curious as to why you wanted to become a vicar, why you chose to come here, though I'm certainly happy that you did, and how it is that a girl from Belfast came to Cambridge? By the way, I'm an Oxford man," he said, with that beguiling smile again.

"Well, I guess I can forgive you for that," she laughed. "I grew up in Belfast. My father is a vicar there, in a city church with quite a mixed congregation. He's still working."

"Brothers, sisters?" he asked.

Annie nodded, taking a sip of her tea. "I have two older brothers, Patrick and James." She sighed. "I miss them, all of them. We were a noisy, happy family."

"And who were you the closest to in the family?"

It was an easy question to answer. She smiled as she answered, "My dad. He's the most wonderful man in the world."

"Hmm, it will be tough for a man to compete with that."

"What do you mean?"

"Well, I mean a husband."

Annie blushed. This man was so unusual; he said whatever came into his head, but he said it in a way that didn't bother her. He seemed to go right to the heart of things. She felt completely relaxed with him and all the things she had planned to do that afternoon totally left her mind. "Oh, well...maybe so," she admitted.

"Tell me about this wonderful man," Matthew urged. He leaned forward toward her with his arms resting on his knees, giving Annie the impression he had all the time in the world to listen to her.

Annie told him all about her family and how she felt so all alone in this big house, away from her friends in Cambridge. She couldn't remember every feeling so intimate with someone she had just met. She felt she could tell him anything she wanted to, that he would understand. She was used to listening, not talking so much about herself, but somehow she found herself revealing more than usual to this man whom she'd only just met.

"You must be homesick," Matthew said, "not only for your family, but for your former exciting life," he said, smiling gently.

Annie inexplicably felt the hot warmth of tears about to emerge and was terrified of it happening. She got up abruptly and taking his cup, said, "I'll go put the kettle on again, all right?" Before he could answer, she was out of the room and into the kitchen. She hastily wiped her eyes, which were full by this time and reheated the kettle.

He didn't follow her and she was composed by the time she returned. "Sorry, I just thought maybe you'd like another cup of tea, I know I would," she said, as she poured him another without his having responded.

Matthew ignored the cup of tea and with a sympathetic look on his face said quietly, "Annie, this must have all been a terrible shock for you, leaving a thriving city like Cambridge and coming here to this huge empty vicarage and not being met properly. I mean, I just want you to know that I understand." He hesitated a moment as she looked down at her cup. And if you need to have a good cry, it's all right with me."

At that, the tears, which had so surprised her, yet, which Matthew obviously hadn't failed to notice, came back. She blinked to stop them and smiled at him rather wetly. "You are so kind—most men wouldn't want a woman to cry, especially one they just met." The tears were still there, but somehow being able to admit they were there, not having to hold them back, paradoxically lessened their demand. "You're an unusual person, Matthew. I usually don't talk so much about myself, but you're such a good listener."

"Well, I had a good teacher, you see." Matthew was silent for a moment, not looking directly at Annie, but somewhere in the distance beyond her.

"Who?" she asked.

"My wife." His voice was soft and he looked down at the floor for a moment.

Annie was astonished. His wife! He wasn't wearing a wedding ring and she had assumed he wasn't married.

"She died last year," Matthew looked directly at her as he said these words and his face revealed his sorrow.

"Oh, how terrible," Annie said, thinking even as she said it what an inadequate response it was. In an instant, there was a role reversal. She had been being helped by this understanding man, this sensitive man who understood how she felt, but now her problems seemed miniscule and she felt foolish. She now realized why he was so empathic. He had been through, was still going through, it seemed, a tragedy. "How, of what did she die?"

"It was a road accident, Christmas Eve before last. The weather was foul and a lorry hit her car on a roundabout." He sighed, "So I miss her very badly and always will I'm sure."

Annie was silent for a moment, and then asked "How have you coped?"

He shrugged, "You simply do, that's all. You put one foot in front of the other and keep on slogging. But there is a giant hole in my life which I'm sure will never be filled."

"Did you have anyone, do you have anyone to talk to about

it?

Matthew nodded, "Yes, fortunately I have a very close friend in London. He's a psychologist, but I don't see him professionally, he's just always, or seems to be always, available to me. We often meet for lunch or dinner after work. He's been wonderful." Matthew looked at his watch and stood up.

The magic moment had passed, the moment when they were intimate, having only just met.

"Look, I know you must have things you need to do, and I have to prepare for my lecture tonight, so I'll be going along."

Annie stood up as well and extended her hand. "Thank you, Matthew. Thank you for being understanding. And thank you for telling me about your wife. I hope I can be of help if you ever need someone to talk to about her. I hope we will be friends."

He smiled that smile again, so disarming, as he shook her hand. "We already are, Annie. We already are."

Dear Emily: Well, today has been very eventful. I met a man, a VERY good looking man with the most wonderful smile you can ever imagine and with a tender heart. But he's a recent widower; his wife was killed in a car accident a little over a year ago. I feel a tad less lonely, but still wish you were here to talk about it. These emails will have to be our substitute. Things are looking up! I told the Lord so tonight in my prayers. I'm sure he is relieved to hear it......"

There was an immediate reply.

Dear Annie: Looking up I guess! You must describe him in every detail; I must get a clear picture of him in my mind. But obviously, he is still grieving for his wife and that can be quite heartbreaking—the idealized dead person who is grander than anyone living—hard to live up to. Still, no one ever said things were supposed to be easy. Happy you're back in sync with our Lord, he certainly has been smiling on me as of late. I'm thrilled with my parish, never lonely for a minute as it is active, bustling, and very involved politically. No handsome stranger has come into my life as yet. But then, I really don't want one. I want to make a difference here on earth—you know, we've talked about this ad infinitum. Wouldn't a husband drag one down? I would like a little romance, can't deny that. But I really want to serve the Lord and I think, for now, a husband would interfere. Sure miss you—write every day if you possibly can. And if things really get bad—don't hesitate to call. I'll share the cost with you. Much love, Emily

The next week was busy. Annie met quite a few of the church members, was invited out to dinner every night, and tried to prepare for her first sermon on Sunday. She was nervous about it. As a curate, she had been responsible for one sermon a month, which hadn't been enough to overcome her fear of public speaking. She liked all the other aspects of serving in the church, but when she got into the pulpit, when she looked down onto the congregation, when everyone was looking at her, expecting to hear something new and brilliant, she was always nervous. She knew this coming Sunday would be a test; she knew that afterward everyone would be talking about her, about what she said, how she said it. And she also knew from growing up in her father's church that what she said could be lifesaving.

Annie's father was an evangelical in the Church of England. He had a booming voice and knew how to organize his sermons so that the main points stuck with his listeners. He knew, and taught Annie, that what he said mattered a great deal. So Annie had a lot to live up to, yet at the same time, she had been given a strong foundation. What was she going to talk about? She had been praying all week and didn't have an answer yet. Sunday was two days away.

Dear Emily: Going to bed, it's late. Can't get going on my debut sermon—any ideas? Yours sounded smashing, but then you always did shine in the pulpit. I'm afraid it's my weakest point and I'm utterly terrified. Dad has been very supportive, as usual, but he simply says, 'The Lord will tell you what to say—it's not for me to usurp him.' Dear dad, I wish you both were here, and I wish you both would tell me what to talk about. It's two days two days away!!!! Haven't seen Matthew again....Lots of love, Annie

Just as she was drifting off to sleep, the phone rang. It was Joy.

"Annie, I'm over at the Hodson's house and their baby is very ill—can you come? I know it's late, but I really think you should come," her voice insistent.

"Of course I'll come. But I don't know which house…"

"It's the white house two doors down from the pub. Lace Lane. I'll leave the porch light on and watch out for you." With that Joy slammed down the phone.

Dressing quickly, Annie walked out into the cold night. It was past midnight and the village was put to bed. A frost was beginning to form on the street and her boots made a crunching sound as she walked. It wasn't that far, but it was bitterly cold and she wished she had driven. She saw the light up ahead. Joy was standing in the doorway as she approached, taking up the entire doorway with her largesse. Annie stepped inside to the empty sitting room.

Joy explained the situation as they climbed the stairs to the bedroom. "The baby Katie has been sick for several days, fever and bronchitis. But now, she's worse and they're very worried."

Annie was greeted with the anxious looks on the faces of the young couple, Norton and Grace. She had not met them previously.

"Thank you for coming, Vicar," Grace said. We just wanted the baby prayed for, that's all. I'm sorry it's so late…" her voice trailed off with a look of helplessness.

Annie smiled. "It's fine, that's why I'm here, to help when I'm needed." She went over to the cot and looked at the baby, her cheeks bright with fever and moist blonde ringlets surrounded her face. "What has the doctor said?" Annie asked.

"He said it was bronchitis. We've been giving her the medicine, but she's not getting any better and we don't know what to do. Her fever isn't going down; it's 104!"

Annie laid her hand on the baby's forehead. It was burning hot. She closed her eyes and looked up to heaven. "Father, we pray for little Katie here. Please heal her from this illness, we ask you to lift the fever, to take it away from her body, to heal her, in Jesus' name and through the power of your Holy Spirit." She remained with her eyes closed and her face uplifted for several moments. The baby stirred, looked up at Annie and began to cry.

Without hesitation, Annie said, "I think you should take her to hospital. I totally believe in God's healing power and I've witnessed healings, but at the same time, I believe we should do all we can to use the knowledge of modern medicine and she's so terribly hot."

"We didn't know what to do, we're so worried, we can't think straight. It seemed cruel to take her out in this cold night, but I guess you're right," Norton said.

"Look, go out and start the car" Annie directed. "Turn on the heater so it will be really warm by the time we get out there with Katie." Annie was in charge. She didn't hesitate to tell each of them what to do next. The young couple were so distracted they needed someone to do this. Joy had done it in the first place, but Annie had been even more masterful. "I'll go with you, would that help?" she asked Grace.

"Oh, yes—would you?"

Joy stood by, watching Annie and nodding to herself. This was a different Annie than she had seen as yet. She was going to be just fine, she said to herself. Meaning Katie as well as Annie. "Should I come as well?" she asked.

Annie shook her head, "No, Joy, maybe you could stay here and tidy up though. I think they'll need some breakfast when they get back. We'll phone you from the hospital and let you know what's happening. All right?"

Joy smiled again. "You are so sensible—so in charge."

They took Annie to get her car and she followed them to hospital. The baby was admitted and Annie stayed all night with Norton and Grace by the bedside. In the grey dawn, when little Katie awoke and smiled up at them, reaching up her arms up for her mother, they knew the crisis was over and wept together. Annie drove home with a grateful heart. Just as she climbed under the covers, barely undressed and exhausted, she looked up. "Thanks," she said.

Buzzzzz. The harsh sound of the doorbell woke Annie from a deep sleep. Surely her head had just hit the pillow. She rolled over to look at her bedside clock. It was eight; she'd had two hours sleep. She was tempted to ignore it, but then it came again. Bzzzzzzzzzzzzzz. Reluctantly, she got up and opened the drapes slightly to peek out below. Her bedroom was in the front of the house, giving her a clear view of the front doorstep. It was Horace. Shaking her head, Annie got back under the warm covers. She was asleep again instantly and didn't even feel guilty. Her alarm went off at ten; she had set it before she went back to bed. It was now Saturday and her sermon still wasn't done or really even started. She put herself under the shower and stayed there a very long time. With dripping hair and a body a bit more awake, she once more heard the buzz of the doorbell. She wrapped a towel round her head and put on her fluffy terry-cloth robe. Padding into to her bedroom, she peeked out of the curtain. Horace again. She shook her head. He seemed to know just exactly when it was a bad time and besides, he seemed to come round frequently. When she opened the door a crack, there he stood, displaying his wet smile.

"Oh, did I disturb you?" he asked. "I was getting worried, I came round earlier and now your curtains are still all pulled, are you all right?"

Well, I would have been if you had let me sleep, Annie felt like saying through gritted teeth. She didn't invite him in. He was still on the doorstep but seemed perched to bolt in at any minute. "What can I do for you?" she asked, managing a tight smile.

"Oh, nothing. I just came round to see if there was anything I could do for you!" he said enthusiastically.

"I was up all night at the hospital with a family and I slept late. Now if you'll excuse me, I need to go get dressed. I'm fine, thank you." With that, she shut the door in his face. She looked up. *"Why me, Lord? Why did you send such an irritating character into my life?"* No answer.

The telegraph system of the village was in full force and by noon, everyone knew about little Katie and about Annie being up all night. And everyone in the church was eagerly looking forward to her first sermon on Sunday morning. No one would have dreamt that the sermon had not even been started.

Annie was exhausted. She was a morning person. She liked to be up early to meet the sun, to wring as much out of a day as she possibly could and she wasn't good at staying up late. The momentum of the crisis had kept her going. Now, with coffee and a solid breakfast, she once more sat at her desk, but nothing came except self-pity. She didn't like the intrusiveness of the village, the way people 'popped round' so often. She felt she had to keep the sitting room, at least, if not the loo and the kitchen as well, looking picked up at all times because of the frequent visiting. She couldn't seem to get herself organized and she already missed the libraries of Cambridge, the coffee shops, the intellectual stimulation of conversations. She phoned her father. "Dad?"

"Hello, Annie. How are ya?" The familiar voice always soothed her.

"I'm terrible. I'm exhausted and my first service is tomorrow and I can't think straight." She told him about the baby, about her early morning intruder, about being stuck in terms of a sermon…it all came tumbling out. "Why do you think I'm here?" she wailed.

"I don't know, Annie, but he does. God knows why

you're there. It doesn't matter so much why, it matters what you do whilst you're there. Think of it as an assignment on the mission field. If you were in India, in a village, would you constantly think about Cambridge?"

She laughed. "Probably. But at least I'd know why I was there. Can you get me started; can you help me a bit in terms of my sermon?"

"What you need to do is put a note on the door asking to not be disturbed, then you need to go have a nice long nap, and while you're doing that, I will pray for you. Sermons just seem to come, all on their own, full blown. If you are filled with the Holy Spirit, and I know you are, he will tell you what to say. Your mum and I will both pray constantly for you from now till tomorrow noon when it will all be over. I am very proud of you, my daughter and so is God."

Annie had tears in her eyes when she hung up. Her earthly father always came through for her.

Chapter Three

Matthew had been invited to Sunday lunch by Ruth Parkinson and her husband Ben. When he arrived, he found two other couples there, which made him suspicious. He knew the main topic of conversation was going to be the new vicar. It was a post-mortem.

"Come in Matthew," Ruth welcomed him, coming out of the kitchen. "I didn't get to speak to you in church this morning, so I'm glad you remembered to come."

He took off his coat, handed it to Ben and joined the others in the sitting room where they were having a glass of sherry. Matthew felt that people in the village didn't seem to know what to do with him. He was one of them in that he attended church fairly regularly, but he had only lived there for two years, was definitely still an Incomer and he didn't seem to take part in the village chatter. He talked about world events, politics, the environment, and literature, those sorts of things. Not that they didn't, but they also talked about each other. Matthew didn't participate, and because of that, he felt that conversations when he was around were sometimes awkward.

Ben poured him a glass of sherry. "Sit down, Matthew, we were just discussing the new vicar and her sermon." The 'her' was emphasized.

"I thought it was superb," Matthew answered, looking round at the rest of the faces, which were a mixed read.

"Ahem," the elderly Sam Jenkins cleared his throat—it always took him awhile to get going with what he was going to say. "It just don't seem right, having a woman up there in the pulpit, is what I say. I couldn't listen to anything she said, I just kept thinkin how she looked like a little kid—being so small and all. It ain't right. Women ain't supposed to be preachers!"

Well, that was certainly blunt; why don't you say what you mean, Matthew thought. He knew he would defend Annie, but decided to wait till he heard from the others.

Sam's wife, Matilda, looked annoyed at her husband. "You know that's nonsense, Sam" she said. "There's not a reason in the world for women not to be vicars. She's just young, that's my only thing. She's awfully young; she looks like she ought to still be in school."

Ruth was in the kitchen finishing the meal preparation, but she could hear the conversation and came into the room at this point, wiping her hands on a tea towel. "Well, I think she's going to be just fine. You heard about how she stayed all night in hospital with Norton and Grace. Now Charles, our previous vicar, he never would have done something like that."

Several of them nodded their head in what seemed to Matthew as reluctant agreement. Then from Sam, "Yeah, but that's the sort of thing his wife would have done, Charles's wife, you know. When you get a female in the pulpit, you only get her, that's it. When you have a proper male for a vicar, you get two for the price of one! Value for money." He looked around with a self-satisfied air.

Matthew remained quiet, but it was hard for him to do so. Internally, he was raging. He felt time never marched on in villages. Nothing changed; no progress was made. He had moved here because of his wife Amanda. Her dream had always been to live in the country, to have a thatched roof cottage and to participate in village life. Having grown up in Dulwich, with the noise, dirt, and impersonality of London, she had yearned for the quiet village life and as soon as they could afford to buy a house, they had looked for and found this village. They had only lived there a year when the accident happened. Matthew was glad she had experienced her dream cottage in the country and she was happy here. She quit her job in London and spent all her time decorating the house and doing things she had never had time for before, such as painting. She learned how to make bread, tried recipes from exotic cookbooks, gardened, and had acquired three dogs. She told Matthew she had always wanted three dogs.

Matthew wondered now as he listened to what seemed to him to be extremely bigoted conversation, if she would still have been happy here, one year later. They had gone to the village church and she had been involved with the typical things women are allowed to do in churches, arrange flowers, serve tea and coffee, and put on church suppers. It seemed to him it had taken awhile for things to surface, for the underlying controversies to poke through the veneer of the outward face of the parishioners. He had only recently been elected to the parish council and had been alarmed, upset even, at meetings. Was this how all churches were when one got inside? Were they all political, struggles for power, for control? He was becoming more and more disenchanted with village life.

He had stayed on after his wife's death for several reasons. One, the village people had been unerringly kind to him. They brought him food, they took care of the dogs, and they had provided a listening ear, though he didn't talk much. The other reason he stayed was the cottage. This was Amanda's dream cottage and even though it was harder for him, since he sensed her presence in all the rooms, he felt it would be letting her down to move. Yet at the same time, he found himself withdrawing more and more from village life. In fact, he had about decided to quit the parish council, but when he began hearing all the controversy about the new woman vicar, he decided to stay, not because he was curious, but because he thought maybe he could be of help to her.

Dinner was ready, so the conversation was interrupted, but only until Ruth's husband had said grace and the roast was served round. Matthew was a vegetarian and many in the village seemed unable to cope with that. He didn't say anything. He just didn't eat the large slab of rare beef that was put on his plate and took extra helpings of the potatoes, parsnips, carrots, and Brussels sprouts. Amanda had taught him to eat this way, but somehow, in this village, it was thought unpatriotic to be vegetarian.

"Matthew, you haven't said much. What do you think?" the loquacious Sam asked.

"Of Reverend O'Donnell?" he asked.

Sam nodded.

"Well, I think she needs to be given a chance. She came here in good faith. It is her first parish after having served as a curate, she knows no one and I think," he hesitated a moment and looked round the table, "I think she's going to be terrific!" he said enthusiastically.

That didn't stop them, however. No one commented on his comment, but Ruth smiled at him and gave him a surreptitious wink. "So what about her sermon? Seemed like we've all heard it before, don't you think? I mean, it's hard for a woman to project; her voice is too soft." This from Craig, a small, red-haired Scotsman who had only lived there for five years, definitely an Incomer.

And so the critique went on and on. Yet at the door of the church, as Annie had stood greeting everyone, people had been friendly and welcoming. Matthew had stood back till most of the others had gone. "Well, done, Annie," he said, taking her hand and holding it a moment longer than he would have held the previous vicar's hand.

She looked up at him and smiled. "Oh, thank you, Matthew. You can't imagine how nervous I was."

"Have you been invited somewhere for lunch?" he asked, not wanting her to go back to the empty vicarage.

"Yes, thank you. Joy is having me over with some of the others in the congregation. But thanks for thinking of me."

Matthew wasn't sure what he would have done if she had said she had no plans, but he knew he wouldn't have allowed her to be alone. Now as he sat listening to the sermon being ripped apart, sentence by sentence, he wondered how she was getting on where she was. Didn't these people get anything out of what she said? Why was how she delivered the sermon more important than what she said? He knew it wasn't the best sermon in the world, but he also knew it was her first. She based it on the Good Samaritan and although it was a familiar theme and it was true he didn't learn anything new—did one need to every time? Besides, with her copper hair, green eyes, creamy complexion, and freckles, he concentrated most of the time on how she looked, rather than what she was saying.

Am I being disloyal to Amanda? He asked himself that when he left Annie's house last week. How can I appreciate a pretty young woman's face when Amanda has only been gone for a year? Would Amanda do the same? He didn't know. But he knew he couldn't help being drawn to this new vicar. And he also knew he would have to be extremely careful, that if he saw her very often, the village would talk.

Meanwhile, Annie was being well stuffed by Joy's excellent cooking. She had only invited women to this lunch, all widows from the church and all older. They were quite a lively group; they met once a week for ostensible Bible study and prayer, which they did, but at the same time, they passed the sherry bottle liberally and had a grand old time.

"You know, Annie, we're so happy to have you here. It's about time the church got round to ordaining women, that's what I say. Such a waste of talent all these years." The speaker was Margaret, someone Annie was to learn had a sharp wit and a discerning eye for judgment of people.

Annie told them about Emily, now serving as an Episcopal priest in New England and how there was no resistance to women there.

"Well, the trouble with the Church of England is the name, in the first place. It's the established church and you know what that means—the church of the establishment. And the establishment means men," Margaret said vociferously.

"How many women were in your class at Cambridge?" another woman asked.

"Oh, there were only ten of us," Annie answered, "and fifty men."

"And how were you treated?"

"All right. Especially after the first year, after they got to know us and found out we were serious about our calling." Annie paused and took a sip of water. "Some of them were disappointed that we weren't after them—as husbands, I mean." She wrinkled up her nose in a mischievous way that emphasized the twinkle in her eye.

The luncheon continued with others shifting the attention away from Annie, onto their own affairs, chiefly because she asked them questions, drew them out. She liked these women. They didn't seem like poor widows in terms of their happiness. They seemed to be leading the type of life that interested them.

Over coffee in the sitting room, Joy asked, "Now, Annie, what can we do for you? It seems like it must be lonely living in that big old house all alone, but I know you don't want people popping in all the time. You're a city girl and you probably won't like the intrusiveness of village life."

Honest, thought Annie. She pondered for a moment and then said, "You know what I would like? I'd quite like a puppy."

"A puppy!" several women said simultaneously. "Well, that's easy," Margaret said. "The shelter is quite close; would you like me to take you there tomorrow?"

"Oh, yes, that would be lovely. You see, in my family we always had a dog or dogs actually. And since I've been away, at school, I've missed that. I would love to have a new little puppy to raise. I think the house wouldn't seem so empty then."

Dear Em: It is Sunday night and the first service is over. My sermon was certainly not sterling and I was a nervous wreck. Thanks for praying. I am sure I was the topic of conversation at all the Sunday lunch tables all over the village and I'm not sure I will ever get over resenting that. But I suppose it's only natural—maybe it would be the very same in a city—I don't know. Went to Sunday lunch with the single women of the village, not what you think—they're all widows. But not terribly old or at least they sure don't act like it; they seem to have a high old time together.

They seem to be very accepting of me—I gather it's the married men who are against women in the pulpit. I'm going to get a puppy tomorrow! How are you? Sure miss our long talks. Love, Annie

The next morning, Matthew awoke to a grey sky and a steady, insistent rain, reminding him of how Amanda always described the rain as shining silver curtains outside the windows of the cottage. He had to be in London all day and hated to leave the three dogs cooped up in the house, but there was no other solution. He couldn't let them stay out in the rain. Three dogs! What a single man was doing with three dogs to take care of, he wondered, not for the first time. It wasn't that he didn't like them. He did and they were a source of companionship to him when he was home. As he pulled out of the driveway, he saw Annie coming down the street under a huge black umbrella. He pulled up beside her and rolling down the window, asked, "Can I give you a lift?"

"Oh, thanks Matthew. I'm just going right over here to Margaret's. She's taking me to the animal shelter today to get a puppy."

"Well, get in, you shouldn't be walking in this weather."

"I don't want to make you late," Annie said, as she dutifully slipped in the passenger seat.

"No, I'm early actually," he said, smiling. He drove the short distance to Margaret's house, stopped and turned off the engine. "Say, do you know that I have three dogs?" he said, looking amused.

"Three! My goodness, that's a lot. You must be a dog lover."

Matthew smiled ruefully. "Well, I like them and all that, but they were Amanda's, you see. She just kept bringing new dogs home from the shelter and we ended up with three of them."

"It must be hard for you to take care of them, being gone all day as you often are," Annie said.

As she spoke those words, a strange feeling was washing over Matthew. He had never been as physically close to her as now in the car and he felt drawn to her in a manner only a physicist could explain. It was if there was electricity in the space between them and he had to fight against leaning forward toward her. Instead, he drew back, trying to recover some normalcy. "It is, especially on a day like today," he finally answered, feeling as if he'd been in a trance, albeit a short one. "I hate leaving them in all day," he said, looking directly into her eyes and not smiling.

Annie made no move to open the door and he made no move to start up the engine.

"This sounds crazy, I know, but you wouldn't like to have the dogs, would you?" He laughed and shook his head. "No, no one wants three dogs, never mind."

But Annie didn't laugh. "I might. You know I always had at least one dog growing up and I've missed them so. Do you mean it, are you serious?"

"Well, here you are, going off to get a dog and I've got a surplus and I wouldn't feel guilty if you had them, somehow, and they can't be split up; they're great pals."

Annie was silent for a moment as if she was thinking. Then she said, "Look, why don't you go on to work and I'll talk to Margaret about it over a cup of coffee. I think you should take some time to think about it as well."

Matthew nodded, "Okay. I'll be back around seven tonight. Are you free? Would you like to come round to see them? Interview them?"

Annie put her hand on the door handle and opened it quickly. Stepping out into the rain, she said "Thanks for the ride. I'll come round when you phone this evening."

When Margaret let her in, Annie told her what had transpired. "Three dogs!" she exclaimed, "I've seen Matthew walking them. They seem to be quite a handful if you ask me."

"What kind of dogs are they?" Annie asked.

"One is a golden lab and one is a tiny terrier, quite a contrast and one is a right old mix, I couldn't say, in size she looks in between the other two."

Annie didn't know what to do. It seemed such a bizarre offer for someone to give you three dogs. Yet she had grown up in a house full of pets and they certainly would fill the house, would make it less quiet, would be companions for her. But would Matthew be sorry he had done it?

"I suppose, if Matthew regretted it, he could always take them back again," Margaret said, as if she had read her mind.

"Yes, you're right. I could take them on a trial basis. I gather Matthew isn't as much a dog lover as was his wife."

Margaret smiled. "Everyone in the village loved Amanda; she was out and about all the time with those three dogs. We all miss her. I wouldn't be surprised if Matthew would rather move into the city. I gather that living in the country was her idea."

Annie felt a stab of . . .what was it. . .fear? Matthew might move back to London. Was that why he offered her the dogs? She brought herself up mentally. Well, why not? He certainly must be lonely in his house, she thought. It was a small cottage compared to her vicarage, but still, if he didn't take to village life and the house, the rooms, the furniture, haunted him with memories of Amanda—-maybe it was too painful for him to live there any longer. *For heaven' sake, Annie, you barely know the man and you're reacting as if his moving away would be a catastrophe.*

She and Margaret mutually decided not to go to the shelter. They would wait until Annie saw the dogs and came to a decision. Still, she had looked forward to having a brand new puppy. Maternal instincts rising up, she asked herself?

Monday was her day off, but since she had the entire day ahead of her, Annie decided to work on her sermon, get it done and over with in case another emergency cropped up. Following her father's example, she began by spending an hour reading

The Bible and praying. She was talking to God about the dogs, about Matthew, and by the way, her sermon, when the doorbell rang. Sighing audibly, she got up and answered the door. There stood Horace under a dripping umbrella. Given the weather, she had to invite him in, she told herself.

"I just thought you might be at loose ends today and would like some company," he said, smiling wetly at her.

Annie didn't know how to handle this man who seemed to have a knack of always coming or calling at the wrong time. Would there be a right time, she asked herself sarcastically. "Well, actually, I'm working on my sermon, thank you. I was looking forward to a day without interruption so I could make sure it was at least begun."

"Your sermon! This is Monday—you don't mean to tell me it takes you an entire week to do a sermon. Why, the last vicar would turn them out late Saturday night after having been round to our house for a rousing party and they were always spot on!"

Annie gritted her teeth metaphorically. "Well, that isn't my pattern, I'm afraid. I like to have it done and then I can move on to other things." She hadn't asked him to sit down. But he did.

"So what do you think of us so far? We're a queer bunch, don't you think? Lots of characters in this village. I've lived here since I was a young man and I've seen lots of changes here. Some don't like change, but I say it has to come."

Annie's heart sank. How was she going to get rid of him? She had lit a fire in the fireplace, she had been sitting there with a hot cup of tea, cozy and warm, talking to God and now here was this pest. She berated herself for being so uncharitable. "I think the village is lovely," she prevaricated. Which isn't the same thing as a lie, she told herself. She was referring to the houses and the landscape.

He looked meaningfully at her cup of tea. What seemed like a long silence ensued. "Well, you sure have the village abuzz. I visit around quite a bit and you're the main topic of conversation."

Annie tried to smile.

"Yes, sir. Your sermon last week was discussed up and down one side and the other."

She didn't dare ask what the conclusions were. She was pretty sure she knew and didn't want to hear it.

"You need to learn to project your voice more," he said, looking at her hopefully.

"I'm sure I do. I will try." Why did this man make her feel so insecure?

Another silence.

"Well, I guess I interrupted you. I'll be going along then—maybe later in the week we'll have a chat? The missus wants to have you round for supper. When would that be do you think?"

"That would be lovely," Annie lied again. "Ask her to phone me tomorrow, will you?" She stood up and finally, he did as well.

"Here, let me get the door for you," she said as she edged ahead of him, afraid if she didn't, he wouldn't leave.

After shutting the door, she sat back down in front of the fire, her mood totally shattered. She tried to pray, but couldn't. Nothing came. Horace's words kept echoing, 'you were the topic of conversation—you need to project your voice more—your sermon was discussed up one side and down the other.'

Where was God in all this? Where was the love of Christ? Everything had started off wrong when she arrived and it hadn't really become any better. Her meetings with Matthew, few as they had been, were a highlight. Joy's helpfulness and understanding, the Sunday lunch with the ladies, otherwise, she felt alone and vulnerable. She sat staring into the fire for what seemed a long time. The house was so empty. The incessant rain beat against the roof, precluding going for a walk. She couldn't call Emily because of the time difference.

Just then the phone rang. She hesitated, knowing she was on the verge of tears and not wanting her voice to show it. The answer machine came on. She recognized Matthew's voice.

"Look, Annie, I realize.."

She rushed to the phone and interrupted his message. "Hello! Sorry I didn't get to the phone in time."

"Oh, I'm glad you're there. Look, I know the offer I made this morning seemed rash to you and I got to worrying that you might feel obligated.."

"Oh, no, Matthew, not at all," she felt so relieved to be talking to him that she interrupted him again.

"I know you said you were going to get a puppy, and here I present you with the alternative of three grown dogs—I mean that was really very presumptuous of me." He hesitated a moment, "I say, Annie,…is something wrong?"

"No" she lied, "why do you ask?"

"Well, your voice…it sounded like…I don't know. Are you sure?"

She didn't answer. There was something about Matthew. It was more than her attraction to him because he was good looking; it was his empathy, his understanding; it seemed to break down all her defenses.

"Annie, are you upset about something?" he asked.

She sighed as she answered, "Yes, I'm afraid I am. Horace was just here and told me the other vicar always gave great sermons. I'm sorry, Matthew. You're at work and I hardly know you and every time I see you, I seem to need someone to talk to. You must think I'm a ninny."

"I don't think that at all," he said quietly. "I think you've come into a very difficult situation and you don't have friends and family to support you, at least not in person. I want you to know that I will always be willing to help you, to listen. What's on your schedule for today?" he asked.

"I was trying to work on my sermon," she answered, sniffing, and feeling less likely to become tearful.

"Well, I have a lecture to give at two. Why don't you drive to the railway station and come to London. We could have dinner and even go to the theatre, if you like. It might help to get out of that lonely house and into the big city. What do you say?"

Annie's mood instantly changed. Getting on the train and going into London was just what she would like to do. She felt a surge of energy…why not? Nothing to stop her. And surely she had all the rest of the week to work on her sermon.

"I would like that very much," she said. "And Matthew,"
"Yes?"
"Thank you."

He laughed. "Thank you for accepting. Can you find the LSE? Take the Piccadilly Line and get off at Russell Square station. When you get to the information desk, ask for me. They'll ring my office and I'll come right down. What time do you think you'll get here; can you phone me on your mobile from the train station?"

As she took a shower, washing her hair and wondering what she was going to wear, she marveled at the lift in her spirits. "Thank you, Lord," she said as the warm water washed over her head and body. *Thank you for answering my prayer—which I didn't even know I prayed."*

She met Matthew in the lobby of the university. This was impressive in itself. She had never been there and he offered to show her around, but it was cold and wet and she said what she really needed was a cup of tea. Matthew opened his large, black umbrella as they stepped out of the building. He hailed a taxi, and getting in, gave the driver the name of the restaurant, Passione. Annie had heard of it and wondered if she was dressed well enough. Matthew, in his suit and tie, looked very professional, every inch a Londoner.

When they were settled in the restaurant with a cup of tea and had their order in, they discussed the dogs. "I know this is sudden," Matthew said, "but honestly, I've been trying to think what to do about them for ages. They really are a problem for me."

"Won't you miss them?" Annie asked.
"Yes, I'm sure I will, but it's not right for them to be

there alone all day and besides, I could visit them often, don't you think?" He smiled.

"Yes, of course, you could," Annie replied, sipping her tea, "but could we do this on a trial basis? I mean, what if I feel overwhelmed, what if they don't like me? It will be quite an adjustment for them and don't you think they might run away, come home again?"

Matthew laughed. "They might well do, but let's just play it by ear."

"All right," Annie answered. "I do love dogs and I've missed having one and they certainly would make the house less lonely."

Matthew smiled broadly. "Okay, so that's settled. Let's move on to humans—us."

What does he mean? Annie asked herself..

"I mean you and me separately—we're humans," he hastily corrected himself.

She realized that her nervousness about what he just said must have shown on her face. It wasn't that she wasn't interested in him, it was that she was too interested in him. She was in a new job, in a new place, a place where people would, and she was certain did, talk. And he was a recent widower, dangerous, Emily had warned her.

"What made you go into the ministry?" Matthew asked. "I'm really interested in that about you, first of all, that is."

This was better. Annie felt on safer ground and she began to relax. "Well, as you know, my father is a vicar in Belfast. So I grew up in that atmosphere, which is very different than if your father is a butcher or something and you just go to church on Sundays."

Matthew nodded, "So he was your main influence?"

"Yes. He's such a role model for me, but I don't know if I'll ever be as effective as he is. He's a wonderful orator and his sermons penetrate to one's soul. I wish you could hear him sometime."

"Well, maybe I will," Matthew replied. "Do you know, I've never been to Belfast."

Annie nodded, "That's not so unusual. I find people all the time who've been all over Europe, but have never been to Ireland, either the Republic or Northern Ireland. There really still is a lot of prejudice against us, don't you think?

"Not amongst the type of people you would want to know," he answered. "But there are people who it seems have to try to build themselves up by feeling superior to others, so they develop prejudices. My own opinion of these people are that they feel powerless in this world, either through lack of education or low earning power, so they try to gain a bit of power by lording it over targeted groups, be it Pakistanis or black people, whoever the current minority happens to be."

"Rather a kick the dog syndrome, you mean?"

Matthew nodded in agreement.

Their food arrived and Annie was quiet for a moment, twirling the pasta on her fork and taking a bite. The food was delicious. Before she took another bite, she asked, "Do you think there are those in the village that feel that way about the Irish? And me?"

Matthew took a deep breath and shrugged. "You know I'm not in on village gossip much. I try to avoid it, mainly by not frequenting the pub."

"It's interesting," Annie said, because I've never felt Irish. I've always thought of myself as British. I just happen to live in the part of Britain that is located in Northern Ireland."

"And the Troubles? Did they affect you growing up?" Matthew asked.

Annie told him how the violence in Belfast had been concentrated in certain neighborhoods and that if one never ventured to those, the Troubles seemed like just another news item, as it would to the rest of England living on the mainland. "Now with the peace treaty, we all hope those days are over." But she also told him there were old prejudices that were deeply rooted, Protestants against Catholics, Catholics against Protestants.

"Well, since political science is my topic, I've always been under the impression it was more nationalism that created the problems, that religion was just an excuse."

"Yes, but that's only part of the picture. This was really one of the main reasons I wanted to get away, to come to England."

Annie was thoroughly enjoying herself. This was the first real conversation she had had since she left Cambridge. She knew she wasn't being fair, that there must be those in the village who talked about the wider world, politics, world problems, philosophy, theology, but in her short time there it hadn't happened until tonight. Here finally was someone she could talk to and she felt certain he was going to turn out to be a friend, if nothing else.

Matthew had grown quiet.

"It's all so stupid," she continued. "We all worship the same God, the only God. Why anyone would care how or where someone else worshipped never made sense to me. Jesus didn't tell us to go out and convert everyone to our particular interpretation of the Bible. He said to go out and tell people about Him and to love each other. That's all!"

"I'm sorry, what were you saying?" Matthew asked, looking embarrassed as if he hadn't heard her.

"Oh, I was just saying of all the prejudices that exist, probably the one that I think is the most stupid, is the one about religion."

"Would you like some dessert?" Matthew asked, "Or coffee?"

"Oh, no, thank you, but go ahead if you would," she answered, in a different tone of voice. Actually, she would love to have a profiterole and a cup of espresso. She was puzzled. Maybe he wasn't someone she could talk to about theology, about God. He seemed desperate to change the subject. It was always so tricky, she lamented to herself, how to act on a date.

Was this a date? She had thought it was at first, but now Matthew seemed to withdraw. Was he just being nice to her so she would take the dogs off his hands? That thought made her a bit angry, so she retaliated by withdrawing as well. The ensuing silence grew embarrassing.

"No, none for me, either," he answered. "Should we get the bill, are you ready to go?"

Annie's mood now shifted from anger to a sinking feeling in her stomach. What had gone wrong? What had she said to make him change the mood of the evening so quickly?

On the half hour train ride to the village they again discussed the dogs and Annie agreed to a trial. He would bring them over on Saturday with all their paraphernalia.

When they got to the station, it was still pouring rain. Matthew walked with her to her car and as she unlocked the door, said casually, "I'll see you Saturday morning, is that all right?"

Annie nodded. He turned and walked away. She stood there for a moment, dry under her huge umbrella, but feeling very wet nevertheless. The evening which had begun so wonderfully didn't end that way.. As she drew near her house, she saw lights on, startling her for a moment before she remembered it had been almost dark when she left that afternoon. Still, the house was empty and quiet. Maybe being greeted by three yapping dogs would be better than this utter stillness. For once, she was too tired and too dejected to write to Emily. I'll tell her about this in the morning, she thought, as she drifted off to sleep.

Chapter Four

Matthew had trouble going to sleep. When he lost track of what Annie was saying, it was because he was noticing how pretty she looked when she became passionate about a subject. She was very different in appearance from Amanda. His wife had been tall, almost as tall as he was and she was strongly built, slim, but not delicate. She was athletic, actually more athletic than he was, and would set him quite a pace when she talked him into going on long walks in the countryside with the dogs. Her biggest desire had been to have her own horse, which was one wish he hadn't fulfilled for her.

Now, trying to go to sleep, all he could think of was Annie's face, her laugh, her look of interest when he was talking, her quickness of mind, and most of all, the look of disappointment on her face when his mood changed. He berated himself. *It wasn't her fault I asked her to dinner—she's an innocent victim of my excessive guilt. Is it excessive?*

He had loved Amanda as much as anyone could love another; he had quite simply adored her. And she had only been dead for a year and a few months, a year that left a terrible pit of loneliness, a deep loneliness he had felt all his life until he met her and was now worse than it had ever been. It was so sudden; she was so young, and they had such plans for a wonderful long life together. One minute their life was proceeding and the next minute it was gone—in a flash. Why? Why, he asked God over and over. He could see no sense to it, a willful accident that he knew God could have prevented. A wet night, the lorry skidding, and in one instant, his life and Amanda's was over.

His instinct had been to flee the village immediately; he didn't want to stay in what had been her dream cottage. She had learned how to make bread and delighted in timing it to come out of the oven just as he walked in the door in the evening, all three dogs beating her to the door to greet him. He couldn't abandon her dogs and he couldn't take them to a flat in London, so he was still here, still struggling with their care, feeling guilty when he left them alone too long, knowing that they missed her too.

And now, he was actually thinking of another woman. So soon. He disliked himself for what he was experiencing. *How could I be attracted to another woman so soon?* He wondered if he had been the one to die and Amanda had met someone new, would she act, feel the same? He didn't think so. He thought something was wrong with him. He accused himself of being shallow, fickle, disloyal.

He got up and switched on the bedside lamp. Amanda's picture was there in a gold frame, and as often happened, he couldn't fathom that she no longer existed. He knew she was buried in the graveyard at the church. There had been a funeral. He had seen her after she had died, as required by the coroner. It was very real at the time.

Now, a year later, it all seemed like a dream, a very bad dream. Here she was in the picture, with her long, golden hair draped over one shoulder, her brilliant blue eyes laughing at him. He had taken the photograph one day when he especially felt how breathtakingly beautiful she was. He had gone inside to get the camera and made her pose several times, taking quite a few pictures. He was so pleased with this one that he had it enlarged and framed it himself. "Oh, Mandy," he spoke to her now, feeling choked. "Mandy, I still love you." It was as if he was convincing himself, rather than her.

He had enjoyed this evening. He had enjoyed it far too much and he didn't like himself because he enjoyed it so much. He also knew he had been rude to Annie; he had turned cold and was sure she was upset by it. He didn't know if she had a boyfriend somewhere. He hadn't had the courage to ask and she hadn't volunteered. He convinced himself she was simply accepting a kind offer of a dinner in town. He made himself a cup of tea and went back to bed with a novel he was reading, hoping reading would make him sleepy.

Two days later a letter arrived for Annie from someone she knew in Cambridge.

Dear Annie:

I hope you are settled in and happy in your new parish. You are sorely missed here, I can tell you. I am writing to ask a very large favor of you. I am trying to help someone from a former parish. She has a distant relative who is a bit down on her luck at the moment. She is betwixt and between and doesn't know what she wants to do with her life, having tried several things and none of them having worked out. She is extremely short of funds and needs a place to stay. As you know, our house is bursting at the seams, and as I heard that you are in a large house all alone, wondered if you could take her in for a three-month period at the most. I think walks in the country and fresh air and time to think will be of great benefit to her. Perhaps she could find work in the village as a cleaner and from that could pay you a small amount, which should cover her food costs. I know this is a lot to ask when you are so new there and all. Please feel free to say no. I am exploring several options for her. Her name is Julie. I don't know much about her background other than that she has been in several foster homes. Her mother died when she was only five I gather she has some contact with her real father. She is evidently a bit mixed up at the moment. Let me know.

God bless you – Kevin

Annie read the letter through several times. Do I want this? she asked herself. She sat down and wrote to Emily immediately.

Dear Em: Just when things couldn't seem to get worse....this friend of mine, you remember Kevin Blakely? He wrote to ask if a girl could come here to stay with me for three months!!!! What can I say? No, I don't have room for her? No, I don't have time for her? Well – I honestly don't think I have time. What do you think? Help!!! Love, Annie

Dear Annie: Isn't email wonderful? Instant answer. I'm wondering if it's God who is sending this person to you. I know, I know—easy for me to say. But look, she needs help, you have this big, lonely house—maybe she could clean it for you, that would help, wouldn't it? You know what the Instruction Book says – Love, Em

Annie received Emily's answer with a wry smile. She looked up to heaven. *"Okay, Father—what is it you have in mind? Could you please let me in on it?*

The next morning she was still mulling over Kevin's letter and still struggling with next Sunday's sermon, when the doorbell rang. Exasperated, thinking it must be Horace, she reluctantly opened the door.

It was Matthew. He was so tall she had to look up at him and his deep blue eyes had a twinkle in them that made her want to respond. At the same time, the sight of him gave her a funny feeling in the pit of the stomach. She didn't have time to dwell on her feelings, however, as he had all three dogs, all on leashes, all barking and eager to come in.

"Hi, I thought I would bring the dogs over to visit for the day, kind of a day trial, is that all right?"

Annie smiled, first at the dogs and then at him. "Sure, should we take them round back? I'll meet you at the gate." She went out the back door and round to the side of the house to open the latch on the gate. Matthew let the dogs loose, shutting and locking the gate behind him. They raced round, sniffing the place out, following each other in hysterical abandonment. Finally, all three came back to sniff Annie. "They sure enjoy each other's company," she laughed, trying to pet all three at once.

"I know, that's why I couldn't bear to split them up—they're each other's family. The lab is named Scout, and the little Yorkie is named Tibby. The mutt here, my favorite, is Daisy."

Annie knelt down and put her arms around each of the big dogs, then picked Tibby up in her arms. He was so small he seemed like a puppy.

"I can see you like dogs," he said, "Just like Amanda. I never could get into them like that."

"But they must be used to you. Don't you think they'll miss you?"

"You know," Matthew said, "I honestly don't think they will. They have always been more interested in women, I guess because Amanda spoiled them rotten. I just feed them and walk them and pet them when they absolutely demand it."

Annie put Tibby down, but he kept jumping up, wanting her to hold him again. "So you want to leave them here all day?" she asked, knowing very well that's what he had just said.

"Is that okay? I'll stop and pick them up tonight when I come home. It may be around ten o'clock. Is that too late?"

"No, it's all right. Did you bring their food?" *He could have phoned, could have given me warning—he just blithely appears with three dogs and expects me to say yes.* They seemed to be really nice dogs and she did miss having a dog. But three, how many people in this world have three?

When Matthew left, she stayed outside and played with them for fully an hour. Then, giving them water, and letting them into the kitchen, she shut the door into the hall because of their muddy feet and tried to get back to what she was doing before Matthew arrived, but she couldn't concentrate. All she thought of was him and how he looked. Am I falling in love with him? Is this what it feels like? She needed to talk to Emily.

Dear Em: You know all the discussions we've had about falling in love and how would one know? You haven't written about it happening to you and I know you would have if it had happened. But I'm wondering if it has happened to me?!!! I can't get the picture of him out of my mind. I think about him a lot.

And it certainly isn't mutual. He treats me as if I was a student of his or another guy. Wouldn't you know it? When it finally happens, it isn't reciprocal? Oh, well – how are you? Hope your life is 'normal' because mine sure isn't. You are probably right about this girl, Julie – I do have this big house and now I have these dogs to deal with and it might be good to have some help here. I just hope she doesn't have too many problems. Love, Annie

Julie arrived on the train several days later. Meanwhile, Annie had delivered her second sermon, a bit better than the first, but still not sterling. The dogs had arrived, with all their paraphernalia, and it was now anything but lonely in the house. They settled in nicely. All three slept in Annie's bedroom with Tibby curled up next to her on the bed. Matthew was right; they didn't seem to miss him a bit. When she took them on walks, they edged toward their old house, but were happy to go on past after a few sniffs around. Annie was enjoying their company immensely.

Julie, however, was a different matter. When Annie picked her up at the train station, she had no problem recognizing her from Kevin's description. She was a large young woman, not overweight, just tall, big boned and muscular, towering over Annie and intimidating her at first sight. Her dark blond hair was carelessly and greasily pulled back in a ponytail. Dark brown eyes were framed by totally incongruous blue eye shadow and unsightly zits spotted her face. Worst of all, she never smiled. Mumbled responses were all Annie was able to get from her. She brought three large suitcases, making Annie wonder if she had come to stay.

After Julie unpacked her things she came downstairs, and without asking permission, turned on the television. Four hours later, she hadn't moved. When Annie tried to talk to her, she was met with an icy stare. After fixing her a cup of tea and bringing it to her on a tray along with some biscuits, Annie left her alone and retired to her study to begin on the next week's sermon. That evening, Annie cooked a meal, but Julie hardly ate anything. Not much of a cook anyway, Annie was invited to parishioner's houses many evenings for dinner and living alone, she usually existed on tinned soups and sandwiches.

Life was certainly not going as she had planned. However, life seems to go on in spite of what one plans and after two weeks of Julie being in residence, nothing had improved. Annie had not yet seen her smile, nor did she talk much. Annie felt as if she were pulling glue off plaster when she tried to engage her in conversation. When she first arrived, Annie had told her to help herself whenever she was hungry to anything in the fridge or cupboards, but she didn't think Julie ate much at all. She didn't say thank you when Annie cooked or did something nice for her, resulting in Annie feeling like an innkeeper, except that she wasn't getting paid.

Julie didn't know what to make of Annie either. When she saw her as she stepped off the train, she couldn't believe she was really into this church business. She was so tiny and pretty and looked far too young to be a vicar, probably biding her time until a man came along to rescue her, she decided. Julie didn't trust anyone, but she particularly didn't trust anyone mixed up with the church. As far as she was concerned it was a job like any other. No one in the church really believed all that nonsense they preached about, did they? It was just the party line, wasn't it? Like a political party, simply a route to power. She had never gone to church and what she had learned in RE classes in school was all she knew about religion. When Kevin told her he found a place for her to stay, she worried about how holy Annie would be. Was she going to make her go to church? Were there going to be compulsory prayers morning, afternoon, and evening? So far, however, she hadn't thought Annie to be very holy at all. She seemed like an ordinary person. She was so friendly, helpful and open, it made Julie trust her less. She realized it made Annie feel uncomfortable that she wouldn't talk to her, but she couldn't help it. If she ever once began talking, she was terrified she would cry. Crying meant she was weak and she simply was *not* going to do it.

When Annie was out of the house, which wasn't nearly often enough as far as Julie was concerned, she wandered around the big house. One of the bedrooms had been converted to a study, where Annie kept her computer and her books. Lots of religious books, lots of Bibles, lots of books with titles such as "How to be a Happy Christian." No interest there. She tried to log onto Annie's email, but was disappointed to find she needed a password. She had no compunction about probing into Annie's private diaries, drawers, and cupboards. She didn't want to steal anything, she was just curious. It never entered her head that she shouldn't be doing it. If Annie had kept a journal, rather than writing all her fears and hurts to Emily, Julie would have known about them in no time at all.

The only living things to which she responded were the dogs. She thoroughly enjoyed them and was especially drawn to the golden lab, who like herself, was large and rather clumsy. After a few days of almost complete silence, Annie asked her if she wanted to take the dogs for a walk and after that, it became a daily routine.

Annie breathed a sigh of relief whenever Julie left with the dogs. It was the only time she was out of the house. Growing up in a benevolent family, with her father's regular admonition that the only reason we're here on earth is to help other people, Annie always thought she possessed a strong sense of altruism. Do unto your neighbor and all that. However, with Silent Sam, as Annie privately called her, she wasn't feeling very charitable. She realized Julie was severely disturbed, but she didn't have the expertise to know what was wrong, much less how to deal with it.

She hadn't heard from or seen Matthew since he left the dogs two weeks ago. He hadn't even phoned to see how they were. She wondered if she had been used, wondered if he was being friendly, asking her to dinner in the city just to get rid of the dogs. Other than Joy, Matthew was the only person in the village in whom she felt she could confide and she was desperate to talk to someone about Julie. Finally, on an impulse, she phoned him one evening. Julie was ensconced in front of the television as usual, so Annie was certain she couldn't hear the conversation upstairs in her study.

Matthew answered right away. "Oh, hello, Annie. How are the dogs doing?"

How are the dogs doing...you haven't cared to ask since they arrived, have you and now you can't even say how are you? So went her internal reaction. Out loud she said, "The dogs are just fine, thank you." Her quick temper threatened to overwhelm her. As a defense, she was silent.

"What can I do for you?" he asked.

Annie took in a long deep breath, not wanting to show her anger, but thinking how infuriating he was. I might as well be phoning a business, she told herself. She stumbled as she began, "Well..I..I just needed to talk to someone, I guess, and I hadn't heard from you...."

"Oh, I've been out of the country," he interrupted. "Guess I should have told you in case it didn't work out with the dogs, but there was a conference in Italy. I hadn't planned to go, but then my colleague fell ill, so I went in his stead at the last minute. Of course, you can talk to me—do you want me to come over?"

Now his voice had changed. He sounded more like she remembered him. "No, you can't come over. I have a guest," she said. "Could I come there?" she asked, surprised at her courage.

"Of course, come right over, I have a nice fire going."

"All right," she responded after a moment's silence, "I'll be right there." Five minutes on her face and hair in front of the bathroom mirror was all she felt she had time for. She squirted some perfume on her neck and wrists just before she left the room. Going downstairs, she talked to Julie's back. "Julie, I'm going out for about an hour—okay?" Julie didn't turn around, mumbled something, and continued watching television. Might as well, Annie thought. She doesn't seem to care if I'm here or not.

It was dark, windy, and cold as Annie walked the short distance to Matthew's house. She was bundled up in her long coat, a hat pulled down over her forehead, and a woolen scarf around her neck. Although it was early evening, some of the houses already had all their lights out and she passed no one on the street. The bare trees bent into the wind, doing a strange dance, making her shiver from more than the cold.

When Matthew opened the door and she saw his face, after two weeks of silence and of being ignored, after two weeks of wondering if she was falling in love, after being furious at him for not caring enough about the dogs to even phone her, she melted. The feeling began somewhere near her face and ended down by her belly button, like pure melted butter flowing. *Don't show it, pull yourself together—don't let him know how he affects you.*

"Come in, come in, it's cold out," he urged her.

She stepped inside and began unwrapping herself, taking off her boots in the foyer.

"How are you?" Matthew asked, and taking her by both shoulders, kissed her lightly, first on one cheek and then the other.

This was the most intimate he had ever been. Other than shaking her hand when she first met him and taking her elbow to help her into the taxi, he had never touched her. She knew it didn't mean anything, that everyone did it, but at the same time, it melted her further. Down to her knees.

"Come on in by the fire. May I get you something to drink?"

"No, nothing, thank you," Annie replied and smiled weakly as she sat down by the fire, rubbing her hands together to warm them. What a lovely cottage, she thought, as she looked around. The fireplace was very wide and deep, obviously it was once the kitchen fire. Little shelves made from the stone and mortar graced on the sides, places for pots and pans.

She guessed the cottage probably dated from the seventeenth century. Wide, irregular beams crossed the ceiling. The room had been decorated beautifully. It was warm and inviting.

Annie realized she hadn't uttered a word other than to reply to Matthew's offer of something to drink. When she looked away from the fire toward Matthew, he was sitting opposite her with an inquiring look, waiting for her to speak. But she was afraid to speak, afraid if she did, all her hurt and anger at the way he had treated her would spill out. What was it about him that stirred up all these emotions in her, negative as well as positive? Around him, she felt helpless and weak.

"Annie?" he quietly urged. "What did you want to talk to me about?"

She turned back to the fire. Maybe this was how she would manage it, by not looking at him. "The dogs are fine," she began. "I really love them already and they seem to be quite at home with me, but I have another guest in the house. The house is filling up fast," she said, glancing at him quickly and then back to studying the fire.

"Yes, I heard. You know this village. Nothing goes on here that everyone doesn't know. I happened upon Joy at the village post office before I left and she told me. What's her name, Judy or something? Your niece?"

"It's Julie and she's not my niece," Annie replied, "she's the niece of someone who knows someone I know, knew, in Cambridge. She needed a place to stay, to recuperate or something, and so I felt I couldn't turn her down, with that big house and all."

"What's she recuperating from?" he asked.

Annie took in a deep breath before she answered. "I don't know. That's just it—she won't talk to me. She mostly sits in front of the television or sleeps. I can't get her to eat much and she responds better to your dogs than she does to me." Annie paused again, still staring at the leaping flames in the fireplace. "I'm just at my wits end. I don't know what to do!"

"Do you know anything about her?" he asked, and then

continued, "Sounds like someone who is depressed, shouldn't she have some professional help?"

Annie shook her head, "No, I don't really know much about her. I phoned my friend from Cambridge who sent her to me. He said she had evidently always had problems and had been sent to a counselor, but it wasn't any use. Julie wouldn't talk to her, so quit going." She turned away from the fire at this point, becoming absorbed in Julie's problem rather than her own, "Her mum died when she was five and she's pretty much been in foster homes ever since, but she does see her father now and then. He lives in Cornwall, I believe, and sometimes takes her on business trips with him when he's going someplace nice. The whole thing is a mystery. I want to help her, I really do, but I don't know how. I simply don't know how and I feel I should know how."

"Why? Why should you know how?" His voice sounded sympathetic.

Annie grimaced and shrugged her shoulders. "Well, because I'm a vicar, you know, pastoral care and all that. If I'm going to lead a church, I should be of use to people in the parish who are disturbed."

Matthew rose from his chair, went to a small table set back away from the fireplace, and came back with a very well worn Bible. Annie was surprised. In her short experience of him she somehow didn't think he read the Bible much. He hadn't been in church the past two Sundays either, but then he had been in Italy, she reminded herself. He leafed through the gospels until he came to John, Chapter 5 and began to read. He had a deep baritone voice and when he read the Scriptures, Annie felt a frisson of excitement.

"There was a man by the pool of Bethesda, who had lain there for thirty-eight years. Jesus said to him, 'Do you want to be healed?' He closed the Bible and looked at her expectantly, silently.

She nodded her head, once more staring at the fire. "Yes, that's it I suppose. I can't help her if she doesn't want to be helped. So what's your advice? Do you have any for me?

Matthew leaned forward, his arms resting on his knees. "I would just let her be. Everyone else has probably been nagging her to talk for a long time. Just let her live with you, let her know what food is available, maybe ask her to do a little housework for you, take care of those three stroppy dogs, and see what happens. Does that sound like sound advice?" He smiled, showing his chalk-white, symmetrical teeth.

Film stars would pay a fortune for such a smile, she thought, as the answered, "Thank you, Matthew. I just needed someone I could trust to talk to. You won't tell anyone else what we talked about, will you?"

He smiled again. "Of course not. I'm not one of the village telegraph recipients or participants. You can always safely talk to me. I hope you know that."

Annie stood up.

"Are you going?" Matthew asked.

His voice sounded alarmed. She shook her head. "Thanks for your time, but I really must be going." She began walking toward the foyer where her coat hung on one of the wooden pegs.

Matthew followed her, took down her coat and scarf and helped her into it.

"Bye," she said, holding out her mittened hand. She looked him full in the face for the first time that evening, met his eyes, and immediately looked away. "And thanks," she mumbled.

Chapter Five

Matthew stood in the open doorway, watching her walk away in the cold, feeling very bleak He wondered why she wouldn't look at him. He had never before had a problem with her actions; it was his that gave him a problem. Two weeks had passed since he last saw her, two weeks since he had made any contact at all. And it had helped. He did think of her now and then, but found he wasn't as preoccupied with thoughts of her as he had been before and he had congratulated himself on his strategy, what he thought of as his self-preservation strategy. He thought of Amanda more as a consequence and felt sure this was the proper way to go. Yet when Annie phoned tonight and he heard the urgency in her voice, he could tell she desperately needed someone to talk to. He couldn't have turned her down, could he? At least that's what he told himself. Maybe she isn't interested in me at all—I'm sure she's not. But I did think she liked me, enjoyed our evening together, but maybe that's just hubris. Maybe it's just because she doesn't know anyone else here, that must be it.

Meanwhile, back at the vicarage, the minute Annie walked out the door, Julie turned off the television and went upstairs to Annie's study. She turned on the computer and began looking into the files. She couldn't go on the internet without Annie's password, but all her files were available and she browsed through them. Most looked pretty boring. Theological data, church organizations, sermons Annie had written. She clicked on Sermons, curious to know what Annie was saying in church. Julie hadn't gone to a church service. She shook her head vehemently from side to side when Annie invited her.

Her curiosity about Annie was growing, near to

becoming an obsession. The problem was that Annie wasn't out of the house often enough, but when she did leave, Julie felt she could be herself; she could quit pretending and snoop around. She had been through all of Annie's drawers, though these were a disappointment. Annie didn't have many clothes and what was there was nothing spectacular. She always seemed to have her diary with her, so Julie hadn't been able to look into that. When the phone rang, which happened often, Julie wouldn't answer, but always listened intently to the messages. She didn't intend to tell Annie anything about herself, but she certainly wanted to know everything she could about Annie.

Why is she doing this, Julie wondered. *Why is she putting up with me? What's her motive?* She was sure Annie wanted to convert her. All clergy had that goal with everyone they met, didn't they? She knew in a vague sort of way that she was testing Annie, that she was seeing how far she could push her, wanting to see what would make her break that niceness which she invariably showed. Julie thought Annie must be pretending; she couldn't really be that good. She had seen her reading the Bible every morning and sometimes asked Julie to give her time to be alone for prayer. At those times, she shut the door to her study. She seemed to be in there an inordinate amount of time and Julie wondered what she was doing, surely not praying for that long.

There were two reasons Julie snooped. One, she was sure she could catch Annie in something that would prove she wasn't as good a person as she tried to portray. She was sure she would find some drug paraphernalia somewhere or erotic magazines, or at the very least, cigarettes. There were no spirits in the house, only a bottle of sherry. Sherry! Julie felt indignant when she saw that was all there was, not even a can of lager in the fridge. So far, however, she hadn't been able to find any 'dirt' on her benefactor. She was very disappointed.

The second reason she snooped was because she felt utterly empty inside, like a hollow person. She needed to fill herself up with other people's lives, else there wouldn't be any-

thing there at all. She heard Annie's key turning in the lock.
She shut down the computer hurriedly and just managed to leap into the bathroom before the heard Annie say, "I'm home, Julie." She flushed the toilet even though there was nothing to flush, and after a minute came out and went into her room. She had thought her benefactor would be out all evening. She wished she was home alone more. She didn't like having to share the house with Annie.

Annie came upstairs and seeing Julie's bedroom door shut, sighed and shrugged her shoulders. *Guess she didn't miss me.* She let the dogs out for a last time before bed and made herself a cup of tea whilst she waited. Her mood was a minus ten on a scale of 10-0-10. The dogs came back in, wet and muddy. She wiped each of their paws on an old towel she kept near the kitchen door for the purpose and left them penned in the kitchen to dry out. She would let them upstairs when she went to bed. At least *they're* glad to see me, she thought.

Her only comfort at times like these was her friendship with Emily, her confidante, her best friend. She turned on the computer and looking at the desk, had a niggling feeling that something was out of place, but then she wasn't most organized person in the world, so she shrugged off the thought and sipped her tea as she wrote.

Dear Em: Another bad session with Matthew. He seemed so nice at the beginning of the evening, he kissed me on both cheeks in greeting me. you know, continental fashion, oh, Em, it was heaven! But then I just couldn't look at him. I was so flustered that I just avoided his eyes and sat there looking at the fire and then everything went sour again. We don't seem to be in sync – when he's nice to me, I'm not nice to him and vice versa. And Julie – she's becoming the bane of my existence— that's why I went over to talk to him. I was at my wit's end. There is something very strange about her and so now instead of living in this big house all alone, I have three dogs sleeping in my bedroom and this almost mute girl hanging about the house. If I had raised her it might be different. I feel like a parent with a teenage daughter going through angst! My life is sure going pear shaped. Glad you're experiencing joy and normality – whatever that is. Write a lot, please. Love, Annie

After Annie left, Matthew sat in front of the fire for a long while, staring at the fire. Although he hadn't thought he would miss the dogs, he did. At least they were some company and now the house seemed very silent. He missed Amanda with every bone in his body. Her picture was in a frame on the table beside the fire; he had caught Annie glancing at it. Reading a passage outloud from Amanda's Bible had brought on a shaft of sorrow that he hoped he hadn't conveyed to Annie.

How cruel God was to have taken her away. She was his happiness, his love, his life. She had so much promise, everyone loved her and he had fallen in love with her at first sight. There were many times when he thought he heard her voice. He knew it was just his memories and his longing for her, but he could remember exactly how she sounded and he especially remembered her laugh…

"Matthew?" Amanda laughed, "What are you doing? You've got paint all over you!"

It was true, he looked down to see peach colored paint splotched on his overalls, his hands, and glancing in the hall mirror, even his face. They were painting this living room before they moved in. It was the color Amanda said she had always wanted for the living area of a thatched roof cottage.

"Here, let me wipe some off," she said, coming close to him and wiping his face with a cloth. But before she could do that, he put his paint brush down and drew her close to him, kissing her, at first just tenderly and then more seriously, feeling that rush of warmth he felt whenever he once more realized how very much he loved her.

They were married for a year when they found this house. He had his doubts about living so far from his work, but Amanda asked if they could try it. "If you don't like the commute, if you're not happy here, then I'll move closer to London. But, Matthew, this is the house I've always dreamt of. Can we have it—please?" Of course she could have it. He couldn't, wouldn't deny her anything.

What would she think of him spending time with the new vicar in the village? What would she think of him, her husband who adored her, dallying with someone new? Come on, Matthew, you're not exactly dallying, he told himself. You've taken her to dinner once and she's come over to your house once, very briefly. This time it was his voice, not Amanda's he heard. That's not the point. You're very attracted to her, aren't you? Wife not dead much over a year, and here you are, trying to replace her. Am I trying to replace her? I don't think so. She isn't replaceable. What we had was so special it could never be duplicated.

Amanda had a deep faith. She prayed every morning, read the Bible, and spent what she called a quiet time with God. He didn't have the kind of faith that Amanda had, but he went to church with her and tried. He knew she wished he had been more excited about the prospect of having a relationship with God, as she put it. He wasn't against it, it just hadn't happened to him. And now, where was God when he needed him? If God was, is, in control of the earth, why would he let someone who was so good and kind leave this earth so soon? Before she had children, grandchildren? Amanda was a budding artist and Matthew had encouraged her in her art. He was certain she would be well known for her watercolors some day. That was another constant reminder for him of her presence, her framed pictures hung on nearly every wall in the house.

I must move away from this house and from Annie, he told himself. In new surroundings, he wouldn't see Amanda in every room. He would be away from the dogs and the temptation to use them as an excuse to drop in on Annie. And, he admitted, he wouldn't be facing this guilt because he wouldn't have anything to do with Annie. He made a decision before he went to bed that night. He would put the house up for sale the next day. He would move away and that would be that. He expected to feel better after having made that decision, but he didn't. Rather, he felt just as dismal as when Annie left.

Meanwhile, the village was busy. There are many things that keep one busy in the village. There is the Women's Institute for the women and the pub for the men. Meetings to plan the church fete, choir practice, the men's bowls team, the cricket team, and gardening. This was the busyness that went on if one was retired. These people were the ones who had time to talk and for now, the main topic of conversation was the new vicar.

It was Saturday morning and the entire village seemed to be outside. Though the sun was shining diamond bright, the wind had not gone away and it was still chilly. Bulbs had sprung through the ground and the branches of the apple and cherry trees were beginning to show a hint of green. People were walking their dogs, visiting the shop, tending to their gardening. The telegraph system was in full operation.

"Did you know the new vicar was at Matthew's house last night?"

"No, really? What about?"

"Dunno. But it was late and she went right in. I don't think that's proper, do you? A young, single woman calling on a single man. A widower. At night. . ."

"Did she stay long?" The voice had a tinge of horror, yet of expectation.

"Well, long enough—if you get my meaning." The arched eyebrow of the male speaker and the smirk spoke worlds.

The woman he had talked to went right over to her neighbor's house. "Did you hear?"

And so the telegraph system buzzed through the village until by noon, Annie had certainly stayed there most of the night. What were they to do? This was a scandal of greater proportions than had ever occurred before, even greater than the previous vicar becoming depressed. No one knew why he was depressed, but the consensus was he must have done something wrong, something he felt guilty about—else why would he be depressed?

And what about this strange girl who lived with the vicar? She was indeed very strange, would hardly speak to anyone. Rumors had even begun in some circles about Annie's sexuality. Well, now that one was laid to rest, at least. She must like men, unless she liked both, of course. Giggles.

So the rumor grew and spread like the proverbial wildfire through the village. It was definite that Annie spent the night at Matthew's house. There was a good deal of shaking of heads and tut-tutting. "These new females in the church—I told you we didn't want someone who was that young, and she's pretty to boot. It was asking for trouble. And Matthew, barely a year since Amanda died and he's vulnerable, that's what. She tempted him—that's what happened. So what are we gonna do? We've got to get rid of her; can't have those kinds of go-ins-on in the village, can we?"

Until the rumors got to Joy, that is. Where they stopped short as if they had hit a virtual cement wall. She was ragingly indignant. Having lived in the village for so many years, Joy knew the harm the gossip could do. "I don't believe a word of it," she exclaimed to her neighbor, Mrs. Clarity. "Not a single word. So what if she went to his house? How does anyone know why or what they talked about? And I can guarantee that she did not spend the night. I will swear to that on the Bible." However, it worried her. She couldn't get the words she had heard out of her mind. Finally, she decided she must go see Annie. She must get at the truth and must let her know what was happening. She phoned first, rather than dropping in as so many of the church members did.

Annie asked if she could come over there instead. "It'll do me good to get out of the house," she said, feeling bleak about Julie, about her sermon, and as always, about Matthew.

She yelled up the stairs to Julie's room, telling her she was going out for a while. Then disappointing the dogs because they weren't invited, she stepped out into the bright sunshine. This village is so beautiful, she thought, looking at the gently sloping hills of green, brilliant in the sunshine of early spring. The gardens were neat and tidy and she was sure would be resplendent in summer when all the flowers were in bloom.

However, tomorrow was Sunday, and she wasn't yet satisfied with her sermon. I must learn to shut problems out and concentrate on my sermon, she told herself, as she walked the short distance to Joys'. *I no longer have the luxury of long hours by myself, uninterrupted in my flat, having arranged the time with Em. This is the real world, Annie—and you must adjust.* She longed for the days which now seemed idyllic at Cambridge. No good looking man intruded on her thoughts, no troubled boarder who didn't help at all with the housework as Annie had anticipated, no meddlesome parishioners like Horace, popping in at all hours. Oh, God, she said, looking up at the blue sky, *I am such a wimp! I could be in a refugee camp, with no food to feed my children, and I'm complaining! Sorry....*

Two women passed as she walked and only nodded briefly, barely saying hello. Annie shook her head and knocked on Joy's door. Joy welcomed her and gave her a warm hug. Annie was grateful for this motherly woman. Whilst she didn't feel as free to speak to her as she did Matthew, at least there was no tension between them. Joy had tea prepared and after settling in one of the large, overstuffed armchairs, Annie asked, "It seems there was something you wanted to speak to me about?"

Joy put down her teacup. "There is no other way to do this except to plunge in, Annie, she began, "you know that villages can be places where people gossip."

Annie's heart sank. What was coming? More trouble? "Yes..," she answered tentatively.

"Well, there's talk about you and Matthew. And I just wanted to warn you, to let you know that it's happening so you will be armed."

"What are they saying?" Annie asked. She had put down her teacup and was leaning forward.

"Well, evidently you went to see him last night after dark?"

"Yes, I did, but only for a very short while. I couldn't have been there much more than half an hour. Is that not allowed?"

"Of course it is allowed," Joy began, "but you see, the rumors have grown. It is now being bandied about that you spent the night with him. Might as well tell you the truth, I know you didn't and I told everyone so, but evidently, the talk is continuing and you need to combat it."

"Spent the night! I've never done such a thing in my life! I've never spent the night with any man—oh, Joy—how cruel! I was only there a short while. Is someone trying to get at me, to destroy me? What is going on?"

"I don't know, Annie. It's next to impossible once these rumors begin to find out where they started, but I do know that they grow and grow. It's one of the prices you pay for the lack of anonymity in a village."

Annie's heart was racing. "I went over there because I was so upset about Julie and I've found Matthew easy to talk to." She didn't think she could confide to Joy that she was drawn to Matthew, to his looks, and to his touch. Only Emily would understand that. "I didn't stay long at all." She stared at Joy, who looked nothing but sympathetic. "What should I do?" Annie asked, the anger hitting her stomach like bullets.

Joy was silent for a moment and then said, "You have to hit this straight on. It's the only way. You will have to address it in the pulpit."

From the pulpit....she hadn't even become established yet, she hadn't even given a good sermon as far as she was concerned, and now Joy was telling her to talk about this gossip from the pulpit? "But aren't a lot of people who gossip like this non-church goers?" she protested. "How would I reach them?"

Joy shook her head as she said, "Well, my dear, you still

don't understand the village. Every single thing you say will be known by the beginning of Sunday lunch. You may as well go on television." She smiled ironically, "Everyone will know."

Annie's first instinct was to flee, to leave this cursed village where nothing had gone right so far. She slumped back in the overstuffed chair, willing back tears. "I've never dealt with anything like this! What do I say? Joy, this is awful. And poor Matthew, does he know people are saying these things about us?"

"I don't know. I doubt it, but since he's selling his house...."

"Selling his house!" Annie interrupted. "How—when did that happen? He didn't tell me he was selling his house." She was aware that the anguish showed on her face. Matthew was leaving. she would never see him again.

"The estate agents sign went up this morning. I don't know when he decided to do it. I've always thought he would sell up some day and move back to London. This village was Amanda's place and I'm sure now that you have the dogs, he.."

"But the dogs aren't mine!" Annie interrupted, her voice rising to a pitch. "They were a trial; he didn't say he was going to abandon them." She hung her head and cradled her face in her hands. Then, looking up at Joy, she said in a calmer voice, "But I must admit, he doesn't seem very interested in them, he hasn't seen them once since I took them two weeks ago." She was silent for a moment, looking out the window at the bare trees, beginning to sway again from a wind that promised a soon coming storm. The sunshine had disappeared behind menacing dark clouds. "Oh, Joy, I don't know what to do. First, there was an obvious resistance to me coming here as vicar, because I'm a woman and because I'm young. And then Julie came. I didn't see how I could say no and I thought maybe she would be a companion and maybe I could help her, but instead, she's a burden." She looked up at Joy, who seemed to loom over her even though she was sitting perfectly calm in her large overstuffed chair. "Please don't tell anyone what I've said about her, will you? I don't want people in the village to talk about her as well as me."

Joy assured her that everything they said was always confidential, adding "You badly need a friend here, I know that. And I want you to know I will always be that friend. You can phone me or come here anytime you like—I'm hardly ever not at home. All right?"

At this, the tears came. Annie didn't even know they were there—they just came tumbling out of her eyes as the anger she had been feeling melded into self-pity. She was grateful, immensely grateful, for Joy's friendship, but she longed for Emily and for her father. They had been her two pillars. Emily for confidences she never would have shared with her father and him as a spiritual mentor. Not that Emily wasn't spiritual, but she was on the same level spiritually as herself. She realized she needed to go back to the vicarage, call her father, and email Emily. She stood up, wiped her eyes with the tissue Joy handed her, gave her a swift hug, and without saying anything other than thank you, left. She saw no one on the short walk back home, but now wondered who was peering at her out of the windows.

Turning the key in the lock, she was struck by the silence. There was no incessant television noise and no greeting from the dogs. Seeing the leads missing from their peg in the kitchen, she was thankful. Julie must have taken them on a walk.

Her father wasn't home. She chatted as best she could with her mother, but this wasn't the type of thing she could discuss with her. Her mum was a simple woman, one who had not wanted a career of her own and had had deep misgivings about Annie becoming a clergyperson. She didn't approve of women standing in the pulpit and Annie's lack of domesticity seemed a great pity to her, as she often told her daughter. No, she wasn't someone Annie could identify with; she never had been. She left word for her father to phone back. So it was just Emily. She wrote all about it to her and Emily replied in half an hour.

Dear Annie: What a mess! I so wish I were there to give you a big hug and talk until the wee hours of the night. Your friend Joy is right—this must be nipped in the proverbial bud—but what a frightening thing to do – especially when you don't feel entirely accepted by the church as yet. I tell you, there are a lot of things wrong with the States and I often long for the sanity of Cambridge and England where there are no guns, but at least I've had no problem being accepted. When you have what you're going to say written, run it by me first, okay? I will be praying for you, my friend, as always, only much more. Lots of love, Em

Chapter Six

When Annie left that morning, Julie turned off the television, snooped around Annie's things for awhile, but finding nothing new or of interest, went into her own room. From her window she could see the fields painted lush green and beige. There were no buildings interrupting or marring the landscape. Julie grew up in a city and other than a few school outings, had never known anything of the country, of fields, of open spaces. She always felt restless, but today, she felt she would burst if she didn't do something. The inertia was bubbling up and threatened to spill over. This was a sign she recognized in herself and it frightened her. She determined to take the dogs for a walk.

She laughed as she attached leads to all three dogs, a feat in itself since their joy at seeing the leads made them all leap about and onto her. No one was there to hear her laugh. She left by the front door with them yapping and straining. She was strong and could contain them, but wondered how Annie could handle them since she was so tiny.

There were times when Julie felt different and this was one of those times. Once they were clear of the village, out into the countryside, she let the dogs off their leads. As they ran free, she began to run after them and with them. Her laughter revealed her delight and since no one was around to see her, she felt free, free to be herself—whoever that was. The animals accepted her, and because of that, she felt comfortable with them. After an hour, she led them back to the village, back to the house and through the back door. She wiped each of the dog's paws thoroughly, gave them some fresh water and a final pat on the head. She thought they were beginning to like her more than they liked Annie and that pleased her.

She plunked herself down in front of the television once

more, but since it was Saturday, her usual programs weren't on and she soon grew disinterested. Annie didn't have cable, so there were only the BBC stations plus one other. Annie was home, but seemed to be busy upstairs, so Julie went back into the kitchen with the dogs. She noticed her cereal bowl still on the kitchen table along with the crumbs from her toast and marmalade. She cleared the table, washed her bowl as well as Annie's, wiped down the table and the counters and felt a sense of accomplishment. Sometimes she did this at one of her foster homes without being asked and had always hoped she would get some praise for it, but it never came. Then she went into the living room where the sunshine was pouring through the windows revealing a thin layer of dust on all the furniture. She poked around in the closet, found a duster and began to dust the tables and bookcases. Next she swept and mopped the kitchen floor and took everything out of the fridge and wiped it down thoroughly. She was sitting on the sofa with Tibby on her lap and the other two curled up at her feet when Annie came downstairs. Julie looked up with a timid smile.

But Annie didn't go into the kitchen where she might have noticed all the work Julie had done. She didn't seem to notice that the dust was gone from the furniture and she didn't smile back at her. Oh, well, it wasn't any use. Annie looked sad, but then what on earth could she be sad about. She had a house of her own and three dogs and a job. Julie turned on the television again.

Sunday morning the church was packed; it seemed as though no one stayed home. For Annie, it came sooner than she would have liked. She had stayed up the night before until she had completed an entirely different sermon from the one she had prepared earlier in the week. As she wrote, her despair turned to anger and she slept very little when she finally went to bed at three.. With a tremulous voice, she began the sermon:

"The text this morning is from the Gospel of John, Chapter 8, verses 1-11." She paused, wondering if her choice of passages shocked them, at least those who had been gossiping and those who knew their Bible well enough to know to what she was referring. Praying that tears wouldn't even come into her eyes, not looking up, not looking at the congregation, she began:

"I want you to imagine being there, on that dusty, Palestinian street when Jesus saw a crowd gathered round, a crowd of men. They were shouting terrible things at someone, He couldn't see who it was for the density of the crowd, at least he couldn't see with human eyes. Before he reached them, he knew who was at the center of their abusive attention. He knew it was a woman, a woman whom they were accusing of adultery. I want you to imagine being there." At this point, she looked up briefly, timidly. She certainly had their attention.

"Take on a role of one of the crowd or be the woman in your imagination. If you decide to be the woman, how would you feel? Think about lying on the ground, being spat at by a group of angry men, knowing that they were probably going to stone you to death, all because you had succumbed to the invitations of someone whom you couldn't resist. Suppose you were married, had been married at age 14 in an arranged marriage. Suppose your wedding day was the first time you saw your husband and suppose he was much older than you, not nice to look at, and even less nice to live with. Suppose he regularly beat you and openly humiliated you in front of others—suppose he often didn't return home at night, having spent his time in a brothel. Think about that woman's life and what it could have been like. And then suppose that five or six years later, a young man, someone close to your age, started paying attention to you, told you that you were beautiful, told you he was in love with you. Of course it would be wrong to succumb to his temptations. And you didn't. You resisted for two years. But he was relentless; he secretly brought you little presents, he told you to run away with him, that he would give you a whole new life. Suppose he whispered flatteries into your starved ear, starved for affection, starved for positive attention. And suppose that once you were caught off guard, alone at home, and he kissed you."

Annie thought she could hear quiet murmuring.

"You couldn't forget how soft his lips felt on yours and you thought about him all day long. Your husband noticed that you had changed—you didn't seem so subservient—you weren't as afraid of him as you used to be. So he began beating you more, to get you back in shape, to make you cower before him. Suppose you cried yourself to sleep every night, yearning for the handsome man you had fallen in love with. And just suppose that one day, when you knew your husband was going to be late coming home, you said yes. Just once, you said yes. And your lover showered you with the kind of kisses and caresses that you had never before experienced. It was bliss—the height of happiness."

Not waiting for more reaction, Annie hurried on. "Then your husband appeared. He had not gone to another village as he had said. No, he was here, waiting, watching, all the time. And he brought a crowd of men to the house, quietly, so as to catch you in the very act."

It seemed as if no one in the congregation was breathing, the silence was as real as a deafening noise. Annie was reading her sermon, something she tried never to do. But at this point in the sermon, she didn't dare look up at the faces in the congregation. She knew she must just get through to the end. And she also knew that it might be the end of her in this pulpit.

"What if you had been dragged out of the house by your hair and by your cloak, to end up lying in the street for all to see? And your lover, where was he? Not in sight—he had fled. How would you feel lying there? Betrayed? Yes, of course. Afraid? Terrified is more like it. Repentant? That is the question for you to decide."

There was no one in the congregation who wasn't paying full attention. Metaphorically, they were holding their breath and at the same time, had open mouths. They couldn't believe what they were hearing.

"Then that man, Jesus, stepped into the circle. He looked

down on you compassionately. The men became silent. They quit menacing you—their attention was full on the man who stood before them with such a charismatic presence. You were sobbing and continued to lie there with your face hidden."

Annie paused. There were no tears, anger was in full domination and her voice grew stronger as she continued. "'If any of you are without sin, let him be the first to cast a stone at her' he said. He stooped down and wrote on the ground. If you had been one of those men, would you have cast a stone? Or would you have realized, understood the hypocrisy, and been one of the first to walk away? The text says that the older ones walked away first; they had had more time to sin, I gather. Finally, Jesus was the only one left. He quit writing on the ground and looking into her eyes with compassion, asked, 'Woman, where are they? Has no one condemned you?' 'No one, sir,' she said. 'Then neither do I condemn you,' Jesus declared. 'Go now and sin no more.'

That's all the text tells us. And this story isn't even in the most ancient manuscripts of John's Gospel. It was likely passed on through an oral tradition from its early days. Many third-century Christian writers refer to it. Later it was included in a sixth century manuscript of the Gospel of John. The story was added to the Latin translation and later versions because it was judged to be a true story and it was consistent with Jesus' compassionate nature."

The congregation was hushed, as silent as fifty people in a small room can be, except for here and there a nervous movement, a shifting in the seat. What was this? Was she admitting to adultery? Well, it wouldn't be adultery, would it—not with her being single and Matthew as well. But it was, you know—that long word that began with an f, fornication—unmarried sex. The worst kind. And none of them had ever had unmarried sex—had they?

Annie paused, looked down at her text, sure she knew what was going on in their minds. Then she began again and this time she looked up. She quit reading. One by one, she looked each person in the congregation in the eye.

"But what if the crowd got it wrong? What if there was only circumstantial evidence—what if they only saw the man go into her house and didn't see anything else? What if it just 'looked like' that is what happened? What if you were that woman and what if you had been wrongly accused? How would you feel? What would you do? Who should be forgiven in that case—the woman, the man, or the people who were willing to stone her? Words can kill. Jesus talked a lot about slander and how he would judge it. I ask you again, who is in need of forgiveness in that case?"

With that, she sat down. The organ began playing the next hymn. She was shaking, but there were no tears. She was very proud of herself and silently thanked God for helping her through it.

When the service was over, Joy was the first to Annie. She hugged her and didn't say a word. The rest of the congregation walked out in silence. Only a few who obviously hadn't heard the gossip acted normal; others seemed to avoid her glance and the church was cleared quickly. When everyone was gone, Joy remained.

"Atta girl," she said. "You were truly magnificent. I am very, very proud of you."

"What do you think is going to happen?" Annie asked. "Do you think this will only cause more gossip?"

"No, I think that one by one, they will realize what they've done, but don't expect them to come and ask for your forgiveness, that would be admitting that they were one of the gossipers. But they won't soon forget this sermon, my girl. You have the makings of a great preacher—do you realize that?"

Annie was taking off her robe. "Thanks, it's always been my weakest point, and since I've been here, I've had even more problems with my sermons. They've been pretty lackluster, I'm afraid."

"Until today," Joy gave a little laugh, "the Sunday

lunches around here will be interesting. Would you want to come to my house, you and Julie today?"

Annie was grateful but declined. "No, I think I'm going to go see my parents. Monday is my day off and Julie can take care of the dogs. I feel like getting in the car and driving fast, like I can't stay here another minute. Do you understand?"

Joy nodded. "Good, I just didn't want you to be alone."

Fat chance of that, Annie thought. With Julie there, I'm never alone. Matthew wasn't in the congregation that morning, for which she was glad. Maybe he didn't know about any of this; she hoped he didn't.

Going to see her parents meant driving to Luton Airport to fly to Belfast. These days the cheap airlines were the least expensive and certainly the fastest way to go. Annie, as she had told Joy, wanted to be alone in her car and drive, so she was glad that it was almost an hour to the airport. The problem was that since her car was an ancient Morris Minor, driving fast meant sixty miles per hour, its absolute limit. She felt better as soon as she was clear of the village. She had phoned home to let them know she was coming. She felt she had to talk to her father and it had to be in person.

Annie was going through a dark night of the soul such as she had never experienced. Thinking back over the past few months, she felt terribly gloomy about her prospects for the future. What had gone wrong? Would anyone else have handled situations differently than she had? She wondered, not for the first time, if the previous vicar had been driven into depression by the personalities, almost the 'forces' in that village. And was that place different than others? Was it a village problem? She didn't know, but she had never felt such a failure.

She knew she would have to tell her father about Matthew, else he wouldn't have the full picture. That was no problem. She had always been able to confide in him, chiefly because he was not judgmental, as was her mother. Her mother would say that a good-looking, young, recent widower was dangerous and that she should have known better.

Known better! I haven't done a thing, nor has he, she ruminated, pushing down hard on the accelerator. *Except offered his friendship, which I thought I could accept, but then I wanted more and was terrified of showing it when it became obvious to me that he really only thought of me as a friend.*

Annie talked to herself and to Emily in her thoughts on the drive up the A414. The countryside was beginning to awaken from its winter sleep. Buds were appearing on some of the trees and the daffodils were blooming here and there, rather tentatively. There was less and less snow in Britain these past years. Global warming had taken hold and instead of snow there was more rain, which caused local flooding and brought chaos to some villages. Cambersham was not in a valley, thus hadn't suffered from that problem. So whilst it wasn't as cold as Annie remembered growing up in Belfast, it was wetter. It seemed to her it had rained almost every day she had been in that cursed village.

She didn't swear, not since she was a young teenager experimenting with a few words. Her father overheard her and admonished her so strongly that she didn't think the words were worth it, but she realized that this was one of those times when it might make one feel better to swear. Not to use God's name—she was too respectful for that.

She couldn't wait to go home. Home to the big city, where there was hustle and bustle, where when you left your house, no one saw you, or if they did, they could care less where you were going. She missed the anonymity of the city, she missed the intellectual conversations she used to have not only at home with her father and brothers, but with almost everyone she knew in Cambridge, at university and theological college. Yes, she thought, it will be good to get home.

The village was all abuzz after Annie's sermon. Every single person in the village heard about it because that was simply all that was talked about. This was certainly some new kind of vicar. She told it like it was. She had gone on the offensive and everyone knew that was the best kind of defense. The effect of the sermon on the women could be summed up as identification. They sympathized with the unnamed woman in the story, and projected that sympathy on to Annie. No doubt she had been wrongly accused. Even if they had been the ones who had gleefully spread the rumors, they were now the first ones to spread the news of the sermon. To hear them, one would have thought they had believed in Annie all along. The men came at it from a different angle. They liked the fighting spirit they saw in Annie—she had some spunk, she was a fighter, and they admired that. It was as if some force outside the village had spread the rumors in the first place and now they were out to defend their vicar.

What her sermon had not accomplished was a sense of shame in those who had been so quick to tear her down. A sense of shame had been there for an instant as she began the sermon. It had hit a few people in the region of their heart, a little stab of guilt, but it evaporated in the mist of the talk afterward. The rationalization process began and to hear them talk, each of them was the only one who had said all along that Annie wouldn't do such a thing.

Of course, there never had been any condemnation of Matthew. It was a little soon, but men will be men, after all. How could he resist the temptation? The men had been jealous of him before, now he didn't enter into the discussion at all.

As everyone noticed, Matthew had not been in church. He had gone to see Amanda's parents. He thought it would do him good to be with them, to reconnect. Just what I need to keep me from straying off with the first pretty woman I see, he reasoned. Amanda's parents had not coped well with their daughter's sudden death. What is coping well, after all? It isn't natural for any of your children to die first, before you do, and Amanda's mother had spoken to her on the phone every day. They had an especially close relationship, with the result that when Matthew visited, all they talked about was Amanda. Matthew didn't know if this made him feel better or worse, but he did know it was nice to have someone with whom he wasn't always wondering if he should quit mentioning her, if he was dwelling on her too much.

What would they think if I married someone else? he wondered. *For heaven's sake—I'm not thinking of marrying her—I'm just attracted to her, that's all.* But the idea had come into his head, came into his head when he was with her parents and they spoke of his loss of a wife; they spoke as if he was to be alone the rest of his life. He told them about the dogs and didn't know if they really understood. They couldn't have taken them on, as they both suffered from various illnesses and he knew the three dogs would be too much for them, but he sensed disapproval. After that reaction, he decided not to tell them he had put the house up for sale. One step at a time.

On Sunday morning, church wasn't mentioned, so Matthew didn't go either. They never had been churchgoers. It was Amanda who became interested in religion when she and Matthew moved to the village. He often wondered if she had a premonition, knew she was going to go to heaven at a young age. He didn't know, but it was a change for her. When he questioned her about it, she said she had always been seeking and hadn't been sure what it was she was seeking. He asked her if she had found it and she had replied that she thought she was in the process of finding it.

There were photos of Amanda everywhere in her parent's house. Pictures of her as a baby, pictures of her when she was four with her first puppy, pictures of her in her school uniform, on and on—each stage of her life was framed and filled several table tops. Then the picture of him and Amanda on their wedding day, laughing, smiling at each other. What a hopeful day that had been! She wore a white flowing dress, a white misty veil, looking more beautiful than he had ever seen her. They were to live a very long life together, like her parents, like everyone expected to.

When he left their flat after Sunday dinner, he decided it made him feel worse to be there. All the pictures, all the talk. They didn't seem to have moved on at all. Not that they should, he told himself. After all, it was different, losing a child. Amanda had been their child, grown up as she was. He had gone there hoping that it would make him stop thinking about Annie. Instead, he thought about her the entire time, which made him feel even guiltier. I tried to run away, and it didn't work, he told himself. Now what? *If I move into London, I won't ever see Annie, will I? And how will that make me feel? Am I in love?* It certainly felt like it; he knew the feeling. He was thoroughly miserable.

When Annie drove away, Julie was elated. She was to have two entire days and nights alone. All that time to snoop, to try once again to get into Annie's private things. She didn't feel particularly guilty about this; she assumed anyone would do that to anyone. It was part of not having one's own identity, being so intensely interested in someone else's life. She looked through Annie's lingerie drawer, places someone might hide a dirty magazine, but there was nothing. It wasn't that Julie wanted to find something, not really. It was just that she expected to find something. Annie couldn't be as perfect as she seemed on the outside. This was a complete mystery to her. Annie never appeared to get angry with her or even annoyed—she always smiled and tried to talk to her. She read a lot of religious type books and seemed to endlessly read the Bible. Julie had not been able to find anything that was different from the image Annie portrayed. She explained this to herself by thinking she just hadn't found anything yet.

That night, lying in bed, Julie thought she heard a noise. It sounded as if it came from the attic. She had coaxed the dogs into her room for the night and just as Annie did, had Tibby up on the bed with her. She lay there rigid, listening. The light was already on—she never slept with the light off. There was a slight breeze outside, maybe it was something brushing up against the house, a tree branch. But no, it sounded as if it was right over her head. She didn't dare move. She hugged Tibby tighter to herself, waking him up, and he began licking her face, thinking she wanted to play. She began to pet him, trying to calm him down, trying to calm herself down. There was no telephone in her room. Annie had left Joy's number by the phone downstairs and told her to call Joy if she needed anything, but there was no way she was going to walk downstairs.

Big tears began rolling down her cheeks. Tears of fright, tears of self-pity, tears of loneliness. Why? Why wasn't she like ordinary people, people who seemed to be busy with their lives, who had a purpose, who had a family. She had gone from one foster care to another and never felt she belonged. Some were better than others, but now she was considered old enough to fend for herself. How? She didn't see how she could get a job when there were those periods of time she seemed to lose, periods where she would find herself in an entirely different setting.

She hadn't told Annie about this; she hadn't told Annie hardly anything. She had learned the hard way not to trust anyone. If you tell someone something about yourself, it will be used against you. Every time. So she had withdrawn deep within herself long ago and simply lived day-to-day, never knowing what the future held for her. There were times when she didn't want a future, when she wanted to go, to end her life of loneliness and misery, but she had never been able to figure out how to do that without pain and she was frightened of pain, she was far too familiar with it.

When she awoke, the sun was streaming in her window. She didn't know what time she fell asleep, but knew it must have been very late and her body ached from sleeping in such a tense position. The dogs wanted to be let out, jumping up, yelping at her. She laughed out loud;these dogs were like having a family of unruly kids. Putting on her robe and slippers, the dogs preceding her, she went downstairs to the kitchen and let them out. The house was cold. She turned up the thermostat and put the kettle on for a cup of tea. The newspaper had been put through the mail slot of the front door—she took it into the kitchen and sat there reading the front page whilst the kettle boiled. This is nice, she thought. She realized she had never been alone in a house before, not alone when she knew no one was coming back any minute. *It's as if this is my house.* Now that it was daylight, she was no longer frightened. She let the dogs back in as soon as they scratched on the back door and made some toast and jam. She had just finished dressing when the doorbell rang.

It was Horace. He had begun ringing the doorbell since Annie had instituted the before unheard of policy of locking her door. He wondered what she was hiding. No one in the village locked their door in the daytime, why, he remembered when no one locked it at night. What was the world coming to when the vicar, even if she was of the wrong sort, locked the door? He liked to just walk in, hollering 'I'm here' and standing in the front hall expectantly. If no one was home, or rather, if no one answered his yell, he wasn't above going on back to the kitchen, just to make sure.

Julie peeked out of the curtains in Annie's office from which she could see the front door. The dogs were barking furiously.

"Hello, I'm Horace" he greeted her. He had been very curious about this person who was living with the vicar. What was their relationship? You never could tell about these women vicars, a lot of them were lesbians, he'd heard. Maybe this was her 'girlfriend' he said to himself. Ever delighted to fuel his gossipy and scandalous mind he found himself excited.

The door was only open a crack. It didn't look like the girl was going to let him in. She hadn't said a word. "Is Annie in?" he asked.

"No, she's not—she's away," Julie answered.

"Oh, where did she go then?" he asked, wondering why

the vicar would go away without telling anyone. She probably wanted to get out of town after that sermon of hers and it had caused quite a stir; he had made sure the topic circulated to its full extent.

"She went to Belfast—she'll be back on Tuesday," Julie answered, making the gap of the door a bit thinner. Meanwhile, behind her, the dogs were setting up even more of a racket.

"So you're all alone here, eh?" he asked.

She didn't answer.

He stood there staring at her. Finally, he gave up. He wanted to come in and chat with this girl, wanted to know all about her, so he could have a scoop on others, be able to tell them something he knew that they didn't. This always made him feel powerful. But it was cold and she obviously wasn't inviting him in. "Well then, tell her I called," he said, reluctantly, still standing there staring.

Julie nodded and closed the door. She went into the kitchen, made herself another cup of tea, then went back into the sitting room, the dogs following her each step of the way. It was like having a little family—three who loved her. Wouldn't that be nice? She didn't have friends. How could she when she couldn't invite them home. It wasn't a proper home, was it? A foster home. Everyone in school knew it wasn't her real home. She was always embarrassed and angry. She was embarrassed around other children, other students as she grew older. And she was angry at the world, at God if there was a god, at fate. Her fate.

Why couldn't she have been born to ordinary parents? Parents who loved their children and took proper care of them? That wasn't so much to ask, was it? She knew there were other kids like herself, but she didn't know any. She was given the money to buy school uniforms by the council, so she dressed the same as others, but she didn't use proper language. She talked like her foster parents talked, an accent that set her apart from the girls whom she worshipped from afar, but treated terribly if they dared to approach her. She had learned early on that it was best not to get close to people. That way, she didn't get hurt.

The phone rang. "Hello, Julie. This is Annie. Is everything all right?"

"Yes," Julie nodded.

"Are the dogs okay?"

"Yes."

"Well, I was just making sure you're okay. You have the phone number here if you need anything—you will phone, won't you?"

"Yes."

"All right, I'll phone again Tomorrow just before I leave here. I should be home by mid-afternoon."

Silence.

"Bye," Annie said.

Julie slammed the phone down and immediately thought she shouldn't have.

Chapter Seven

Annie grimaced, as she hung up the phone in the kitchen.

"What's the matter?" asked her mother, who was doing the washing up.

"Oh, nothing, only I can't get Julie to talk to me. I want to help her, but she won't let me in—you know?"

"Well, if you ask me," her mother said, turning around from the sink, "and you haven't, it was a bit much to take in a stray girl when you've got so much else on your plate. You should have said no."

Annie nodded. "Yes, with hindsight, I can see you're probably right. But there I was with this big empty house; it seemed selfish not to let her stay. And I honestly thought she would be some sort of companion for me, but as it's turned out, she's only a companion for the dogs." She gave a wry smile, knowing as soon as she said it that this was simply an opening for another reprimand from her mother.

"And that's another thing, Annie—why did you agree to take on three dogs, for heaven's sake! Three dogs! The nerve of that man. He was simply taking advantage of you, probably because you're a woman. What nerve."

Annie always felt about ten years old in the presence of her mother. Her mother never seemed to understand her; she could only understand things from her point of view, which was pretty insular. For relief, she left the kitchen in search of her father. He was in his study, as usual. She envied him. He fixed himself a cup of tea when he awoke and went into his study for his morning reading and prayers. Everyone knew he was not to be disturbed during this time—it had always been so. If the phone rang, her mother answered it and took a message unless it happened to be an emergency. Then he dressed and went back into his study to clear up any unfinished business from the day before, answered telephone calls, etc. Then, he took his morning walk This walk, he told Annie when she was old enough to be interested, was his thinking time. It wasn't just for exercise. It was part of his meditative process, of his preparation of sermons. Then after a light lunch, fixed for him by his wife, of course, he once again retired to his study to work on his sermon for the next week, at least two hours a day. Again, his wife fielded phone calls for him during these sacrosanct hours.

Wouldn't that be nice, she thought, to have someone doing the housework, the meal preparation, and having someone answer the telephone? Maybe she wouldn't have so much trouble with her sermons if she was relieved of all her other duties. Maybe I should get myself a househusband, she thought wryly, as she tapped on her father's door.

"Come in," he said, in his pleasant, deep voice.

"Am I disturbing you?" Annie smiled at her father, a smile of deep affection. Timothy O'Donnell had a rich mane of snow-white hair and his eyes were exactly like hers, a saucy green. He had been a redhead in his younger days and was a large-boned man, not overweight, but broad. Annie inherited her small frame from her mother.

"Of course you're not disturbing me, my little one," he smiled back. "Come, sit. Let's have a good old natter. I want to know all about your parish, all the troubles and all the bright spots. And...I want to know how you are doing with our Lord."

Annie sat down in the easy chair opposite his. This was such a comfortable room; she had spent many hours here talking to her father. She knew she was very blessed to have a father like him. It wasn't that she idolized him, she didn't have him on a pedestal, but she thoroughly trusted him to be the good man that he seemed to be. He wasn't just good on Sunday preaching to the congregation, he was good all the time. Not good in terms of being so saintly that he wasn't fun. He was lots of fun, they roared with laughter in their house because of his wit, but he wasn't someone other than who he pretended to be. He was transparent.

"Well" Annie began, "there haven't been too many bright spots, I'm afraid."

"Tell me about those first—if there aren't too many then we'll dispense with them in a jiffy."

Annie thought for a moment. "There is Joy. She is aptly named, Dad. She has been wonderful to me, not intrusive, but warm and welcoming. And then there is Matthew, but he's been both a blessing and a source of trouble." She had told him the night before about the rumors and how she felt about Matthew as well.

"Yes, it's difficult. You know, if you were male, and there was a young widow in the village that was nice to you, paid attention to you, everyone would be delighted. They would be at their matchmaking at once and give you their entire blessing. But, unfairly, because you're female, there's the idea that you are doing something wrong. I'm afraid our society still has to evolve more before it gives true equality to women."

"And all of this has affected how I'm doing with the Lord," she said, looking down at her hands in her lap, playing with her fingernails. "I'm having trouble praying and God seems very far away lately. I'm really in trouble, Dad, and I don't know how to get out of it! I wish I'd never heard of this village. I think I belong in a city."

He was silent for a moment, looking at her. "One of your problems is that you look so young, You're twenty-six, but look sixteen, and it would be so much easier if you were a man with a booming voice. You probably would be happier in a city, after all, that's all you've ever known, but that doesn't mean that's where God wants you right now. I think he put you there for a reason, we just don't know the reason yet. Remember, Annie, he knows what he's doing, even when we don't. I've learned over the years that he's far more intelligent than I am," he smiled.

"Oh, I know that, Dad," picking up on his irony, "it's just that it's so hard. I don't feel welcome and I'm not doing a great job in the church. No one likes any of my ideas. They don't want to change anything at all, and my sermons haven't been very good—well, not unless you count the last one. And then there's Matthew. Oh, Dad, I think I'm in love with him! And now he's moving away and he doesn't seem to care a scrap for me. I've never felt this way before about anyone; you know how I went through boyfriends at a huge pace. They were just guys I liked, but liking is sure different than being in love!" she wailed.

He stood up and took her hand, drawing her up to him, enveloping her in his arms. He was so comforting, big and warm, like a friendly bear. When she was ready, she drew away, smiled, and sat back down.

"Well, he hasn't moved away yet, has he," her father asked rhetorically "and maybe something will happen that he won't. Or maybe he will and he will still see you—in the city, away from the prying eyes of the village. We don't know. All I know for sure is that if God wants the two of you to be together, he will make it happen. And if not, then he has someone even better in store for you."

She didn't feel very comforted by these words.

"When you were seventeen, right here in this room, you told me you wanted to study for the ministry, that you wanted to dedicate your life to God. Do you doubt that decision?"

Do I doubt? she asked herself. She knew her father wasn't challenging her, that he was asking that question in the most loving possible way. Maybe I am, maybe I'm not cut out for this. She felt as if she had been plunged into a deep pool of ice-cold water. The reality of the cold was much worse than anything she had dreamt of. It was one thing to be in theology college and listen to wonderful lecturers on the Bible and church history, to have debates with a real intellectual challenge. It was another to be thrown out into the world, with no one on your intellectual level to talk to, to a church where worshipping God seemed to be the very last thing anyone talked about. Rather, the next fete, the car boot sale, whether they should get rid of the pews and put in chairs, whether or not to buy a new organ—those things were what was talked about.

"There doesn't seem to be any love in that church or in that village. I don't know what it is. It's not a feeling of evil. It's apathy, indifference. It's like the church functions and the costs of the heating bill are what are important. I wonder if Jesus returned to earth and came in on Sunday morning if he would be welcome."

Her father's eyes twinkled. "Um, sounds like a good sermon topic."

"You're right, it would be. But I think I shook them up so this week, I'll have to downplay any theatrics for awhile."

"What do you mean, theatrics?"

"Well, my impression is that they want dull sermons, which is certainly what I've been giving them. Until last Sunday, I would have graded my sermons with a C-, but they seemed to like them. You know, the kind that don't say anything new, the kind you can sleep through. I don't think they want to be shook up."

The senior Rev. O'Donnell leaned forward, resting his elbows on his knees.

"All right, let's get to the heart of this. What is the worst thing that could happen if you did shake them up. What if every sermon was a ground shaker like your last one. And what if in the parish council meetings, you told them what you really think, that there is no love in that church, that their eye is way off the ball, that they aren't being Christians, in the New Testament sense, but custodians of a jointly owned building and a social group. What is the worst thing that could happen?"

Annie looked at him wide-eyed, "I'd be asked to leave I guess. That's the worst thing that could happen."

"And if you were asked to leave, what would you do next?"

"I don't know, probably try to get a position in a city, but that would be a black mark on my record. And I would feel like a failure."

"Would you? Or would you feel like a failure if you don't shake them up. It seems to me that you can't win in this situation if you buckle under to their criticism, their gossiping, their lackluster Christianity. That would be failing. But my question to you is—are you strong enough? Can you stand up to them?"

Annie sat silently for a while, looking past her father through the window out into her mother's garden, looking rather sad now at the end of winter. The trees were still bare here in this more northern area and stark against a grey sky. But spring was just around the corner—there was hope that soon the world would be bursting again with life. "I don't know if I'm strong enough, Dad. I guess time will tell."

"Annie, you're a fighter. You always have been. And it seems like until this Sunday, they were winning, and you were giving in, but now you've unsettled them, thrown them off their feet. I know it shouldn't be this way; I know that churches should be places of understanding and love and caring, but very, very often they're not. The last vicar gave in, ran away. Try to stay there, try to make a difference, my pet. I have complete faith in you and what's more, I know our Lord has faith in you."

At these words, Annie let all her hurt feelings burst forth and she cried. He said nothing, just moved closer and touched her on the shoulder. He just let her cry. He knew she needed to.

Matthew returned late on Sunday evening, drove past the vicarage, surprised, and disappointed, to see that Annie's car wasn't there. On Monday evening when he came back from London, he once more noticed it wasn't there and wondered about the dogs. He decided he'd better go check on them, but just as he was about to walk out the door, the phone rang. It was Joy.

"Hello, Matthew, I need to speak to you about something important, could you come over here for a minute?"

"Sure, I was just about to go out anyway. I'll be right

there," he answered, "and say, do you know where Annie is? Her car has been gone and I wondered if the dogs were all right."

"Annie is what I want to talk to you about," Joy said, in a softer voice than was normal for her.

"Oh, is she all right?" Matthew asked anxiously.

"Yes. Come on over and I'll tell you all about it."

He was there in a few minutes and Joy was standing in the doorway waiting. "Come in," she greeted him, but she was not smiling.

"Is something wrong?" he asked, as he sat down on the sofa in her comfortable living room.

Joy sat down opposite him and began, "Matthew, you know, you must know, how this village talks."

He nodded, not having any idea what she was leading to, other than it obviously involved him.

"There are rumors going around about you and Annie." She looked at him with a sympathy written all over her face.

"Me and Annie? Why, what are they saying?" He looked as incredulous as he felt.

"I might as well come right out about it. The rumor is going around that Annie spent the night at your house last week." She rushed on before he could react, "Now Matthew, I know you and I know Annie and I don't believe the talk, but you should know what they're saying."

Matthew was indignant, "Of course it isn't true. Annie came over one night last week because she needed to talk to someone and didn't feel she had privacy with that girl in her house, but she didn't even stay an hour. She left and I haven't seen her since." He got up and walked around the room, "Damn," he let out, not loudly. "What are they trying to do, get rid of Annie? Who would start a rumor like that, do you know? And does Annie know? I noticed her car isn't there—are the dogs still there?" He thought she might have left, for good. The lights were on in the vicarage, but that could be the girl there. He was furious, not for himself; he didn't care what people thought of him—he was furious for Annie. And frightened. What if she had gone away for good?

"I have an idea who it was. You know your strange neighbor across the street, Trina. She must have seen Annie go in and not seen her leave."

"So are they trying to force Annie to leave? She's had such a hard time. She hasn't been given a chance. And here I put the additional burden on her of keeping Amanda's dogs—gosh, I'm an idiot. Do you know where she is? Has she left?" He was leaving the village; he had already made up his mind to that, but he hadn't expected her to leave. She might go far away, to her friend in America where he might not ever see her again.

"She just went to see her father in Belfast," Joy reassured him. "She'll be back tomorrow and Julie is taking care of the dogs. She had to get away and I don't blame her. But Matthew, she gave this congregation a whopping sermon on Sunday. It was all about being wrongfully accused. It was a stunner. She showed some real fighting spirit. I know you would have been proud of her." She went on to tell him in detail about the sermon.

He was very impressed. "And what was the reaction?"

"Well, since I don't enter into the gossip with relish, I'm often the last to hear, but I gather it made some people feel ashamed, others miffed, and others relieved—a mixed bag. I don't know what will happen when she returns and what's more, I don't blame her if she leaves, do you?"

"No," he answered hesitatingly.

They both were silent for a moment. Then Joy said in a very kind voice, "Matthew, you know I've been a good friend to you and I hope I'm becoming a good friend to Annie. What people tell me doesn't leave this room. I won't tell anyone, not even Annie," she said, in a hesitant tone.

"What is it?" he asked, wary.

"I just want to say that if you and Annie are interested in each other, there is nothing wrong with that—it's normal and all right."

Matthew felt a mix of emotions. Was it so evident? Is that why she was asking? Did it show on his face when he was around Annie? He had tried not to show it; he had tried not to admit his interest in her even to himself. He felt disloyal to Amanda even thinking about Annie, much less doing anything about his interest. He looked down at the floor, his elbows on his knees, leaning toward the warm fire. "Thanks, Joy. But nothing at all has happened between us, nothing at all. We've just had a few talks, not many for that matter. Most of them about the dogs. I...I was just being welcoming, she seemed so alone when she arrived. He knew he was lying, but since he hadn't really admitted to himself how he felt about Annie, he sure wasn't going to tell someone else, even someone as understanding and sympathetic as Joy.

Joy nodded and changed the subject. "So you're selling your house and moving away?"

"Yes, I think it's the best thing for me," Matthew replied, "to live near my work. A new start. You know, Joy, I see Amanda in every room, in every picture on the wall, in all her paintings. It's not that I'm trying to forget her—I'll never forget her. But the house was her house; she picked it out, she decorated it, she loved it. So it doesn't seem right without her there. Maybe I can move on a bit in my life if I'm in new surroundings."

"The geographic cure," Joy said, as she smiled. "Well, we will miss you. You and Amanda were a breath of fresh air to the village, but you're right, it's your life now, not yours and Amanda's and you need to take care of yourself. Look, I will do my best to quench the rumors about you and Annie and she has done a lot herself. She is a very brave young woman. I admire her tremendously. I don't know though whether she'll stay and I wouldn't blame her if she didn't."

Matthew stood up, not to leave, but just to relieve the tension he had felt ever since Joy asked him to come over to talk about Annie. He went over to the window looking out on the street, deserted at this hour. He wondered what people were talking about behind those closed doors. Without turning around, he said, "I'd like to talk to her about the village gossip, but now I'm afraid to go to her house, afraid of more talk. And she certainly can't come to mine again. I guess I'll have to talk to her on the phone."

"Yes, I'm afraid that would be best," Joy answered. As he turned around, she said, "You know, Matthew, the Bible talks about the existence of evil something like this kills just as surely as murder. Jesus had something to say about that. He said that if you call your brother a fool then you are in danger of losing your salvation. That seems pretty harsh until you apply it to what's happened here, evil talk done with apparent glee, knowing the harm it would cause."

Matthew didn't know if he believed the Bible was true or not. He believed that Jesus lived, was a historical figure, and he certainly espoused a good philosophy by which one should live, but he didn't have the faith that Amanda had, nor Joy, nor Annie. And when something like this happened, when people who were supposedly Christians acted like this, he became thoroughly disillusioned, at least with the church and certainly with this church in this village. He longed for the anonymity of the city, which is what he was used to. Not because he wanted to live a wild life without anyone knowing it, but because it allowed one to live one's life as one wanted to, not having to worry about what anyone thought. He felt lonely here in the village, but he had never felt lonely in the city. There was energy in the city which didn't exist here. People were in a hurry, going places, doing exciting things. He would prefer to live in the city and have a country place for a respite. He loved the theatre, the symphony, the opera. He even loved the big churches, not in terms of building size, but in terms of the size of the congregation—not because he could get lost in it, but because, again, there was an energy about it. Yes, he resolved, the sooner his house sold, the better. He thanked Joy for telling him and went out into the night to his darkened cottage, wondering who was peering at him through those ubiquitous lace curtains.

Chapter Eight

Annie drove home, or to her house as she thought of it, (she had just left home) with trepidation. She felt stronger after being with her father, having him listen as well as give good advice. What would she do without him? She couldn't imagine how terrible it would be to have a father you either didn't respect or from whom you didn't receive love and affection. She didn't feel the same about her mother and often felt guilty about that. She just wasn't of the 'same cloth' as Annie. They didn't understand each other and since she had always been so close to her father, she often wondered if her mother was jealous of their relationship.

She didn't know what was inside her parent's marriage. Because her father was always gentle and non-confrontive, he seemed to let his wife's bickering slide off his back and always tried to appease her. Now, as an adult, Annie wondered if her father truly was in love with her mother anymore. She knew he would remain loyal and faithful, no matter what. How terrible for him if this were true. Now that she had had a tiny taste of what being in love was about, she wished her father had that same feeling for his wife. Maybe he did in the beginning, she thought. Yes, he must have had in the beginning. That was a scary thought, what happens to relationships over time. People change. Resentments build up. Love goes away. All these thoughts filled her mind as she drove to the village from the airport.

As she steered the car into the driveway and stopped, she heard the dogs barking in the back garden, recognizing the sound of her car. Rather than put her key in the front door, she went round to the back gate and was greeted joyfully by all three, jumping up on her and all wanting her attention at once. At least someone in the village loves me, she thought, laughing at their exuberance and taking them with her through the back door. "Julie, it's me. I'm home."

Silence. Annie walked on into the living room, having noticed that the kitchen was sparkling clean. Everything was in order there as well. Calling out Julie's name again, she climbed the stairs, with the dogs running on ahead. Julie wasn't in her room. Her things were gone from her room. There was no note—nothing.

"Oh, I sure didn't need this, Lord" Annie said out loud, looking upwards. Everything was spotless in the house; even her own bedroom had been dusted and vacuumed. This certainly wasn't like Julie. Going downstairs once more, she saw that the dogs had been fed and there was still plenty of water in their bowls. She realized Julie must have left this morning, knowing Annie would be home by noon. She couldn't believe she wouldn't leave some sort of note and went all through the house looking once more, but there was nothing. Going out the front door, she got her small bag out of the car and was bringing it in, when almost running up to her door she saw Horace. Exactly who she didn't want to see. On the other hand, he was so nosy, maybe he had seen Julie leave.

"Hello, Vicar, have a nice time away?" His wet smile sent an actual shiver down her spine. The only way to treat someone like this was to meet them head-on, she decided, following her father's advice. "Yes, I went to my parent's home. I've been there since Sunday."

"Oh," he responded.

Probably disappointed, she thought. He probably thought I was having a wild weekend with Matthew. "Horace, Julie isn't here. She seems to have left. Did you see her go?"

"No, I've been out visiting in the village. When did she leave, where did she go?"

"She must have left this morning, because the dogs were all right." She didn't answer him regarding where Julie went and she stood in the doorway, blocking him from entering and not inviting him in.

He looked confused for a moment and then said, "Well, I'll ask around the village if anyone saw her this morning."

"Thank you, Horace that would help." After another awkward silence, he finally turned to leave. She sighed with relief; at least she didn't have to deal with him right now. The phone rang as she closed the door. "Hello," she said, hoping it was Julie.

"Is this the Rev. O'Donnell?" a female voice asked.

"Yes.."

"I'm a friend of Julie's," the rather tremulous voice interrupted. "And she wanted me to phone you to tell you not to worry about her, that she's all right."

"Where.." Annie began when the voice again interrupted.

"And she said to tell you she took good care of the dogs."

"Yes, I can see that she did. What is your name?"

"I'm called Corinne."

"And do you know where Julie is? Is she with you?"

"I..I can't tell you that. But she's okay and that's that." And with that she hung up.

Annie immediately dialed 1471 but heard the impersonal voice say, 'the caller has withheld their number.' She sat down on the sofa, leaving her bag in the hallway and leaned back into the soft cushions. *"Oh, Lord—what now? I seem to lurch from one problem to another—what are you trying to teach me?"* She had dreaded coming back to the village. On the way home she had thought how wonderful it would be to be free from her obligation to the people there, to the church there. to be once more free, as she had been in the period even before she was made a curate. She dreaded coming back to the stares, to wondering what people were saying behind her back, and let's face it, to Julie. Am I responsible for her? I should be glad she's gone; she was another problem I didn't need. But Annie knew herself too well; she couldn't help feeling responsible for her.

She took her bag upstairs and unpacked it, looking again

into Julie's room and struck once again with how immaculate the house looked, realizing she must have cleaned the entire time she was gone. As she was putting away a clean pair of underwear she hadn't worn in her lingerie drawer, something struck her. The piles of underwear were perfectly straight. Annie wasn't that kind of person; her lingerie drawer wasn't a mess, items weren't thrown in willy-nilly but she wasn't this neat. Had Julie been through her drawers? The thought made her cringe—what else had she been looking in?

She immediately went to the computer and wrote a long email to Emily, telling her exactly how she was feeling, oppressed, picked on.

"I'm feeling right sorry for myself, my friend. Why is my life taking such a turn? Do I deserve it? I really don't think so—I haven't even done anything fun enough to deserve punishment! Help!!!!! Love, Annie"

By the time she had fixed herself a cup of tea and sorted through her mail, she checked the email again, knowing that if Emily was at her desk she would have replied right away.

"Oh, Annie-of course you're not being punished. And I don't know why all this is happening. I feel guilty—my life is going so well—but other than let Kevin know about Julie, I think you can't take on responsibility for her actions. She obviously has a lot of emotional problems and needs professional help. Chin up, honey, as my dad used to say. It isn't like you not to fight. Love, Em.

Annie knew she had to meet with the parish council that evening and dreaded it. It had now been two days since her sermon and she was certain the topic of the evening would be about it, but it was necessary. Em was right—she was a fighter.

She found the house curiously lonely without Julie there. Even though she had been a problem, a worry, a source of a great deal of frustration, it was another human being in the house. The dogs had taken to Julie and at times, Annie found herself a bit jealous. But now, their loyalty was back. They followed her from room to room, sometimes almost making her trip. Poor little fellows, Amanda must have given you lots of attention, you seemed starved for it. The thought of Amanda led to thoughts of Matthew, which made her feel even more melancholy. She wondered if he knew yet, knew about the rumors and about her sermon. She phoned Joy to ask..

"Yes," Joy responded, "Matthew came over Monday evening. He had gone to visit Amanda's parents and he noticed your car gone, so he came over to ask about you, and the dogs, of course." She added that almost as an afterthought.

"How did he react?" Annie asked.

"He was angry, of course. He said it made him want to leave the village even more, I'm afraid. But he admired your pluck in standing up to the church. I told him about your sermon."

Knowing he admired her pluck, as Joy put it, made her feel good, but hearing he was even more determined to leave the village certainly didn't. "Joy, I feel funny about even phoning him now, almost as if my phone is tapped—it's a horrible feeling. Other than you, he was one person I felt I could talk to and now, he's been cut off from me." She knew as she said the words that she wasn't being truthful, but she didn't want to confide in Joy, not yet anyway. She had told her father and of course, Emily knew everything. Two people were enough in terms of Matthew. But Joy was the one person who understood the village and she knew she wouldn't pass on anything she said to her. *Thank you for Joy*, she breathed a prayer.

"Annie, there was a time when everyone listened to everyone's conversations in this village, when I was a girl and there were party lines. But of course you can phone him. I think he would love to hear from you, would love to try to help you."

"Um, well, I'll think about that," Annie replied. "But Joy, I have a new problem now. Julie has disappeared." She told her about the telephone call and about Horace. "And I have to meet with the elders tonight. I sure do have a lot on my plate!"

"You have a lot to pray about, if you ask me. I'll pray for you tonight during the meeting. Listen, Annie, I would like to be your prayer partner—would that be all right? Whenever you have anything difficult coming up, let me know and I'll talk to God about it. On my knees. And you know it will never go further."

Annie smiled into the phone. "Joy, you are aptly named. I'm so thankful for you."

"And I for you," she said sincerely. "How did it go with your father?"

"Oh, he's wonderful, as always. Lots of good advice. If you're going to pray for me, please pray for me not to slip into the sin of self-pity. I've never been prone to that, but I sure feel I'm getting dangerously close."

"All right, I'll make a note of that. And Annie, no one is going to talk about you if you come to my house. So come over anytime you feel like talking. We'll have a cup of tea or even a glass of sherry and a good ole natter. Okay?"

"Thank you Joy. I'll take you up on that. Bye." She felt a bit cheerier as she hung up the phone. It was now close to five. Matthew wouldn't be home until at least seven from London and the meeting was at half seven. She fixed herself something to eat in the kitchen, noticing that there wasn't too much in the fridge, and gave the dogs a lot of attention for awhile, drawing comfort from their eagerness to be with her.

She had never been this lonely or depressed. It was a new feeling for her and she didn't like it. Going upstairs to her study, she turned on her computer, hoping Emily had written. There were several emails, but none from her. She clicked on the first one:

Hello. I'm a friend of Julie's—a guy friend. Has she told you about me? I don't have your phone number, Julie wouldn't give it to me, but she did give me your email address. I haven't been able to get in touch with her and I'm worried about her. She phoned me once, about a week ago, and gave me this email address—then nothing since. Is she still with you? Please let me know. Joe Smith

Amazing. Julie was even more complicated than she thought. And how did Julie get her email address? Annie realized she must have been fooling around with her computer. Well, only natural, she guessed, home alone with nothing to do. Still, it bothered her. It meant Julie had to have come into her study and sat at her desk. Was she snooping? She wrote back:

Dear Joe: I'm sorry, Joe, but Julie has left and I don't know where she's gone. If you hear from her, will you let me know? I'm worried about her. No, she hadn't told me about you but I'm glad she has a friend. Please tell Julie that I didn't want her to go and thank her for leaving the house in such a nice condition and taking care of the dogs. Annie O'Donnell

Was I telling the truth, Annie asked herself? Or did I really want her to go. She had phoned Kevin when she first came home and now she decided to phone him again. He said he knew nothing of a boyfriend. "She is a strange girl, Annie. Please don't feel you didn't do right by her—she has this history of running away. She seems to be able to take care of herself. She surfaces now and then. We don't contact the police anymore because she's not a missing person. She is classed as a runaway and since she's eighteen, can do what she likes."

"All right, Kevin—I just needed reassurance. Let me know if you hear of anything." As she was reading her other emails, the phone rang.

"Annie..."

It was Matthew. She felt a surge of relief going thump to the bottom of her stomach. Why did even the sound of his voice make her feel this way, all hormonal, as Emily would say. "Hi, Matthew, I'm glad you called," thinking what an understatement that was.

Matthew wasted no time in greetings. "Joy told me what you've gone through all on account of me. I'm so sorry, Annie, and so angry."

"Oh, Matthew, it isn't your fault. I'm angry too, but not at you. I don't know whether I'll weather this storm or not." She stopped talking for a moment, being unsure what to say to him. Then, "I guess I don't know whether I want to or not."

"Um, I don't blame you," Matthew replied in a sympathetic voice. "I wouldn't blame you if you packed your bags and went roaring out of here. I wish I could come over and talk to you, but I guess it isn't a safe thing to do anymore."

"No, I guess not. But if we could talk on the phone, I would like that. Would it be all right?" That way, he can't see me blushing or the beginning of tears, she thought.

"Of course we can. I would like that. Feel free to phone me anytime you want. Look, let me give you my office phone and I'll call you as well. All right?"

Annie sighed and smiled into the phone. "Yes, that will help."

"So how are you doing?" Matthew asked. "Joy told me you went to see your parents in Belfast."

"I'm all right. It's always good to talk to my dad—he's so wise. But when I got home Julie had left, did Joy tell you?"

"No. Where did she go?"

"Evidently she has a friend in London. This friend phoned me to say that Julie was okay. She wouldn't tell me where she was. She had taken good care of the dogs and had cleaned the house, which was a surprise. She left it sparkling. She must have left right after she fed them this morning."

"So now you're back to having an empty house," Matthew replied. "Maybe it's just as well. She was a problem."

"Yes, because she wouldn't talk to me, but without knowing it, I had formed an attachment to her. She seemed so lost and so troubled."

They talked on and on. Annie lost all track of time until she heard the doorbell downstairs. Looking at her watch, she jumped. "Oh, my gosh, Matthew. I've got a PCC meeting to go to. Someone is ringing the doorbell downstairs. I've got to go."

"Probably Horace. I'm not going to it. I think I will resign in light of things. Bye, Annie, I hope the meeting goes well."

"Bye," she said softly. The doorbell rang again insistently. It was Horace demanding to know where she was, telling her they had all been waiting in the church hall.

Annie had very soon learned that there were several who had lived in the village all their lives and who had seen vicars come and go, whilst they remained. This was their church and they were going to run it. No one was going to come in and change things. And she sensed that since she was a woman, and young, they didn't anticipate any trouble from her. Her father counseled her to just go along with things for quite awhile. "Give them a chance to get to know you and then you can begin quietly introducing changes you think should be done. It is your church, Annie, but it is also theirs. And above all, it is Gods. Let him lead you."

The meeting went like many parish council meetings. There was an agenda: Should we switch from pews to chairs, should we buy a new organ and if so, where was the money going to come from? Annie's sermon or what prompted it was never mentioned. The parish council was made up mostly of men. They were polite to her, but she didn't feel she had any authority with them. She found herself bored stiff by all this talk of pipes and building structures. She knew someone had to worry about things like that, but didn't see what it had to do with her. Or with the Lord, for that matter. As she sat there, mostly listening, not taking part very often, she thought back to the early church as recorded in Acts. What has happened to the church? It all seems to be about other things rather than about spiritual growth, spiritual sustenance. Annie thought they had lost the plot.

She had opened the meeting with a prayer for unity and love, but there didn't seem to be any unity displayed. People had strong opinions which seldom seemed to match up to anyone else's opinions. A couple of times two men locked horns over an issue and when it came to a vote, were upset when one of them didn't get his way. Was this what a church was supposed to be? Surely not.

The early church had everything in common. They met in homes and whilst they had deacons who did what this meeting was supposed to do, she sure hoped they acted in a more spiritual manner. What had gone wrong? Annie found her mind wandering as the meeting progressed, or regressed, as she told herself. She began fantasizing—what would happen if Jesus walked into the room right now? Would he be welcomed? Or would each person there complain to him that he or she wasn't getting her way. Would they enlist him, or try to enlist him, into their way of thinking? Would Jesus care about the building with which they were so overly involved? That wasn't what he meant by his church, this wrangling bunch of uncaring people. A tiny smile came on her face as she pictured Jesus with a whip in his hand, driving them all out. "This isn't what you are supposed to be doing!" he shouts. "Doesn't anyone here know what my message was? How you are to love one another in spite of your differing opinions? She smiled even more to herself when she pictured the looks on their faces—shock, dismay, anger. Would they be angry at Jesus for 'interfering?' Would they ask him what right he had to be there, when after all, he hadn't been elected to the parish council? Would they have him locked up as a lunatic?

As soon as her fantasy was ended, she once more grew dismayed at the petty in-fighting, the arguments, the power struggles, the need to control what went on in the church. When the church went democratic, was it a mistake? Should the leader of the church make all the decisions? She didn't know, but it wasn't very inspiring.

She looked at her watch. It was getting late and she hoped the meeting would stop soon. No one had mentioned her sermon, no one had asked her where she had been. No one had done much of anything, other than nod to her and say hello when she came in. She felt dismissed, unimportant. And wondered what would have happened if she were a man—would it have been different?

After the meeting, she wrote to Em just before she fell into bed, exhausted. She told her all about Matthew's phone call and about the meeting.

Hi Em: "Does this happen in your meetings? Do you feel invisible? And what would Jesus think if he attended one of these....I don't know, Emily, I'm sure discouraged. I'm supposed to be here to preach the gospel, to pray for people, to evangelize—and it's as if everything is working against my doing that." Love, Annie

When she awoke the next morning she had a reply.

"Hi Annie—my poor beleaguered friend. I, too, wonder what it would be like if you were a male vicar. Let's do a little role reversal here—what if a male vicar, young, good looking, had been seen to enter a young widow's house at night. Would the rumor have gone around that he had spent the night? I doubt it. And if it had—would the men think 'wish it had been me?' You know, I think you are a threat to those men. They probably are all attracted to you and can't admit it—even to themselves, certainly to each other. So they try to ignore you—all except your one pest. Know that you are always in my prayers, my friend. I hope your praying is picking up." Love, Emily

She also had another email—from Julie's friend.

"Dear Rev. O'Donnell: I heard from Julie—she's okay. Julie said to ask you how the dogs are—I guess she really liked them. Anyway she's okay. But I haven't seen her and she wouldn't tell me where she was. Please answer me if you can. Joe

She didn't answer his email—in the first place, she was highly suspicious of his name, Joe Smith. And secondly, she couldn't deal with Julie right now

Chapter Nine

A few days after Annie came back from Belfast, Joy phoned to say there seemed to be a difference in the village since her sermon, at least amongst the women—that they seemed able to put themselves in her place. Joy told her she made sure she talked to lots of people after the sermon, because she wanted to influence them in regards to Annie's reputation. "Now they're saying that you didn't know anyone here, that you're so young and pretty and must be vulnerable, that Matthew is certainly good looking and that if he is easy for you to talk to, of course, you would have sought him out and just because you went into his house, it didn't mean you didn't go out again—it was just that no one saw you go out."

"Do you know who started the rumors?" Annie asked, in an anxious voice. "Do you know who saw me go into Matthew's house?"

"No," Joy replied, "And no one knows or cares, it seems to me. The telegraph system in the village is such that it's impossible to trace gossip back to its origin once it starts and I think it's like a cloud that passes from house to house, a dark cloud that brightens up the day of people whose lives are small, you know? If one's sphere is small, it's exciting to have something spicy to talk about, isn't it? No one really meant any harm—just an arched eyebrow here, a rolling of the eyes there," she said in a facetious tone. "What's their motive, why do they want to bring people down, down to a much lower level than themselves? I think it gives them a feeling of power over the one who they're talking about, that's the motive for all gossip, I think, especially if you're the one with the scoop. Rumors have a life of their own, Annie, they grow and grow, and get a little bigger in the telling each time."

"Do you think someone has it in for me?" Annie asked, "Is there one person who doesn't like me and doesn't want me to succeed?"

"No, I don't think so, Annie," Joy answered immediately. "I think the women actually want you to succeed. Whilst they wouldn't call themselves feminists, they want to have equal rights and want other women to as well, but they wouldn't have put a name to it. Yet, they are guilty of talk, what seems like harmless talk to them. These same people read their Bibles rather often, read through the Gospels at least once a year, read right over the passages about slander and judgment. To be fair, the whole church wasn't involved with the gossip and it wasn't the whole village who was gossiping either, but there was a substantial proportion in both who loved *to discuss*, as they would have called it, discuss matters pertinent to the village."

Joy continued without Annie saying anything, "A village is a microcosm of the world; there are all types of people in a village, but there aren't that many Incomers and a new vicar is always an Incomer. Other than perhaps two new families a year, the village, being small, without many houses going up for sale, is by its very essence a stagnant group, you know, like a pond with no inlet—the waters grow murky and still."

"Thanks, Joy," Annie replied. "That is helpful. I'm afraid I'm woefully ignorant of village life, but you know, even before all the trouble with Matthew, I've come to realize the condition of the church here as being church-centered rather than Christ-centered. Do you know what I mean?"

"That's right, Annie. You may not know much about villages, but you're right on about the church here. It's a place to gather socially, to greet one another on a Sunday morning, to chat over coffee afterward together. What happens in between is routine, the prayers, the sermon, the music—it's a ritual carried out every Sunday morning and it's called worship."

"But do they? Do they worship?" Annie asked rhetorically. "I don't think so. It doesn't look like it to me."

After that conversation, Annie decided she would

'convert' the church and she would begin with the women. So with Joy's help and blessing, it was announced in the church bulletin there would be a women's Bible study on Wednesday mornings at the Vicarage. All women of the village were welcome, even those who didn't attend church.

It was now Wednesday morning. A week and a half had passed since her bombshell sermon and Annie wondered if anyone, other than Joy, would show up.. At ten o'clock, the doorbell rang and kept ringing for another fifteen minutes as more and more women came through the door. By the time it stopped, there were twelve women squeezed into Annie's front room. She was very pleased.

"Thank all of you for coming. I hope this will be the beginning of a journey for all of us, a journey of learning to know the Bible better and a journey of learning to know our Lord better," she said, smiling at them. A few smiled back. She thought most of them looked nervous.

"Has there ever been a Bible study in the village?" she asked, looking around hopefully.

Heads nodded from side to side. No, there hadn't.

"Well, we will start a new tradition then—how exciting," Annie exclaimed, whilst thinking how appalling that this was the first. She opened the meeting with a short prayer and then introduced the lesson from the gospel of Luke. Everyone seemed to have a different version of the Bible, some didn't have a Bible, and some still read the King James Version. Annie didn't let that be an obstacle and remained cheerful throughout the morning, even when it was tough slogging getting them to interact.

When it came time to pray at the end, she explained, "This is a time to ask for anything that's troubling you, anyone in your family who needs prayer for healing, whatever." With any other group, she would have added the caveat, and whatever is said here is confidential, but decided against it for now, as they might think she was making a dig because of what had happened to her. A few people asked for prayer. They were duly prayed for and then Joy brought in coffee and biscuits from the kitchen.

After they left, Annie and Joy sat at the kitchen table over a bowl of tinned soup. "Well, I think you scored a success this morning," Joy beamed.

"I hope so. You know, Joy, I wanted to run away, to start over somewhere else because everything has seemed to go wrong here, but after praying and talking to Emily and to Dad, they both advised me to stay and fight, but to fight in love—that's what Jesus would want me to do. And I know they're right. I could feel in that room this morning the emptiness of some of these womens' lives. They may have gone to church nearly all their lives, but are they Christians? Do they have a real relationship with the Lord? I think not in some cases. So that's what I'll try to build, a solid foundation of the church built on the women and hopefully, this will spread to the men, to their husbands."

Joy nodded, "Yes, because you can't do this with the men. It's not fair, a male vicar could have a women's Bible study here and no one would think a thing of it, but you have to stick to the women." Her eyes twinkled. "Maybe if you get married, your husband could lead the men."

Annie looked at her fondly, compressing her lips into a shrug. "Oh, Joy, I don't need a husband to complicate my life right now. It's messed up enough, thank you!"

Matthew didn't know what to do. A buyer had put in an offer on the house, a very generous offer, in fact, exactly what he was asking. But now he didn't know if he wanted to leave the village or not. He had many doubts about his attraction to Annie, besides his guilt over it being too soon. He also had doubts about her profession. What kind of relationship could you have with a female vicar? She didn't seem to be holier than thou, but maybe he just didn't know her well enough, maybe she would be in prayer all day, maybe she didn't believe in s ex except for procreation, how was he to know? All he really knew was that when the estate agent phoned, elated about the offer, Matthew didn't reflect the same feelings, but rather he panicked. "Give me a few days," he pleaded with the agent.

"Why? Do you not want to sell?" he asked, incredulous, probably seeing his commission slipping away.

"No—I mean—yes...just give me a few days. Can you do that?"

"Well, I suppose I can stall them. But only for two days. You will let me know in forty-eight hours?"

"Okay, forty-eight hours. Yes." He put the phone down and sank into the easy chair by the fire. Indecision was new to him. He felt foolish; he had always been a decisive person, he had always known his own mind.

Born in London to a rather prosperous family, he went to a posh public boys' school and lived in Chelsea. Holidays were spent abroad, usually in France. His father was a minor minister at Whitehall and his mother spent her time spending the money she had inherited from her grandmother. She went to endless teas, shopped almost every day in high-end stores and frequently went through a series of cooks and maids because she was so demanding. His father was not home much of the time; he either was working late or on government business abroad.

He was an only child and whilst some of his friends were shipped off to boarding school at an early age, his mother rather liked having him around when she felt like it, he supposed. She told him once that it would be inconvenient for him to be away. He noticed a difference in the homes of his friends. His mother never really wanted to know his friends and if he brought someone home, they were consigned to Matthew's room or the small, perfect garden in the rear of the house. This wasn't much good because one was not supposed to do anything on the neatly trimmed lawn other than tiptoe over it. Throwing a ball would have instantly brought his mum to the window to 'halloo' at them. So he usually went to their homes instead and garnered affection and noisy interaction from the size of other families

families and the warmth of their parents. As long as he reported in after school, he didn't really have to be home until seven, when dinner was served.

No one ever told him to do his homework. He just did it, mainly because he very much liked school. He liked to study and there was one teacher, Mr. Ambrose, who took an interest in him, encouraged him. Matthew vowed that when he grew up, he would be a teacher. This was one decision that got his mother's attention. "A teacher! They don't make even a living wage—why on earth would you want to do that?" She was so upset, she almost stopped reading her magazine. He tried to explain to her, but she soon dropped the subject. His father said he should do whatever he liked, but he did encourage him to teach on the university level, not because of the pay, but because he thought Matthew was too intelligent to be wasted on the young.

He read Political Science at Oxford and thoroughly enjoyed his years there, free from his home environment. It was at Oxford he met Amanda. She didn't know what she wanted to do with her life and was pursuing a degree in Art History. After she met Matthew, she didn't want anything else in the world but to marry him and make a home for him. She told him she sensed what he had lacked growing up, especially when he brought her to meet his parents. It made her heart ache for the boy Matthew, growing up in such an immaculate and silent house. That's what it was, she told him, a house, not a home.

As soon as he got a job teaching at LSE, they were married. Amanda wasn't anxious to live in London, but in the flush of honeymoon love, it didn't really matter where they lived. Within a year, however, she began agitating for a move to the country. She loved pets, she wanted to cook and garden, she wanted to live the village life, a life she was used to and loved. Matthew wasn't crazy about commuting, but he was crazy about Amanda and agreed. They had lived in the village only a year, when the accident occurred and his life collapsed. He had been paralyzed for a long time, going to work like an automaton, trying to take care of the dogs as a legacy to Amanda, trying to decide what to do.

When Annie came to the village, his life seemed to clarify a bit. Some of the fuzziness he had been feeling lifted. He had mixed motives in offering her the dogs. He did think they would be better off, but he had admitted to himself it would give him a connection to her, a reason to see her.

However, when the village telegraph spread such horrible rumors about her, he felt protective and knew nothing was going to work with him in the village. Yet if he moved into London, would he ever see her? Only if she came to see him and maybe she didn't want to do that. All these thoughts went round and round in his head like a merry-go-round. After dinner, having ruminated all day, he decided to go talk to Joy, to confide in her, to ask for her advice.

After the inevitable cup of tea had been served, Joy said, "Well, now Matthew, it seems to me you have something on your mind. You know I don't tell secrets—I'm like a tomb—so shoot!"

He told her the entire story from his point of view and when he finished, Joy went to get the sherry bottle. "This calls for something a bit stronger," she said, pouring them each a glass. She sat down opposite him and began, "I think Annie is a gift from God to this village. She's a breath of fresh air and I don't want to lose her, but I also want her to be happy. And you as well. If Amanda was alive and it had been you who died, would you want her to be alone all her life? Mourning you?"

Matthew drank the sherry down in one gulp and got up, going over to stand next to the fireplace. He was wearing a grey blue cardigan and navy cords with a light blue Oxford cloth button down shirt.

"I don't know," he answered, not looking directly at Joy. "I guess if I'm honest, I kind of would like her to mourn me longer than I'm doing. But they're separate—do you understand, can you understand that? How I feel about Amanda is a separate thing than how I feel about Annie. I can't explain it, but it is. It doesn't mean I didn't love Amanda and miss her like hell, every day, every hour, but the house—every room, every piece of furniture, all shout Amanda. I don't think I can move on as long as I live there. And I'm attracted, heavily attracted, to Annie. And I barely know her. And…I don't know if you can understand this or not, Joy, but I don't like the idea of being married to a female vicar!"

Joy smiled wryly. "You men, you're so different from us. That's a news flash, by the way," she said, laughing. "Most women would kill to marry a clergyman..in a matter of speaking, of course. Why would it bother you?"

"Well, I guess I would have to become holy, don't you think? I mean, I could never go off and play golf on a Sunday morning, if I felt like it….gosh, that sounds selfish, doesn't it?"

"It sounds like someone who isn't a committed Christian."

"Don't committed Christians play golf?" Matthew asked, wtih a worried look.

"Of course they do, but Matthew, committed Christians *want* to go to church on Sunday morning to worship. They don't have to go; they just want to go. Why don't you tell me about your faith—do you have one?" she asked in a gentle manner, smiling softly at him, as softly as Joy could do anything.

Matthew sat back down opposite her before he answered. "I never went to church much after school ended, you know, the compulsory chapel, until I met Amanda. She always wanted to go. I guess you're right; she never said I had to go, but she always went. So most of the time I went with her."

"And did it mean anything to you?" Joy pressed, "Or was it just empty ritual?"

Matthew was sitting with his arms resting on his thighs, looking down at the floor. He was silent for a few moments before he answered Joy's question and then in a quiet voice, he said, "Well, it was always good to be with her, I liked to kneel beside her to pray and take communion with her at the altar. But it seemed to be the same every Sunday. I have to confess my mind wandered a lot, especially because, as you know, the vicar that was here before was pretty boring."

"That's one thing no one has accused Annie of being," Joy exclaimed.

He looked up at her and smiled. "No, I'm sure not. I would think the men would just enjoy looking at her—which makes me angry, by the way…"

"Because they find her pretty, just as you do?"

He nodded, "Yeah, double standard there."

"Let me tell you something about Christianity, Matthew. Maybe you've heard this before and maybe you haven't. Sometimes people can live their entire life going to church and never really hear the message. Christianity is not a religion."

"It's not?" he looked at her with surprise.

"No. It's a relationship with Jesus Christ. And until you turn your life over to Him and begin a relationship with him, it will seem boring, perhaps untrue, and certainly irrelevant."

Matthew nodded, "Boring and irrelevant, that does describes how I often feel about it."

"Well, it isn't boring and it certainly isn't irrelevant, once you have that relationship with Christ. Lots of people go to church every Sunday and never quite 'get it.' If you make this decision, and it is up to you, then I predict you won't have any trouble at all being romantically involved with a vicar."

"What do you mean, it's up to me?"

"Well, some people have dramatic conversion experiences, like Paul in the Bible, where God breaks through into our time and space and appears in some form or other, usually a miraculous manifestation of the Holy Spirit. With others, it is just a conscious commitment to God, believing in him and asking him to come in and take over your life."

"It's that simple?"

"Yes, it is. And I'm not surprised that you don't know that. I'm afraid that our state church here in England has rather stultified until it has become simply a traditional ritual with little meaning." She took a sip of her sherry and poured more for Matthew. "But once you've become a Christian, a real Christian, that is, the words of the ritual take on meaning. You realize that the men (and they were all men) who wrote the Book of Common Prayer were in touch with God. They had a relationship with him. I understand because I used to be like you, I used to go to church every Sunday and left feeling rather better because of the hymns and the prayers, but also wondering what it all meant. And this warm feeling never lasted. I would soon return to feeling empty."

"Yes empty, that's how I've felt since Amanda died. Except..." He stopped talking and looked down at the floor.

"Except when you're with Annie?"

"Yes, isn't that awful? Am I just a dirty old, young man Joy?"

"No you aren't and what I'm wondering is if Annie isn't a gift sent to you from God. You know in Genesis, God said it's not good for man to be alone. Some people like to interpret the Bible in today's terms in regards to gender, but it's been my experience that women get along pretty well alone. My friends and I here in the village, we're all widows and we're all fine without a man. But I don't think men do too well alone. I think God knew what he was talking about."

Matthew was silent. Joy knew she had given him a lot to think about. "Look, you go home now. I'm an early-to-bedder."

"Oh, I'm sorry, Joy," he said, standing up. "I didn't even realize what time it was."

"You go home and think about all that I've said. And if you want to talk to me about all this again, I've always got a listening ear."

"And you won't tell Annie what I've said?"

"Of course not. I learned a long time ago that the only way to stay sane in a village is to keep everything everyone tells me inside. And try not to listen to the gossip."

Matthew kissed her lightly on both cheeks. "Thanks, Joy—you're a peach."

"I know I am—whatever that means. Matthew, God is reaching out his hand to you. All you have to do is take it."

He looked at her quizzically and went out into the night.

Chapter Ten

A week later, about three in the afternoon, the phone rang in the vicarage. It was Julie. "Julie! Where are you?" Annie asked.

"I'm okay, I just wanted to talk to you," she said, in a very quiet voice.

"Oh, I've been so worried about you. Are you all right?"

"Yes, I'm fine. I..."

"Yes..go ahead," Annie urged.

"I wondered if I could come back."

Annie didn't hesitate, but answered immediately, "Of course you can, Julie—you are totally welcome. And Julie, your friend Joe has emailed me. Have you contacted him?"

There was a moment's silence before she answered. Then, "I don't know anyone named Joe."

Annie didn't know what to think. "Well, I don't know how he got my email address and he seems to know you."

"I'm sorry," Julie responded, her voice sounding cold. "I don't know anyone that would email you."

Annie noted the change in her voice and decided to drop the subject for now. "When are you coming?"

"I could be there by tonight. Can you meet me at the station?"

"Of course, and Julie," Annie began.

"Yes?"

"I'm very glad you're coming back." As she hung up the phone, Annie wondered if what she had just said was true. She was very glad someone would be in the house with her, but was she glad it was going to be Julie? *Have I forgotten how frustrating it was to have her here?*

Julie looked much better when she alighted from the train

than she had previously. She had a new hairstyle, cut short and bouncy, and the makeup was toned down. Annie attempted a hug, but she shrank back.

"Welcome!" she said, smiling broadly, wanting Julie to believe she really was welcome. "Here, let me help you with the luggage." Annie noticed there was more of it than when Julie left. "I thought we would have supper here at a restaurant. I haven't had time to fix anything." Julie looked disappointed, but Annie persisted. Her fridge was empty and she hadn't had time to get to the supermarket.

"McDonald's would be fine," she answered.

"Oh, all right. I haven't had a hamburger in a long time myself," Annie said, realizing Julie probably didn't want to sit across from her for a long chat at a restaurant. They quickly ate their take-away food with Julie not speaking much. "So can you tell me where you've been?" Annie asked, smiling in what she hoped was an encouraging way.

Julie stared out the window, taking a bite of her chips and not answering.

Annie tried again, "Well, you look like you're okay. I worried about you, that's all."

Julie finally looked at her for a moment. "I don't like people asking me questions—okay?" Her voice sounded belligerent.

Annie took in a deep breath before she responded. "Look, Julie, I have a lot of my own problems and it's not that I don't want to help you, because I do, but you have to help me, you have to help me to help you. Do you understand?"

Julie went back to looking out the window. She hadn't eaten much of her hamburger.

Annie gave up and finished her meal in silence. When they got home, the dogs were overjoyed to see Julie. She seemed to warm up, thaw out a bit, at their response. She even let out a small laugh.

"See, they missed you, missed the walks you took with

them." Annie helped her bring her luggage to her room. "I'll be in my study, why don't you get settled and then I'll come down and we'll have a cup of tea and watch television, all right?" The last thing Annie wanted to do was watch television, but it was something she could do 'with' Julie; it was a reason to be in the same room with her.

She went into her study and turned on the computer. There was an email from Emily and one from Joe. She clicked on his first.

"I know Julie is returning to you. I hope she stays this time. She has many secrets which she needs to divulge. Please keep me informed as to how she is. Joe.

Annie shook her head in wonderment. What a mystery all this was! Then she clicked on the one from Emily.

Hi Annie: How is your relationship with Our Father going? Remember, he knows everything and knows how it will all turn out. My message for you is Trust. Trust him, keep close to him, I know you are a special person and of course, he knows it. So it is all going to be all right—trust me! Things are busy here, but good. Worried about the usual world issues, of course, and praying a lot. Have joined a women's prayer group—very different than any I've been in before. We sit in silence after all the prayer requests have been made—pray deeply for half an hour. Very holy. Hope you have some type of resource like this. Miss you – love, Emily

Annie felt a pang of envy as she read about Emily's prayer circle. Oh, how she needed something like that! She didn't feel she could share her problems with the women's Bible study group she had started. She was their leader; she couldn't tell them all about her doubts as to her ability, her loneliness, her problems with Julie, and of course she couldn't share her feelings about Matthew. The only person she felt safe with in the village was Joy. She breathed a prayer of thanks for her. At least she had her for a prayer partner.

She tried to work on the church bulletin for the next week and soon could hear Julie downstairs with the dogs. She hadn't tapped on her door as Annie had asked. Mentally shrugging her shoulders, she went downstairs and found Julie playing with the dogs in the kitchen. "Are you hungry? You didn't eat much in town," she said.

"No, I'm all right," Julie answered. "Have the dogs been fed?"

"No, would you like to do that? I'm afraid I'm almost out of dog food. Matthew supplied it when they first came here, but I guess I'd better buy some tomorrow." She went on into the living room and turned on the television. Julie joined her after a few minutes. During a commercial, Annie switched the sound off. "Julie, I had another email from Joe. He said he knew you were returning here. can't you tell me anything about who he is?"

"I told you I never heard of anyone named Joe," she said angrily. "Stupid name anyway. I never heard of him," she repeated and looked back at the advert playing silently as if it was the most interesting thing in the world.

Annie had a lot of work to catch up on and if she was going to relax, she would rather be reading, yet she sat with Julie for another two hours, fixing them each a cup of tea, and trying to stay silent. Julie did not say another word the entire time. When she finally gave up and went to bed, leaving Julie downstairs alone, Annie's spirits were low. Her bedtime prayers had always been short. She did her serious praying in the morning when she was awake. For several years now, she had simply reviewed the day and said thanks for what had happened. But tonight, she was too downhearted to do that. *Goodnight, Lord*, was all she said.

When Annie awoke, the sun was streaming in her window and Tibby began licking her face. She gave him a hug.

"You just sit there waiting for me to wake up, don't you?" Getting out of bed, she went quietly down the stairs and let them out. She watched them run in the long back garden. Daffodils planted by other occupants were beginning to bloom. Annie's mother had a beautiful garden in Belfast and whilst she enjoyed looking at flowers, she didn't have a clue as to what to do to make them grow. And I'm certainly not going to have time to keep this garden up, she thought, as she fixed herself a cup of tea.

She heard Julie coming down the stairs just as she opened the door for the dogs to come back in. She came into the kitchen with a smile on her face for the dogs, not for Annie. They greeted her joyfully and she knelt down to pet them.

"Good morning, how did you sleep?" Annie asked.

"Great. I guess I was tired and didn't know it," Julie responded.

Annie was surprised, not by the fact that she slept, but by the entire sentence she used to answer her question. This was something new. As she watched her playing with the dogs, smiling, even laughing a few times, it struck Annie that not only was she acting differently, she actually looked different. Her voice was different as well, it was lighter, higher. The time away must have done her good, wherever she was, thought Annie.

"Tea?" Annie asked.

"No, I prefer coffee, thank you," Julie said, looking up from the dogs.

Coffee, she had always had tea, never coffee. Annie found an old jar of instant coffee in the cupboard and made her a cup.

Meanwhile, Julie was looking in the fridge and pulled out the carton of eggs. "I fancy a scrambled egg, would you like one too?" she asked, smiling at Annie.

"Yes, that would be lovely," she replied, startled by this unexpected event. What was going to happen next, she wondered?

Julie expertly made enough scrambled eggs for them

whilst Annie made two rounds of toast in the toaster.

When they sat down to eat, Annie said "It seems like you're a lot happier than when you were here before. I'm so glad—it's wonderful to see you smile and hear you laugh." After taking a bite, she said, "And these eggs are delicious—where did you learn to cook?"

"Well, scrambling eggs isn't necessarily cooking, is it? Julie replied.

Annie fought back the questions on the tip of her tongue. I need to let her be, an inner voice told her. Just let her be and enjoy this new Julie. Later, when Julie had left with the dogs for a walk, Annie ventured into her room. The bed was made and everything was neat and tidy.

Meanwhile, even with Julie's return and new, pleasant personality, Annie still felt lonely. She emailed Emily daily, phoned her father so much she was afraid she was becoming a pest herself, and saw Joy as often as she could. All that helped, but she missed Matthew. His house had a Sold sign on it and she had not seen him nor heard from him for two weeks now. Joy told her he was moving to the city soon.

A week after Julie returned, she picked up the phone and called him at his office. She heard his voice on the message machine and even that made her feel better. She didn't leave a message.

Later that afternoon, he rang. "Hi Annie, did you phone me earlier?"

"Yes," she said, embarrassed. "How did you know?"

"Oh, I'm a terrible curiosicat. I dialed 1471 when there was no message."

"Curiosicat—I've never heard that expression before."

"I made it up," he said, laughing. There was silence for a few seconds. "Are you all right?" he asked.

"Um, yes, I guess so. I just haven't seen you or talked to you. You haven't been in church, so I just wondered how you were, that's all."

"I guess you know the house sold."

"Yes, Joy told me and I saw the sign. I guess you'll be moving soon."

"I haven't found a flat yet. I've been spending all my free time looking."

Annie was silent. She couldn't think of anything to say, but she didn't want him to hang up. She felt desperate.

"Look, Annie, you know with all the trouble—about us, I mean, I can talk to you on the phone or you could come to have dinner with me again down here, or …." His voice trailed off.

"I would like to talk to you, Matthew. The truth is, I'm feeling rather lonely…"

"Oh, Annie, I know that feeling all too well. I don't want you to feel lonely. Do you want to come down for dinner?"

"No, I can't tonight. But could we talk for awhile? Do you have time?"

"Yes, I have an hour before my next class. So you can talk for an hour and I'll listen, okay? Would that help?"

Annie sighed, hoping it wasn't audible, "Oh, yes, I'm sure it would help."

So they talked for exactly one hour until Matthew had to leave for his class. She told him about Julie's return and transformation, about the dogs, about her loneliness. "I don't have anyone to talk to on my intellectual level other than you. That sounds elitist, doesn't it? And you're the only one I can say that to, but Matthew, I'm not used to this. I'm used to the people in Belfast, in my father's congregation there were lawyers, bankers, professors, people of intelligence who had been to university, women as well as men who had interesting philosophical discussions. Here in this village, other than occasional political discussions, people simply talk about each other."

"I know, Annie. I guess that never affected me. I have my work and my colleagues here in London and of course, I used to have Amanda to talk to when I was home. But since she……now, I just come home and get into bed with a good book. I can see where you don't have any other outlet. It must be rough."

Annie wished they could have had one conversation without Amanda coming into it, but she was grateful he understood. She decided to change the subject, "Julie is such a worry to me. She seems to have changed so much she even looks different."

"Look, I have a friend who is a psychologist. Do you want me to ask him if he could help out with Julie?"

She liked the sound of his voice. He had a definite Oxbridge accent, not Received Pronunciation, but authentic, from his parents, she supposed. Julie needed help and she certainly knew that she needed help with her.

"Annie? Are you there?"

"Yes, I'm here. I was thinking about your offer. I don't know if Julie will agree, but it won't hurt to ask her, will it. All right, I'll ask her and get back to you. And Matthew—thanks. Thanks again."

"Anytime. I'm always available at the end of the phone. Bye for now."

"Bye," she said softly, and hung up the phone. She stood still by the phone for a minute and then went downstairs to see if Julie had returned. She saw her outside through the window with the dogs. She opened the kitchen door and stepped out into the sunshine, where the dogs instantly changed loyalty and almost bowled her over.

Julie looked up. She was bending over some of the daffodils in the garden and she smiled at Annie. "Could I do some gardening for you?" she asked.

"Of course, that would be wonderful. Do you know anything about flowers?"

"No, not really, except that I love them. I could buy some seeds and plant them and see what happens."

"That would be fun. Look, I'm not busy at the moment, should we drive to the garden centre in town?"

Julie nodded and soon they were on their way. They not

only bought sunflower, cosmos, daisy, and foxglove seeds, Annie splurged and bought several potted flowers, ready to be put out. "It would be easy to have an instant garden if you had lots of money, wouldn't it?" Julie had been talkative the entire time, not revealing anything about herself, but easy to be with and they actually laughed together several times.

When they reached home, it was late, so any further gardening was postponed until the next day. Annie wanted to keep up the new affiliation they seemed to have garnered that afternoon and so fixed some pasta for them and set the table.

Over dinner, she brought up the fact that Matthew had a friend who was a psychologist. When she said that word, Julie stiffened up visibly. Cautiously, Annie continued. "I know you have had a rough time in your life, Julie, and I know that it wasn't your fault and I just wondered if you might benefit from seeing someone to help you."

Julie's head bent down over her plate. "But he would tell you everything I say," she almost whispered, "because he's a friend of Matthew's and Matthew would tell you everything. Besides, how do you know it wasn't my fault?"

"I just don't think anything is ever a young person's fault," Annie replied. "You're not old enough to have caused the things that have happened to you."

Julie's voice rose in anger, "How do you know what's happened to me?" She put down her fork and stood up.

"Oh, Julie, I didn't mean to upset you. Sit back down please, I don't know what's happened to you. I just know that you've been in a lot of foster homes and that that usually isn't pleasant. You didn't have the advantages I had, a family and all."

The old look was back on Julie's face and before the last words were out, she stormed out of the room and ran upstairs to her bedroom, where Annie heard the door slam shut. The dogs had followed her, but were stopped by the shut door. Annie heard them scratching and whining to be let in. Annie hung her head in despair. *Oh, you idiot—things were going so well and you've gone and ruined them!*

The next morning, Julie remained in her room, telling Annie through the door that she didn't want any breakfast. Annie had to lead the women's Bible study that morning. She certainly didn't feel like it, didn't feel like praying, didn't feel like being enthusiastic about God's word, wished she wasn't a clergyperson at all and wished she was with Matthew in the city. But somehow she got through it and when it was over, she found that Julie was out in the garden, planting the seeds they bought. Annie decided to leave her alone. She hoped the new Julie was back.

Horace had quit coming round quite so often since he always found the door locked, but unfortunately, thought Annie, he was here again this morning. She saw him go round to the back and accost Julie. Why did the word 'accost' come to me, she wondered? That's exactly what it feels like. Her father told her there was one like him in every church, but in a city and in a large church, it didn't matter so much, those kinds were diluted with the mass of people and couldn't gain control.

As Annie watched from the upstairs window, Julie jumped when Horace came up behind her and touched her on the shoulder. She could hear both of them through the window, which was open a bit.

"Scared you, huh?" He laughed. Julie straightened up abruptly and almost ran into the house, locking the kitchen door behind her. Horace looked amazed for a moment, then taking the opportunity to look around, inspected all the neglected flower beds and even went into the garden shed and disappeared for a moment.

Annie shook her head as she went downstairs to comfort Julie. The man was impossible. She met Julie coming up the stairs looking frightened. Without a word and without looking Annie in the eye, ran into her room, shut the door. Annie heard the bolt click. She stood at the door. "Are you all right?" she asked. There was no answer.

Annie was furious. Just when she was making some progress with this girl, this man who seemed to always do the wrong thing came along and set her back again. With her Irish temper marching forth, she stormed out of the house and caught Horace just as he was leaving the shed. He beamed his wet smile at her and seemed to show no shame at all about looking round her garden.

"Horace, you don't seem to have any of the normal rules of propriety at your disposal. You frightened Julie and I forbid you to come onto my property without permission. Why were you nosing around in my garden shed? Don't you have any sense of privacy, of decency?" she shouted.

Horace stared at her, mouth dropped wide open for a moment before he spoke. "Well, it's not your property, you see. It's church property. And as one of the elders I have an interest in what needs doing around here, always have. No one ever bothered about it before."

"Well, I am bothered about it. And I am ordering you off this property—as of now!" she continued, her arm pointing toward the gate. Horace put down the spade he had picked up and walked away, looking back at her as he went out the gate.

Annie went back inside, trembling with anger. Maybe she had won a battle with Horace, she thought, but she felt she was losing the war. She went upstairs to her study and turned on the computer to write to Emily:

Dear Em: What is it about a village? Are villages anachronisms, is that why the dynamics are still the same as they've always been? And if so, is there any hope at all for things to change? If the people who like to live in a small village are the only ones who continue to live there—if there is no new blood because people who are used to a broader life don't stay long, then what is the future? And hasn't this impacted the church? You have a vicar who has been trained in theology college and then he or she is plunked into an assignment like I've been, feeling alienated from the ways of the village, not having anyone to talk to and so never staying long. It looks like to me that the only hope for the village church is to make sure the vicar is a 'country boy', one who came from the country and wants to return after college. It's a stagnant pond, with no new water flowing in, no new life, so life is simply repeated, over and over and over and over. I'm not talking about intelligence. The people here are intelligent—it's the zeitgeist, you know? The small mindedness that must be a village disease. I honestly don't know if I can stay here—so much of my time is taken up with petty affairs that I am beginning to wonder about my calling, as well as my mental health. I didn't become a vicar to manage church affairs. If I had wanted to do that I would have taken a business degree or got a masters in human resources—how to settle petty quarrels, how best to run the annual car boot sale—do you get the picture? Do you think if Jesus returned to our village he would get the whip out again?!! Even if there hadn't been the vicious gossip about me and Matthew, I would be upset being here. Other than my women's Bible study, I don't feel I am getting anywhere. The church is an institution—that's all it is. It's where the social life of the village is conducted. No one is interested in evangelizing—after all—everyone already is a Christian, aren't they? After all—they're not Muslim or Buddhist, or even Jewish, heaven forbid, so they must be Christian. They don't get it—they don't understand what Christianity is all about. Oh, Em—help!

She answered right back:

Dear Annie: I don't want to sound unkind—I am absolutely brimming over with sympathy for you my friend. But I want to take up where you left off. If they don't 'get it' then it's obvious that is why you were sent there. Do you think Our Father is laughing at the predicament you're in? Of course not. Do you think he made a mistake? Of course not. He put you there for a reason—you are there to make them 'get it.' Don't you see? I know it's tough slogging, I know you feel isolated, as would I. And I would complain just as much if not more than you are. You have been put on a tough mission field. Of course you don't understand the natives. Just because you speak the same language doesn't mean they are the same type of people as you are. If you were in some jungle, you would try to reach them—wouldn't you? Sermon over. About Julie—I think you need to get some professional help with her, she sounds seriously disturbed to me. Does she have some type of amnesia, do you think? God bless you my friend—may the Lord make His face to shine upon you. Lots of love, Emily

Annie shut down the computer and sat there for a few minutes thinking over what Emily had written. She was right, of course, she always had been the most pragmatic of the pair. I must change my attitude. I have been wallowing in self pity, she told herself. And I must get some help for Julie. Thinking she should follow up on Matthew's offer to have her see his friend in London, her heart lightened because it gave her an excuse to phone Matthew. You are such a fraud, she told herself. So you're concerned about Julie, are you? At any rate, she picked up the phone and rang his office number. His voice mail came on and she left a message.

Chapter Eleven

Matthew wasn't happy about the house selling, but he found himself so indecisive lately, that he simply found himself carried along with the tide. And, he told himself, it was for the best. Then why don't I feel relieved, why don't I feel better if it is for the best?

He found a small flat in Islington. The rent wasn't exorbitant and it seemed to be a friendly type of neighborhood, but it was small. He was going to have to get rid of a lot of furniture as well as all the things in the attic and even a lot of books. Deciding he couldn't possibly accomplish all this in two weeks without taking time off, he quickly arranged for a temporary leave and began planning what to do. He was in such a hurry when he left his office that day that he didn't see the light blinking, telling him he had a message.

When he got to the cottage that evening, he phoned Amanda's parents before he did anything else, asking them if they wanted some of the furniture. They still lived in a three bedroom house and whilst they really didn't need any other furniture, they didn't want Amanda's things to be sold off to strangers, so agreed together with Matthew that he would hire a removal company to bring the things to them the next Saturday. Now all he had to do, he told himself wryly, was to decide what to give away and what to keep.

The house was so quiet. Times like these, he regretted giving the dogs to Annie, even though he had found them a blasted nuisance much of the time. At least they were happy to see him when he came home, at least they were alive. Poor choice of words, Matthew, he told himself, as he sunk into gloom. He had signed the papers for the sale and he had signed a lease for the flat. This is what one is supposed to do, isn't it—move on? They always say that. Have those people who say that moved on? Do those people who give that advice know what it takes to move on? How it wrenches your guts? Am I saying goodbye to Amanda by leaving her house, the house she loved so much? Or am I saying goodbye to Annie?

He had eaten a quick meal before leaving the city. He now sat down with a large sketch pad (Amanda's, he thought wryly) and made a floor plan of his new flat. He hadn't measured it, but he had a good eye for dimensions and starting with the bedroom, made tentative sketches of what furniture he would have room for. When he was finished, he realized how much was left. He knew it would be difficult for Amanda's parents to sell off any they could not handle, so phoned them again and asked if they could come there in the next couple of days in order to decide what was to go on the lorry. Maybe the new people would be interested in what was left.

He went to bed exhausted and yet was unable to sleep. He didn't know if he had made the right decision, but it didn't matter now. He had no choice. Oh, Amanda, why did you leave me, he cried out in anguish, knowing how ridiculous it was to say that. There was no one to blame, except the stupid lorry driver and even then, it was dark and rainy and his brakes failed—no one to blame at all. But it didn't matter, his life as he had planned it was ruined. Nothing seemed to matter anymore. Why do I find it so hard to move on? Is it Annie? He didn't know the answer. He simply knew he was very, very unhappy.

Two days after Annie had phoned Matthew, Julie came down the stairs one morning and said, "Could you take me to town to the supermarket? I'd like to buy some ingredients to do some baking, would that be all right?"

Annie was surprised, but readily agreed. "All right, Julie, we can go first thing if you don't mind. I have a busy afternoon."

Julie looked at her perplexed. "You keep calling me Julie. I don't like that name. Can't you call me Rhonda?"

"Rhonda? Sure, I guess so. You've never told me before you didn't like the name Julie. Is Rhonda your middle name?"

Julie didn't answer, she just smiled enigmatically.

That afternoon, Annie was out in the village, calling on two sick people, trying to remember what Emily had advised her. She noticed that Matthew's car was in his drive, but felt hurt that he hadn't phoned her back, so didn't phone him.

When she got home, the smell of fresh baked goods met her. Julie was in the kitchen, flour on her face, hands, and apron, and the kitchen was a mess. There were fresh baked scones on a plate on the table and she was just removing a cake from the oven.

Annie smiled, "I didn't know you liked to bake. I would have bought you these ingredients a long time ago. Um, smells good."

"Would you like a cup of tea and a scone?" Julie asked.

"Yes, that would be delightful. Thank you, Ju....I mean Rhonda." She seemed perfectly at home in this baking atmosphere. "Where did you learn to bake?" Annie asked her, biting into a very tasty scone.

"I really don't remember," Julie answered. She had washed her hands and sat at the kitchen table with her.

The dogs clustered around them, hoping for a handout. Annie tried to keep the conversation light because whenever she asked Julie questions, she seemed to retreat into her silence or even worse, her anger. "You could get a job in a bakery, had you thought of that?" Annie asked.

Julie took a sip of her tea before she answered, "Yes, but I don't know if I would like to bake if it was every day. Annie, is Matthew moving away?"

"Yes, I'm afraid so. You must have noticed his house for sale."

Julie nodded. "He seems nice, I'm sorry he's moving."

Annie hoped she wouldn't show any emotion. Julie certainly wasn't someone she could confide in. "So am I," she replied.

Annie decided to drive to Cambridge on her day off and see some of her old friends, peruse the libraries, and have a meal in one of her old haunts. So it was that on Monday morning, she drove off in her Morris Minor and left Julie in charge of the dogs. She saw the removal lorry parked in front of Matthew's house. Was he going away without even saying goodbye? Should she stay in case he dropped by? No, her stubbornness took over and she drove away, feeling that Julie, or Rhonda as she was now called, would be okay in her new, happier mood.

It was over an hour's drive and Annie felt good to be out of the village. She realized she always felt better out of the village than in it. She felt free. She had phoned a few friends and arranged to meet them for lunch at Brown's Café. As she drove into the city, a wave of nostalgia hit her. So many wonderful memories associated with this place, such happy days. *Maybe I should have stayed on and taken a teaching post, maybe a country vicar is the last place I'm supposed to be.*

She parked in the Lion Car Park and as she had some time until the lunch hour, walked down to the river. It was now April and the wildflowers weren't out as they would be in May, nor were many punters on the river. In May, the meadows on the Backs of the colleges would be radiantly dressed in an array of wild flowers and the river would be full of tourists hiring punters who told them all about the colleges as they went down the river. Traffic was always impossible in Cambridge, but here, all was quiet and peaceful. She found a favorite spot where she had often sat studying on warm days, where she often prayed.

She thought a lot these days about her prayer life. It was so different now. In the beginning, she had been extremely idealistic. It had been like falling in love, knowing that God loved her and responding to that love. It was a little like how she felt about Matthew, but not quite. *Is that what's happened? Am I so disillusioned that I don't think God loves me anymore?* She certainly knew she didn't feel close any longer, not like she used to. She decided to just sit there and concentrate her mind. She was remarkably alone. She closed her eyes and visualized Jesus sitting on the ground in front of her. She always 'saw' him as a very handsome, muscular type of man, one who exuded strength, yet with extremely kind soft brown eyes. His attention never wavered, he always looked straight at her and he was always smiling.

"Hello, Jesus" she began. "*I'm happy to be back here, a place where I learned all about you, learned about you in depth from people whom I respected. But I'm not happy where you've sent me, you know that. And I don't think I'm doing a very good job, either. I'm lonely, I'm miserable because of Matthew, and I don't have any self-confidence. Please, please help me, Lord.*"

She remained quiet then. She didn't expect an answer other than through circumstances. She knew that the Holy Spirit sometimes guided her with a strong thought, something out of the blue that she never would have thought of, but unlike others who had told her of their experiences, she had never had an answer whilst she was praying. Rather, she seemed to get answers at times when she most didn't expect the Lord to speak to her.

After awhile, she rose, wiping away a few tears that had leaked out. *Time to go—time to go meet these interesting and interested friends.*

They were already seated at the table. Jeremy Bornley, who had been in her year at theology college and Jill Worster, who was several years ahead of Annie and had taken a position as dean of women at St. Catherine's. They both rose and kissed Annie on each cheek in greeting.

"Well, Rev. O'Donnell," said Jeremy, "you look even better than you did when you left. Country air must be good for you."

Annie grimaced. "I think city air is better for me. I sure miss Cambridge and I've missed you two." They all sat down and Annie smiled, "First, tell me about your lives, what's happening?" They ordered lunch and both Jill and Jeremy filled her in on what their work lives were now. Annie knew she could confide in these two and she did, telling them everything—about the village dynamics, about Julie, and about Matthew. By the time she finished, they had finished their lunch and hers was hardly touched.

"You eat now and we'll advise." Jill laughed.

Annie laughed with her, "Oh, how I miss you two. Emily and I keep up almost daily on email, but I don't have this kind of supportive, and I must say it, intelligent, conversation to help me out. I feel as if I'm drowning in the pond, as I've come to call it."

"I'll start with Matthew, if you don't mind," Jill said, looking at Jeremy, "since I'm the expert in this crowd about relationships."

Annie knew that Jill had recently married and she smiled at Jeremy, whom she knew went from woman to woman, rather too frequently for his own good.

"It sounds to me like he's very interested in you" Jill said, "and that he feels so guilty about it, that it makes him act strangely. That coupled with the vicious gossip, don't you think? I mean, if he simply thought you were a nice person, he would have no problem being around you. I think he's afraid he's being disloyal to his dead wife. It's a minefield, Annie, stepping in when someone has died. That person gets idealized. I am sure she was a lovely person, but I bet in his eyes and memories now she was absolutely perfect in every way. Tough to compete against that."

Jeremy just nodded his head. "I agree, not that I've had that experience, but I have had that relayed to me on two occasions from widows and widowers. To hear them talk, that person who died was incapable of doing anything wrong—ever."

"So what do you do, do you think I should give up?" asked Annie.

"No, but I think you should be patient," said Jill. "Don't worry, if he's interested in you, he'll contact you no matter where he's living. And maybe it will be better if he's not there, no prying eyes, you know?"

"I agree. I know it will be hard," Jeremy added, "but it

doesn't sound like he'll lose touch with you altogether. Men love to chase, you know. Just back off and let him do all the contacting."

Annie nodded with her mouth full. She wanted to protest, but by the time she swallowed the bite of salad she had taken, Jeremy was again speaking.

"But now about Julie, I think you need some professional help with her. She could be seriously disturbed," he said, looking over at Jill for support.

"Do you know anyone in London?" Jill asked. "A psychiatrist or a psychologist?"

"No, I've never looked into anything like that," Annie answered.

"I've always thought the church drops the ball in terms of mental health," Jill said, "it's as if once you are a Christian, you aren't supposed to have any problems, so why bother with people who fix minds?"

"Um, I know," Jeremy interrupted. "I think it's a hangover from the days of Freud, who wasn't exactly religious. I think the clergy is generally wary of sending someone to a professional who isn't a Christian because when someone says 'God told me to do this', they may lock them up."

"I do know of a charitable trust in London," Jill said. "they liaise with churches to find competent therapists, ones they feel they can trust. Would you like me to ring you with their number after I get home?"

Annie nodded with her mouth once more full. After that, she gave up, the conversation was much more important than food. "Thanks for advice on both things. Gosh, I miss you two and others as well. I miss what I took for granted here, the constant intellectual stimulation, the lectures, the musical events. All those are gone. The only thing to look forward to is the church fete."

"Sounds elitist to me" Jill teased, smiling.

"Yes, it is elitist," Annie admitted, "but not for socio-economic reasons. There are people in the village who are wealthy. It's because of a lack of interest. One of my parishioners said to me, "I hate London. Wouldn't go there if you paid me. All that traffic, all the noise." But that's where the action is, the theatre, exhibitions, museums. And Cambridge, to me, is the seat of learning. Here people talk about ideas, not about each other."

"All I can say is I'm glad it's not me," said Jeremy, smiling at her. "I've forgotten the reason you went there, did you feel called?"

"No, not really. The whole thing was weird. I was told the vicarage was empty, had been for a year and since I've never lived in a village, I thought it might be fun, you know, all that. It sounded restful. It's been anything but."

"So what is your goal there," Jill asked, with a serious look on her face. "What do you hope to accomplish?"

"What do you mean?" Annie asked.

"Well, you obviously aren't going to be there the rest of your life. That's one good thing about the restless life we're called to lead as clergy. We know we aren't ever going to be anywhere forever, so when you leave, what legacy would you like to leave? How will the village be changed by your serving them?"

Annie looked at Jill with eyes wide, silent for a moment. Then, "You know, it just came to me. All I've been thinking about the entire time I've been there is how I like it, what I want to do. My focus has been all wrong, hasn't it? You're right, Jill, I won't be there forever and I would like to leave a legacy."

"So what will it be?" Jill pressed.

Annie was silent, pondering her response for a moment. "I guess...I guess I would like to be sure that every person who is in the church now is well and truly a Christian, that each of them has a personal, vital relationship with Jesus, and that their lives are transformed, and in so doing, that the village will be transformed."

Jeremy and Jill applauded softly, smiling at their friend. "Good, now go do it. Be a leader, Annie" urged Jeremy. "Make a difference in that village. You're not going to change their intellectual tastes. They're not going to become museum buffs all of a sudden, but if you can leave behind a happy village, having stopped gossiping, you will have completed your mission."

"Well, that would be nice, wouldn't it?" Annie said with a smile, as they got up to leave, pushing their chairs back from the table.

"That's the whole point, isn't it?" asked Jill, laughing. "I've got to run, but I'll phone you tonight with that contact in London." As she walked away, she turned back and said, "And Annie, try to be good about Matthew, will you? He sounds worth waiting for." She looked at Jeremy and nodded her head sideways at him. "There aren't that many good fish in the pond, you know!"

Jeremy made a face at her. As they left the restaurant, he put his arm familiarly around Annie's waist. "You know, my pet, I think I've made a huge mistake about you."

She pulled away, wondering what on earth he was up to. "What do you mean?"

He again firmly put his arm around her waist as they walked onto the sidewalk. "I just think I made a good friend of you instead of seeing you as a beautiful, charming, romantic woman.." He smiled.

Annie's heart sank. She liked Jeremy hugely. Liked, that was it. He wasn't her type; she loved having him for a friend, now was she going to lose him as well? She knew Jeremy never had a problem with self-confidence. He seemed almost always to have any woman he fancied fancy him back. "Are you coming on to me, Jeremy?" Annie laughed.

He looked hurt. "Don't laugh. I'm serious. I just realized what an attractive woman you are."

"And why did you just now realize?"

"I don't know—dumb I guess. Anyway, can't you give me a chance? I bet I'll make you forget about that Matthew guy in no time at all."

Annie shook her head. "You can't be serious, Jeremy.

You must be in between ladies or you wouldn't even look at me."

"Well, I am 'in between' as you put it. But all the time we were talking today, I kept looking at you—at that wonderful copper-colored hair, your eyes, your complexion."

"My freckles..." Annie laughed again.

"That's right—your freckles. I love them. I don't know why I hadn't noticed them before." He stopped and faced her. They were now on the Kings Parade, outside Kings College. He grew serious. "Do you have to go right back? I can take the afternoon off. Wouldn't you like to walk around our old haunts, stay for dinner, stay the night?"

"Whoa....what are you asking me?"

"I'm asking you for a date, a long date, since you live out of town. You could stay the night with Jill and I could pick you up for breakfast early in the morning. I'm telling you that I'm immensely attracted to you and I want to spend more time with you."

Annie looked at him intently, "Why all of a sudden, Jeremy?"

"I don't know. But I do know I want to be with you. Please?"

She didn't know what to do. Jeremy was one of her best friends, had been for years. She never thought of him in any kind of romantic way. He was fun and interesting and charming and very spiritual. His girlfriends had always been rather lightweight in the area of brains. If she had thought about it at all, she would have said he liked women like Jill and herself as friends, in a different category than his girlfriends. She really couldn't think of a way out of his invitation and so reluctantly, she agreed, first having phoned Jill and left a message saying she would be spending the night on her sofa.

"So, what would you like to do the rest of the afternoon?" Jeremy beamed at her.

Why am I not excited? Annie asked herself. She always enjoyed Cambridge. "I think I'd just like to walk around, go to the market, and walk around the Backs—is that all right?"

"Sure, anything you want to do. My time is yours."

Annie wondered if he had planned this; it was odd that he just happened to have the afternoon off. They lingered over the stalls in the market and walked around the cobblestone streets of the city. Cambridge, the name taken from the River Cam where a bridge was built at that spot on the river, hence the name.

Annie had always felt very comfortable with Jeremy, they had been buddies. She had looked upon him as a substitute for her older brothers, but now she felt awkward with him. She silently prayed, *'Oh, no Lord, not another problem—please!"*

But Jeremy didn't feel awkward, or at least he certainly didn't act like it. He was on his best form. He was a brilliant conversationalist and also had a wicked sense of humor. He kept Annie thoroughly entertained all afternoon. They ended up hiring a punt and lazily drifting down the river to Grantchester, where they tied the punt to the bank and explored the village. They had tea at The Orchard where Virginia Woolf and the Bloomsbury crowd used to go and ended up back in Cambridge when it was almost dark.

In an extremely enthusiastic voice, Jeremy proposed, "Now, how about a quiet dinner at my place."

"Your place?" Annie was suspicious. She had often been to Jeremy's flat. They all had been there often, studying, having long theological discussions, and it had been fun. Jeremy was an excellent cook and she knew he loved showing off his culinary skills. She was hesitant. Surely Jeremy hadn't changed that much. Surely she could trust him—couldn't she? "Jeremy, tell me the truth. Did you have this all planned?"

He nodded and tried to pull her close to him. They were standing on the bridge on Silver Street, having just turned in their punt. Annie pulled away.

"Yes, I must confess I did. I took the afternoon off when you said you were coming down. So, what do you say, can I fix you a good Italian meal? ."

Annie was torn. This afternoon had been like a holiday, a

holiday from her life in the village which she thought was stifling. Coming here, being with Jeremy and Jill, having deep, intellectual discussions—why break it off early? She knew there really was no reason for her to be home until noon tomorrow and she could make that easily. "All right," she laughed, you've talked me into it. But I must call home and let Julie know I'm not coming back."

She dialed home on her mobile. Julie didn't answer, but then she never did. Annie left a message and asked that Julie phone her back. They drove the short distance to Jeremy's flat in Annie's car and Annie tried to relax whilst Jeremy began to fix dinner.

"That's the nice thing about pasta, you know?" Jeremy said, having just put a large pot of water on the hob to boil.

"What is?" Annie asked.

"Well, you always have it around and the ingredients can be stored in jars, so you can always have a really good meal on the spur of the moment."

Annie stood in the doorway of the small kitchen. She remembered from other meals at his place that he didn't want anyone to come into the kitchen. There was barely any place to turn around. "It gets me out of my rhythm" he always said.

"But I thought you said you planned this," she teased.

"Well, I did actually. I did pick up an aubergine this morning and some fresh lettuce for a salad, but the other things I always have around."

"Just in case you meet a new prospect?" Annie asked, in a teasing tone.

Jeremy stopped chopping the aubergine and looked at her with a serious look. "Is my reputation that bad?" He appeared to try to look hurt.

Annie smiled. "Well, you did manage to go through quite a few women in a short time, if I remember correctly."

"And you're thinking that I just want to add you to that list, is that right?" He wasn't smiling.

He had beautiful brown eyes. It wasn't that Annie didn't

know that, she had always known it. But somehow she had never thought about the way Jeremy looked. He was already balding on top, with a goodish fringe of light brown hair surrounding it and he wore spectacles, always of the latest fashion. He was not what one would call good-looking, but he was suave, in a manner that engaged others immediately. Annie had never been attracted to him; he was just one of her friends, almost in a gender-free manner, one of her pals. Now, however, he was looking at her with such a serious expression on his face that she felt as if she could dive into those deep brown eyes.

He wiped his hands on a tea towel and came over to where she was standing. Without a word, he drew her to him and kissed her very gently on the mouth. Then he drew her closer and kissed her deeply for a very long time. They stood, holding each other until finally Annie broke away. She went over to the sofa and sat down, looking up at him with a helpless expression on her face. He didn't say anything, but sat down opposite her in an easy chair. Neither of them said anything for quite a long while—they just continued looking at each other.

Annie was a jumble of emotions. She was amazed at her response to him. It was as if she had been hungry for a long time and he had provided the food she needed. That kiss had been wonderful, absolutely wonderful and she wanted it to happen again. Yet, this was Jeremy! Jeremy, who must have had this very same effect on fifty women by now. He was very polished and as she knew, very experienced. Just because he was a priest in the Church of England didn't mean she could trust him. He could drop her tomorrow just like he seemed to drop all those other women. And what about Matthew? She had thought she was in love with him and if she really was, then why did she respond to Jeremy so wholeheartedly? All these thoughts raced through her mind and all the while, she never took her eyes off Jeremy's deep brown eyes.

Finally, Jeremy smiled and reached out for her hands with both of his. She took his hands in hers and smiled back. "I don't know what to say," she began.

"You don't have to say anything. Just enjoy it."

And with that, he moved over to the sofa and kissed her once again and once again for a very long time. She broke away and stood up. She was terrified of the feelings she was experiencing and was realizing that she really didn't trust Jeremy any longer. Besides, she wasn't sure she could trust herself; she didn't know what would happen if she stayed. "I think I'd better go," she said, gathering up her handbag and coat.

Jeremy didn't argue as he stood up as well. "I wish you would stay," he said, brushing her hair with one hand lightly, "but I understand." He kissed her lightly on the cheek and then opened the door.

Annie's car was parked right in front of his building. She got in the car and drove rather blindly to Jill's flat. Jill wasn't home, but had left the key under the mat. Thankfully, Annie went in and after making up a bed on the sofa, tried to go to sleep. She was glad she didn't have to talk to Jill about this. She would get up early and drive home, and then she would write to Emily. She was really the only one who would understand. Jill and her husband were still asleep when Annie woke up at six. Dressing quietly, she wrote Jill a quick note thanking her and telling her she would call her soon. She knew Jill probably didn't have a clue. Jeremy and Annie had simply had a fun afternoon and dinner together, the way they always had—right?

Chapter Twelve

On the way home Annie began to feel apprehensive. She tried to phone Julie again, but there was still no answer and she wondered if she had she run away again. When she got to the village, she noticed there was no car in Matthew's drive.

However, when she opened the front door of the vicarage, Julie and the dogs were there to greet her. Julie even showed a tiny beginning of a smile and in answer to her query, said everything was fine. Annie decided not to scold her for not ringing her back; she didn't want to spoil the little bit of progress being made with Julie's new attitude. "Were there any calls for me?" she asked, as she went to the message machine in the kitchen.

"Yes," Julie replied, "they're all on there."

Annie's heart leapt. Maybe there was a message from Matthew. Maybe he wanted to say goodbye and was disappointed when she wasn't home, but no, nothing but several parishioners calling on church business.

"Would you like a cup of tea?" Julie asked.

Annie was surprised, but pleased. "Oh, yes, that would be lovely," she responded, smiling at Julie and giving the dogs the attention they were asking for. She sat down at the kitchen table and let Julie wait on her. "I decided to stay over with a friend last night. Were you all right here alone in the house? I wouldn't have stayed if you had phoned back and said you were frightened."

Julie took the pot of tea she had made to the table, then fetched two cups and saucers from the cupboard, before she answered, "I was a little frightened, but I wanted you to stay if you wanted to. It seems to me you don't have much fun, so I thought you should enjoy yourself."

Annie was amazed. This was the first time Julie had ever

shown any concern for her as well as it being the first time she had spoken in a paragraph, rather than a short sentence.

"Thank you, Julie. Did you sleep?"

"Please call me Rhonda—remember?" she said, in a rebuking tone. She poured the tea for both of them before she continued. "No, I didn't sleep, as a matter of fact. I finally came down and slept on the sofa, so I guess I did sleep a little towards morning."

"Was it because you were frightened being here alone?"

Julie nodded, "Yes, I am frightened to stay alone. I guess I never have before except when you went to Belfast, but it's okay. I enjoyed part of it and after all, I'm not a baby, I need to get used to it."

"I feel terrible now. I shouldn't have left you here alone. I was acting incredibly selfishly."

"Well, you told me to phone that lady Joy if I needed anything, but I didn't want to."

Annie took a sip of the hot tea and said, "I really think this village is a safe place; since I've been here I haven't heard of any crime. And the dogs would bark if anyone was trying to break in." She knew she was sounding very rational and that Julie's fears were emotional. Again, I'm failing in my role of pastoral care, she told herself. Julie seemed almost chatty and Annie lingered after she had drunk her cup of tea, but was anxious to go upstairs and write to Emily, to tell her about Jeremy. When Julie went into the garden with the dogs, she went upstairs.

She turned on her computer and saw there was another email from Joe.

Hello Rev. O'Donnell: I wish you would write to me more often—since I am Julie's friend and since you're taking care of her, I wish you would write. I haven't heard from Julie either—is she okay? Joe

Annie didn't know what to think of these emails. They

seemed like one more problem added to all the others, but she clicked Reply and wrote:

Hello Joe: Julie says she doesn't know you, so I don't know what to think of that or your emails. Did you used to be her boyfriend and she wants to forget you? She is all right, by the way—seems happy. Please tell me what your relationship with her was, is. God bless you. Annie O'Donnell

There was one from Emily. She wrote back, telling her about the new developments with Jeremy and that Matthew had moved without saying goodbye. She had to answer several phone messages, mostly annoying problems which seemed huge to the people who phoned, but were minor in reality. Not personal problems, instead, things such as the fact that someone had moved the notice board which had always been in the same spot and what was she going to do about it, the on-going quarrel between Horace and several others about who was to decide on the prayers at certain services.

Why wasn't the business of the church getting people to come to know God and to serve him? It seemed to her she was only called on to settle disputes within the church. Power struggles, her father had told her. "They exist in every church, every organization, for that matter, but we like to think the church is different. If you give people a democracy, where they all have a say, then they all want their own way." She remembered his words today and rolled her eyes heavenward as she listened to one complaint after another on the machine.

It wasn't as if nothing good had happened since she arrived. There were some people who told her they were grateful for the time she spent with them, for the understanding she had when there were crises in their lives. The young couple whom she had helped the night their baby was so ill had been regular churchgoers ever since and Annie appreciated their receptive faces when she was in the pulpit. And there were several women from the Bible study group that now met at Joy's house, who had come to her to talk over their problems and expressed their gratitude. Yet she had been there four months now and she didn't think she had accomplished all that much. After her bombshell sermon, she thought she detected more respect from the men. She surmised they liked the fact she had fought back, refusing to be scandalized for something she was innocent of, but the incident hadn't endeared her heart to the village. She thought in some ways she was in an adversarial position with them.

It was only Tuesday, but the dreaded sermon needed to be begun, at the very least. How could she be inspired, she asked God, when this place didn't inspire her. *Was what was wrong with Christianity, the church? What would Jesus think about all their petty quarrels?* Just then the doorbell rang and peeping out of the curtains, she saw her old nemesis, Horace.

Two times out of three when she saw it was him, she simply didn't answer the door, but she had used up her other two times and she knew he would simply be back in an hour. She opened the door, making sure she was blocking the door with her body, preventing him coming in unbidden. "Yes, Horace?"

He beamed his oily smile. "Hello, Annie," he looked at the blocked door meaningfully.

"What do you want?" Her voice sounded exasperated and she knew she was being rude, as well as conducting herself in a manner unbecoming to a vicar, but she didn't even care.

Horace acted affronted. "I need to speak to you. No other vicar has ever not let me come in before."

"Well this vicar is different. And I've learned that letting you in means I'm in for a very long time of hearing your complaints and I'm just not in the mood!" With that, she shut the door, went into her study, shut that door and sat down at her desk. Putting her head in her hands and looking out the window across the fields, she tried to pray, but couldn't. She knew she had just treated Horace terribly; she knew she needed to try to be nicer to him and she knew she needed to be forgiven. But as often happened these days, she simply felt overwhelmed. She went into her bedroom, lay down on the bed, and was instantly asleep.

The next day, feeling rested and less emotional, she phoned the psychologist Jill had found in London. She had talked to Julie about seeing someone again and she had agreed hesitatingly, but only if it was a woman, so Matthew's friend was out.

Julie was as nervous as she had ever been as she and Annie sat in the waiting room for her appointment with the psychologist. She hadn't wanted to come here at all, but Annie had insisted, telling her it would be good to have someone to talk to about her past, that it would help her to know what to do with her future, and that no one would know what she revealed in the session. She had refused to see Matthew's friend, because he was a man. So Annie had rung the number Jill gave her and made an appointment with a female psychologist.

"Hello, Julie," a woman who looked to be in her sixties said, extending her hand to her. "I'm Dr. Evans."

Annie introduced herself and said she would be waiting for Julie.

"Come on through to my office, Julie" she said kindly.

Julie was relieved by the way the doctor looked; she was a bit plump, had grey hair, and seemed grandmotherly. The time went by quickly, although she didn't talk much. Dr. Evans told her she didn't have to say anything if she didn't want to, with the result that most of the hour was spent in silence. Dr. Evans also told her that she wouldn't tell Annie what she said and strangely, Julie felt comfortable with her. Dr. Evans just chatted about the weather and asked questions about the village, telling Julie that when she was ready to talk to her, she would and that until then, they just needed to get to know each other. She was gentle and Julie found herself warming to her. Maybe there was someone else, besides Annie, who was kind. Being given permission not to talk, not to confide her terrible past, paradoxically made her want to confide. She actually was disappointed when Dr. Evans said that their time for today was over.

Annie looked up from the magazine she was reading when Julie came back into the waiting room. She smiled at her and didn't ask any questions other than when her next appointment was. "Do you think you could come here alone next time?" she asked.
"I think so, now that you've shown me how to do it. Or maybe, could you come with me one more time, just to make sure?"
"Of course I can, no problem," Annie assured her. She was relieved, she had been afraid the whole thing would be a disaster and that Julie would refuse to come back. Maybe this was going to work; maybe this was something which would help Julie. Knowing the circumstances, Dr. Evans had lowered her usual fee.

Meanwhile, Jeremy phoned her at least once a day, emailed at least once a day and wanted to see her again soon. She didn't find his attention intrusive, in fact, it helped a great deal. He was different from Matthew in that he was willing to talk about spiritual and church matters. They had their Christian faith in common, which she sensed Matthew was either lacking or just didn't want to talk about. She also had a vast memory pool with Jeremy; they had known each other for years and knew a lot of the same people. He was a brilliant orator and was already becoming well known in Cambridge not only as a preacher, but as a writer. He had two published books to his credit and was working on a third. They were the type of theological books only other clergy read, but they were brilliant theological discourses and he seemed to be growing in his ability to grasp and struggle with tough theological issues.

Annie admired him. It was just disconcerting, that was all. He had stepped out of the box she had put him in. She and Jill and Emily as well as other females at school had made sarcastic remarks to each other about Jeremy and his romances. Am I going to become someone everyone is talking about, one of his women—past tense? She asked him that directly one evening when they were having a long chat.

There was a moment of silence on the line. "I don't know Annie. Don't think for a moment that it hasn't bothered me that I've not stuck to one person. I just seem to lose interest after awhile. It's a characteristic I don't like about myself one bit."

"Well, how do I know I'm different? Why wouldn't you lose interest in me?"

"I don't know, but I sure hope I don't. You're everything I've always wanted in a woman and besides, the fact that we have been such good friends for such a long time can't hurt."

Annie laughed. "You mean you already know all my faults."

"Yes," he interrupted, "but that's just it. You sure don't have many, other than that I'm sure all the men in your parish are in love with you. That makes me jealous."

"Well, I can assure you they're not," Annie responded. "I think most of them don't approve of me at all."

"I think I need to put in an appearance in your village. Besides, I can't wait to see you again, to hold you in my arms. It's been almost two weeks—I need to see you."

Annie grew warm all over as he said those words. I should be outraged, she thought, but admitted to herself that she would quite like to be in his arms once again.

"Annie?"

"Yes, I'm here."

"Your silence, does that mean you don't want me to come there?"

"No, I think I would quite like you to come here. When are you thinking of?"

"What about Monday, on your day off. I'll drive up very early, be there by nine and we can have the entire day together. How does that sound?"

Annie smiled into the phone. "It sounds wonderful, Jeremy."

Matthew hadn't been back to the village. He phoned Annie once or twice a week and certainly noticed that she had stopped phoning him. He told himself she no longer needed him, that the interest had all been on his side anyway. Telling himself that didn't help, however, he still wanted to see her. He had tried to phone her several times when her line was engaged for inordinately long periods of time. He knew she talked to Joy often, so he didn't think much of it. He had called several times this evening before he got through. When she answered, he once more felt the attraction, even to her voice. "Hi Annie? How are you?"

"I'm fine, Matthew, how nice to hear your voice."

They talked about Julie for awhile. "She now goes on the train alone and I really think it's helping her."

"Have you spoken to Dr. Evans? Have any of the mysteries about Julie been enlightened?"

"No, the doctor made it plain to me when I first spoke to her that her time with Julie was confidential and that only with Julie's permission could she tell me anything."

"I guess that makes sense. That would give Julie the confidence to talk to her. So does that mean you'll never know anything about her?"

"I don't know. I gather that if Julie begins to feel better about herself, more comfortable, she may begin to volunteer information—I don't know."

"Look, I haven't been back to the village and I was wondering if you'd have time to come down here for dinner?"

There was silence for a long moment, then "Yes, that would be lovely," Annie said in a quiet tone of voice. "When?"

"That's entirely up to you. My social calendar isn't exactly chockablock you know. Maybe Monday, I know that's your day off," he responded.

"No, that won't work for me," Annie said, "how about the next Friday evening?"

"Sure, anytime. I...I've missed seeing you and talking to you." He really hadn't meant to say that, but it came out.

"All right, at seven? At your office?" she asked.

"Yes—and Annie…"

"Yes?"

"Dress up; I'm going to take you to a very special restaurant."

"Oh, Matthew, you don't need to do that…"

"Yes I do," he interrupted. "Yes I do."

Now what did he mean by that, she wondered as she hung up the phone. She looked up to heaven, *"Wasn't my life complicated enough, Lord—is this a test?!!!"* He didn't answer.

Annie was amazed at her reaction. Yes, she would like to see him, but it wasn't the same anymore, she didn't feel overwhelmed with relief, with gratitude that he wanted to see her and she didn't think about him obsessively anymore. *Should I have dinner with him? Will that make me even more confused about Jeremy?* At least with Jeremy it's reciprocal, with Jeremy I don't feel miserable, like I do every time I'm with Matthew.

Monday arrived and Annie was up early getting ready for Jeremy's visit. She knew he would be noticed in the village, but she didn't know how to show him around without his being seen. At least maybe this would diffuse the gossip about her and Matthew.

She was very pleased to see him. He stepped in the door and immediately took her in his arms, kissing her for a long time, which seemed to be his way, until she pulled away, flustered. "Goodness, Jeremy, good morning!" she said, laughing. "Here, give me your coat." He certainly did know how to kiss and she certainly did enjoy kissing him.

"Annie, I'm so glad to see you. I knew I wanted to see you, but now that I'm here, I realize how very much I wanted to see you."

Annie just smiled at his words and didn't say she was glad to see him as well, although she was. "Come on in and have some breakfast, then we'll go from there," she said, leading him into the kitchen. She didn't know what reaction Julie was going to have to Jeremy, but she seemed to still be asleep. Annie was quite good at scrambled eggs, so that's what she fixed for him and tried to keep him from being amorous at least whilst she was cooking. She reminded him that Julie was in the house and that seemed to work.

After breakfast, they toured the house, in silence upstairs, and then set off to see the village. He didn't need to be told to keep his hands off of her while out and about. Soon after they began their walk, they met Joy coming out of the shop. Annie had not told her about Jeremy and now introduced him as simply a fellow student from Cambridge. He did not have on a dog collar and certainly didn't look like a clergyman. Joy welcomed him to the village and went on, not asking any questions, which wasn't like her, Annie thought.

After the short walk through the village, at Jeremy's suggestion, they went back to get the dogs and took them on a walk along the public footpath which began on the outskirts of Cambersham. It was evident from the moment he arrived that Jeremy loved dogs. He laughed as Scout pulled hard against the lead. He had Scout and Daisy, whilst Annie carried Tibby much of the way as he couldn't keep up with the others with his tiny legs.

"I don't know how you handle all three of them," he said, looking over at her.

"Actually, I don't walk them that much. Julie does it most of the time."

They walked a long way and Jeremy kept his distance ."You know, I grew up in a small village, so I understand the the dynamics. T'hat's why I've avoided them since," he said.

"There are some really good people here," Annie said, earnestly, "but there seems to be a disease, or maybe that's too strong a word, maybe it's like a malaise, you know? Does the village do it to them or are they attracted to stay in a village because they're prone that way in the beginning?"

By this time, they were back home sitting in the kitchen. Before Jeremy could answer, Annie heard Julie coming down the stairs. She got up to meet her so that she wouldn't be surprised. "Good morning, Julie, come into the kitchen, I want you to meet someone, a friend of mine."

Julie looked hesitant. Annie urged, "He's very nice. He's a vicar from Cambridge, someone I went to school with."

Julie followed Annie into the room and in response to Jeremy's greeting, gave him a nervous smile.

"You look familiar to me, Julie. Have we met before?" he asked.

"No, no, not at all," she said in a flustered manner. "Glad to meet you." And with that, she hurried out of the room and back upstairs.

Annie followed her, saying "Julie, come on down and have some breakfast. We'll go into the living room and we won't bother you." Motioning to Jeremy to follow her, they settled themselves in the living room and Annie shut the door to the hall. After a bit, they heard Julie slowly come down the stairs and heard her talking to the dogs.

"Maybe we should go somewhere. How about a drive in the country and a pub lunch?" Jeremy said, in a hopeful voice.

Annie agreed and they were soon on their way. "She is such a strange girl, Jeremy. Do you really think you've met her before?"

"Yes, I'm sure of it. Only..."

"What?"

"Her name wasn't Julie."

"Was it Rhonda? She's told me she would rather be called Rhonda, though she won't tell me why."

"No, it wasn't Rhonda—I can't remember her name. All I know is, it wasn't Julie."

Jeremy changed the subject and they had a lovely afternoon. When he left her around five o'clock, he came in, and after making sure Julie wasn't around, held her for a very long time with a very long kiss. "Bye, my sweet. I will miss you the moment I drive away."

Annie didn't know what to say. When she was with him she enjoyed him immensely. They talked about things of mutual interest, people they knew, spiritual matters, church matters. He had a depth that was far beyond hers. And when he kissed her, she realized what the word 'melted' meant when reading about a love scene in a novel. No wonder he had been so successful in acquiring women. He was totally self confident. He never asked her how she felt about him; he seemed to assume it was mutual. Was it? She really didn't know.

No sooner had Jeremy driven away, than she found a note from Julie. She had once more gone away. The note simply said thank you for the help she had given her and that she would be in touch. It was not signed. Annie raced up to her room. Everything was gone. How could she have packed up so quickly? Annie had only been gone from the house three hours.

She phoned Joy and asked her to inquire around the village. She must have phoned a taxi from the neighboring village—that was the only way she could have taken all her things. Annie knew she didn't have much money; she really had no income of her own, but Annie gave her a bit of pocket money from time to time, all she could afford, really.

She phoned Dr. Evans and left a message, asking her to phone her if Julie contacted her. And she phoned Matthew. He wasn't in either. Taking the dogs upstairs with her, she once more entered Julie's room to make sure there weren't any clues.

The wardrobe was empty, the bed was made. On a hunch, she felt beneath the pillow. She saw a small notebook and removed it. She didn't know if she should open it or not. If Julie had been here and she found it, she wouldn't have dreamed of reading it. Now, though, she felt she must; perhaps it would provide a clue to what was going on with Julie. She went back downstairs and sitting in the kitchen, read through it. It was not full and the jottings seemed to have been random. She read the first one, hearing Julie's voice as she read:

3 May I don't know where I am, nor how I got here. I only have three pounds in my wallet and a bus pass with my name on it. I must be in London, since I see red buses, but I don't know where in London. It's almost six o'clock in the evening by my watch. I'm dressed too warmly. I have on a wool coat and it's a warm spring day. I know what day it is because I looked at a newspaper at the newsagent. I'm embarrassed to ask anyone where I am...they will ask me where it is I want to go and I don't know! The last thing I remember was being with my dad. No, I don't want to think about that. But we weren't in London. We were in Torquay—so how did I get here? I must have run away. I always run away from him. I hate him.'

4 May I found Corinne's address in my journal and took a bus to Hackney where Corinne lives. She said I was welcome when I phoned and she lets me sleep on her sofa. I don't have any clothes. I don't know where I left them. She said Dad had phoned, wanting to know if I was here. She told him no, because I wasn't yet. She's promised me she won't tell him. She says not to worry, that she will help me get a job and she'll loan me some clothes—we're the same size. She calls me Rhonda. I don't know why, but I don't like to say anything. It's so good to be able to write in this journal, it helps me keep my head straight. I hide it whenever I'm staying with anyone. That's a joke. I'm always staying with someone—I never get to be alone. I've never had my own place, even my own room. But I left one journal somewhere.

31 May Corinne says I must tell the social services

where I am—she talked to them and told them I was frightened of my father. They told her I'm of age and don't have to go with him, but I need to hide from him.
1 February I'm back at Corinnes. I left this journal hidden in between the mattresses of her bed and I've been gone—I disappeared again. The thing is I disappear from myself. I don't know where I went unless someone tells me.
Another uneventful day, but I don't know what day it is. My life is one non-event after another. Where am I going? Why do I even exist? I don't know who I am.

Annie turned the page and breathed in shock as she looked at a very ugly drawing in black and red ink. Annie couldn't make out what it was of, because it had marks all through it as if Julie had decided to erase it, but couldn't since it was in ink.

She quickly turned to the next page which was blank. Several more blank pages and then:

Joe says he loves me—he doesn't, because he doesn't really know me. If he really knew me, he wouldn't love me, would he.

So Joe did exist! Julie was lying. Annie read the rest of the journal without finding anything particularly remarkable. There was no mention of Annie or the dogs or of anyone in her past life. The very last page had the simple sentence: I feel empty.

As she sat at the kitchen table, mulling over the journal, the phone rang.

"Hi Annie" Matthew said, "Is anything wrong? Your voice sounded rather frantic on the message."

Annie took in a deep breath before she answered, "Yes, very wrong, I'm afraid." She told him Julie was gone again and about the journal.

"What can I do to help—do you want me to come there?"

"No, that wouldn't help, I don't think. But could you phone your friend, the psychologist, and talk to him about her, see if he has any advice?"

"Sure, sure I can do that, but I'm not so worried about Julie as I am about you. Are you all right?"

Annie once more felt the warmth of tears backing up in her eyes. *My body melts when Jeremy kisses me and my eyes melt when Matthew talks to me.* "Yes, I'm all right. I..."

"What? Tell me, Annie. I've got all night to talk if you need to."

"Well, it's just that I'm feeling tired, I guess. Life isn't turning out to be as simple as it used to be."

"Other than Julie, how do you mean?"

"Julie has a lot to do with it, but also it's this village. I don't feel a part of it. I'm supposed to be the vicar, a respected person in the community, and instead, I feel as if I'm constantly pushing on the door and it's only opened a crack—does that make sense?"

"Yes, I know exactly what you mean. I felt the same, particularly after Amanda...after Amanda died."

Amanda again—that dreaded name. Yet she had to respond to what he said, so forcing herself, she asked, "Did she feel that way? Did she ever talk about it?"

"No, not really, but she was a very unusual person, Annie. I wish you had known her. She accepted everyone on their terms. She wasn't judgmental, and I guess, because of that, everyone accepted her."

Annie was torn. She wanted to provide a listening ear for Matthew just as he did for her, but she didn't really want to hear how wonderful Amanda was. Jealous of a woman who is dead, pretty pathetic, she told herself. This is exactly what Emily had warned her about, the idealized dead person.

When she didn't respond, Matthew went on. "You're not thinking of quitting are you?"

"No, I'm not a quitter. I will finish out my time here not matter what, but I'm supposed to be here five years. That seems a very long time to feel this way. You know in any other job, you can quit and move, but I'm here to make a difference and all that's happening is that I'm different than I was when I arrived."

"I don't think you're different," he said quietly.

"Well, I am. I'm afraid my faith is wavering—that's very different for me."

"Well, I can't help you in that department," Matthew said briskly. "But, look, I'll ring off now and see if I can reach my friend."

Annie hung up the phone with mixed emotions. She loved even the sound of Matthew's voice and she wanted him to keep on talking, as long as he didn't talk about Amanda, that is.

After making herself a cup of tea, she phoned her father to let him know about Julie. She also told him about Jeremy. He had met Jeremy at the graduation ceremony in Cambridge.

"Well, he certainly is a bright young man and seems to be going far in the church at a young age. So are you confused?"

"Yes, terribly. It's wonderful to be with Jeremy when he's talking about theological matters. He has such an intellectual grasp of doctrine and Scripture."

"Does he love the Lord?" he asked.

"Well, of course he does....why?"

"I just wondered. You know Annie, you can be a minister of the church and be brilliant in theological discourses and not love the Lord."

"Oh, I know that, theoretically I know that, but I guess I just took it for granted that he does." She thought for a moment, "Actually, when I think back on the things we've talked about, he doesn't say much about his own relationship to Jesus."

"All I'm saying is," her father replied, "look out for that, try to find out about his personal faith. But now, about Julie, don't you think you need to go talk to her psychologist?"

"Yes, I do, Dad. Thanks."

Dr. Evans phoned her later that night and they arranged an appointment for the next Monday. She couldn't call the police, because Julie was of age and she left a note saying she was going away. She wasn't a missing person.

Friday evening seemed to come quickly and Annie took the train, all dressed up as ordered, to have dinner with Matthew. She hadn't seen him in almost a month and somehow had forgotten how she responded to how he looked. But her body remembered and she found herself smiling widely automatically. He really was gorgeous and she wondered why someone didn't snap him up immediately.

He took her to the Connaught. The doorman with his top hat and beige livery opened the door of the taxi for Annie and inside, the maitre-de ushered them to a corner table in grand style. Annie looked around the room, marveling at the dark mahogany paneling, the stiff white table cloths, the crystal glasses sparkling in the light of the chandeliers. This was pure luxury. As several waiters hovered nearby, alert to their every anticipated need, she noticed that the prices weren't on the menu, at least not on hers. Matthew ordered an expensive bottle of wine, or at least it certainly looked expensive, and tasted divine.

Annie had never before been to a restaurant like this and she ate it up—not just the meal, but the ambience as well. The service was superb, the food was delicious, Matthew was wonderful to look at and talk to and she found herself thoroughly absorbed, as if she were a different person. After they had ordered dessert, Matthew reached across the white linen tablecloth and said, "Annie, may I have your hand?"

She was startled. He had never held her hand before. She tentatively put her hand across the table and he clasped it firmly. She felt a bit tingly—must be the wine, she told herself.

"Annie, I've been miserable since I moved," Matthew began.

The expression on his face held her mesmerized and she couldn't look away. "Oh, I'm sorry. Is it lonesome for you here?"

"No, what I mean, is, I've been miserable since I moved away from you. Look, Annie, I'm botching this up, but I thought if I moved away that I wouldn't think about you anymore, I thought I'd get over you."

Annie was astonished; she had no idea he had any feelings for her at all other than as a friend. "I didn't know you were thinking about me."

"Oh, Annie, ever since I met you, you're all I've thought about. But I've felt guilty. I felt so drawn to you, just like I was to Amanda, and I didn't think I should feel that way, and I've been so excited about tonight, you can't imagine, and now I feel like I'm frightening you, from the look on your face—look, I'm sorry—you probably think I'm an idiot." He never quit looking into her eyes and he never let go of her hand.

She didn't' know what to do. She didn't know what he wanted her to do. All this time she had thought her feelings for Matthew were one sided and now Jeremy was in the picture. "I don't know what to say, Matthew, this is such a surprise to me."

"Surprise, oh, Annie, I thought it was written all over my face. And I didn't think I would every feel this way again about someone, after Amanda, I mean."

Rather than being grateful to hear he was thinking about her, Annie felt her Irish temper rising. Here he was proposing something, she wasn't sure what, and he still brought Amanda's name into it. He couldn't say a whole paragraph without mentioning her! She was sick of the name.

Just then the waiter cleared his throat. He had been standing there for a moment and neither of them had been aware of his presence.

Matthew quickly let go of her hand and she wast relieved. She picked at her dessert and didn't look up at Matthew. Her dream date with Matthew was actually happening and all she wanted was to go home. She rolled her eyes heavenward in her mind and prayed. *I hope you know what I'm doing, Lord, because I sure don't.*

The silence grew between them until it was becoming a wall. Matthew signaled for the bill and as soon as he paid it, Annie rose from her chair. Matthew had no choice but to follow her into the lobby, where she was already retrieving her coat. She mumbled a thank you to him, quickly went outside and not looking at him, mumbled another thank you and almost leapt into a waiting taxi

All the way home she berated herself.. Here he was trying so hard to be nice, to start a relationship, evidently, and her temper had risen when he brought up Amanda. She had blindly followed her emotions; she hadn't even displayed good manners, ordinary good manners. She felt miserable and knew Matthew must be thoroughly puzzled. She knew the dinner must have cost a fortune and she had thoroughly enjoyed herself until....until he compared his feelings for her to how he felt about Amanda. Before Jeremy, would she have acted this way? What has happened to the intimacy I used to feel with Matthew and why wasn't I thrilled when he held my hand and said what he said? It must be Jeremy, she told herself. *Am I in love with Jeremy? Or am I just in love with the attention he gives me, and with the way he kisses me.* How does anyone ever know their own mind in terms of romance, she wondered, not for the first time. What she did know was she owed Matthew an apology—a big one.

Matthew stood on the curb, not only devastated, but clueless. He had no idea what went so terribly wrong—he only knew that Annie must think he was an utter jerk. I shouldn't have asked her to come here, he told himself. It was just asking for trouble. Yet when he first saw her waiting for him in the lobby of the LSE, he had felt overwhelmed and realized how much he missed her. And it seemed she was thoroughly enjoying their conversation, until he told her how he felt about her.. He must have read the signals wrong all along. She evidently didn't care a scrap about him other than as a friend.

He vowed he would never approach her again other than in platonic friendship—which made him feel even more miserable.

Chapter Thirteen

When Annie arrived home, there was another email from Joe. *Strange that I get emails from Joe only when Julie isn't her.* Could Julie be sending them and pretending to be this Joe? That was the problem with emails. No one knew the location they came from. No postmark, no telephone number to trace—anonymous cyberspace.

Dear Rev. O'Connell: Is Julie okay? She hasn't wanted to see me lately and I don't know what to do about her. She won't answer my emails and she told me never to phone her at your house—she always phones me. She keeps comin in and out on me—you know? Please answer me. Joe

Annie shook her head, another couple having problems. This romance business isn't what it's cracked up to be. There didn't seem to be happy endings except in novels. She wrote back to Joe, telling him what she knew, asking him to let her know where he was writing from, and spelling her last name correctly at the end.

There was also an email and a phone message from Jeremy. She smiled as she read the email. He had never told her he was in love with her, at least not explicitly. But he did have a way with words. His messages were a mixture of romantic charm and little spiritual nuggets. And he had never mentioned another woman; he had never said one word about how he felt about this one or that one. When Annie was with Jeremy, or as was more often the case in this long distance relationship of theirs, talking on the telephone, she felt important to him, as if she were the one person in the entire world who mattered to him.

She was too tired emotionally to respond to him tonight or even to tell Emily all this momentous news. My life is far, far too complicated for my liking, she thought, as she drifted off to sleep.

On Monday, Annie traveled to London to meet with Dr. Evans. She was ushered her into the inner office, where the old fashioned furniture, although not shabby, gave a comfortable atmosphere to the room. A massive antique desk was framed by the bowed windows looking out to the street. Two overstuffed chairs were placed facing each other with a small table in between. Dr. Evans gestured for Annie to sit in one and she took the other.

"No news from Julie?" Dr. Evans asked.

Annie shook her head, "Nothing at all. Just an email from Joe. Did Julie tell you about him?"

"No….who is Joe?"

"Well, I really don't know," Annie replied, "but every time Julie disappears, it seems I get an email from Joe. Julie told me she didn't know anyone named Joe, but as you will soon see, she does know him."

Dr. Evans reached for a pad and pen. "And you say he only writes to you when she's not there. That seems strange. Does Julie have a computer?"

"I don't think so. She never mentioned having one. I had never gone into her room because I thought it was so important for her to have privacy, a room of her own, you know?"

"So she could have had a laptop that you knew nothing about?"

Annie thought for a moment, "Yes, I guess so. She doesn't have much money, so I guess it never occurred to me she would have a laptop. She did bring three large suitcases though, so she certainly could have had a computer in one of them."

Annie reached into her bag, which she had placed on the floor beside her chair. "I did look around the other day and I have to show you this journal I found under her pillow." She handed the notebook to Dr. Evans, feeling a bit ashamed of what she'd done.

Dr. Evans looked at it briefly and then asked, "May I ikeep this?"

"Yes, please do. I don't feel very good about snooping in her room, but I thought I might find some clue as to what troubles her so much she feels she has to leave."

Dr. Evans smiled. "Don't worry about it. I'll look it over and if there isn't anything of consequence in it, you can have it back and put it where you found it. However, if there is some important information in there, I'll have to tell Julie. Do I have your permission to do that?"

Annie could see why Julie seemed to respond to this woman. She had a warm, kindly way about her, a non-threatening manner. Not like me, Annie thought, I blunder in bluntly. She wondered if she could come to see Dr. Evans as a client; maybe she could help her sort out her romantic life.

Dr. Evans smiled again as she said, "It's wonderful that you've taken Julie in and tried to give her a good home. She does appreciate it—do you know that?"

Annie shrugged, "No, not really. She's such a puzzle to me. I never know what to expect from her."

"What do you mean by that?" Dr. Evans asked gently.

"Well, she seems to be different at times, not from one moment to the next, but she sometimes even looks different."

Dr. Evans nodded. "You know, Rev. O'Donnell, I can't reveal anything Julie tells me unless I know she is going to harm herself or others, in other words, suicide or homicide. That's our ethical code, but it would help me a great deal if you can tell me everything you've observed about her, your impressions of her. As you have probably guessed, she's not terribly forthcoming in our sessions, although each one gets better and I did feel she was beginning to trust me a little."

Annie nodded and proceeded to summarize all that had happened when Julie was there. She was honest with Dr. Evans as well, telling her how exasperated and discouraged she had been at times with Julie. When she finished, she asked, "Do you have any idea where she went and why she disappears so regularly?"

"I don't know where she went, but I think I do have an idea why she leaves and comes back," Dr. Evans responded. "I can't share that with you yet. Hopefully, Julie will at some point give me permission to talk this over with you. She has my phone number and I will certainly phone you immediately if I hear from her."

"Meantime, what do you think I should do?"

Dr. Evans smiled again, "Nothing. You've already done far more than would be expected of someone. Just try not to worry and I am almost certain Julie will reappear. She has a lot of inner strength, am amazing amount, in fact. That much I've been able to ascertain."

Annie left the office with mixed emotions. She was glad Dr. Evans thought Julie was probably all right, and yes, she actually had done a lot for her, so she felt better about that. But she didn't think she could quit worrying. Somehow, strange as she was, Julie had become a very important part of Annie's life. She missed her.

The village now had something new to talk about—Jeremy. He had been observed aplenty. And they knew he was a vicar, they had got that out of Joy. Hard to get information from Joy these days, but it had been accomplished. Their little vicar seemed to be quite popular with the men, didn't she? And she had been going to London a great deal, what was that about anyway?

To be fair, this talk wasn't going on with everyone. The women in Annie's Bible study group were becoming fiercely loyal to her and were beginning to quash anyone who began talking about her. Annie's sermon on John 8 had sunk in deep. They were also grateful to her because their faith was beginning to grow; it was taking root as it never had before. The women were sharing their problems more freely and Annie now said something each week about the importance of confidentiality.

"The only reason we're sharing is for the purpose of praying for each other. No one in this room has the right to tell even one other person, not even her husband, what goes on here in terms of our prayer time. Think of yourselves as priests, you have a solemn duty to only talk to the Lord about what we say here."

The next week, Annie's parents arrived for a few days. She had looked forward to their visit immensely. She thought her father, especially, needed to be in the village to truly understand the zeitgeist and perhaps be able to help her cope. There had been no word from Julie and Annie had quit worrying so much about her. She had phoned Matthew and left a message on the answering machine, apologizing for her behavior. He had not responded.

Jeremy had been introduced to Annie's parents at her Cambridge graduation ceremony, but told her he was anxious to get to know them and was coming for dinner that evening. Annie wondered why he was anxious to get to know them. Was he going to get serious?

Her mum toured the house and gave it a minute inspection. Annie was an indifferent housekeeper and had tried to spruce it up a bit before they arrived, but it wasn't sparkling.

"Very nice, Annie. So huge! Like you've said, it must be impossible to keep it all as it should be."

Was this a backhanded compliment? Annie never knew. It probably was her mother's way of trying to make her feel all right, but she always reverted to feeling like a little girl around her mother.

"And all these dogs must complicate your life."

"Yes, sure they do, Mum, but I honestly don't know what I'd have done without them. They've been a substitute family, they make the house seem not so lonely; they fill it up," she said, reaching down to pick up Tibby and holding him in her arm

Annie knew that everyone loved Rosie O'Donnell. She

had been a good vicar's wife, fielding calls for her husband, making pastoral calls on the sick of the parish, serving on different committees of the church. People always told Annie how kind and caring her mother was. But she treated Annie differently than she did other people and most markedly, she treated Annie differently than her two brothers. Her mother praised them to high heaven, not only when she was with them, but when she was without them. They could do no wrong. Whereas with Annie, she was critical. Annie loved her mother and had tried hard all her life to please her, but it seemed she always got looks of disapproval. None was more apparent than when she decided to go into the ministry. Females in the pulpit were not something Mrs. Rosie O'Donnell approved of—not in the least. She didn't often tell people that her daughter was a Cambridge-educated vicar of a church.

After the house inspection, as Annie thought of it, she took them out to tour the village on foot. They visited the church first (her mum approved) and then walked around, stopping here and there to introduce them to people they saw out and about. When they passed Matthew's house, Annie pointed silently to her father and mouthed 'Matthew' to him. She hadn't told him about the latest episode with Matthew. She didn't think anyone other than Emily would understand. When they got to Joy's house, Annie knocked on the door. She very much wanted them to meet Joy.

"Come in, come in" Joy enthused, "you must have a cup of tea with me, I am so happy to meet you, you don't know how much I like and admire your daughter, yes—she has been quite a blessing to this village, come on in, just sit down over there and I'll be right back with the tea."

Annie smiled at her parents. She had warned them of Joy's method of communication. She had known that Joy would praise her effusively and that was all right; she wanted to be praised in front of her mother.

Joy began talking again as she brought in the tea and cups on a tray and served it around. "And aren't you both proud of your daughter—following in her father's footsteps and helping a village like this become on fire for our Lord? Why I don't have any children, but I tell you if I did, I would want my daughter to be exactly like your Annie and I hope you don't mind, but I think of myself as her adopted family, since you two are so far away."

It didn't take long in Joy's presence to learn to wait until you were certain she was through speaking, though it didn't take too much discernment, since she didn't seem to breathe in between her long soliloquies. Rosie O'Donnell smiled weakly and took a sip of her tea, but Annie's father nodded and responded, "Yes, I would be proud to have Annie for a daughter no matter what she chose to do with her life, but you're right, Joy, it is gratifying to know that having a vicar for a father hasn't put her off, that I had some influence in her decision."

Annie just smiled and remained silent.

"And Annie has told us all about how kind you've been to her. We greatly appreciate that, don't we, Rosie," he asked rhetorically. Rosie nodded and once more smiled feebly.

They didn't stay long, but Annie felt her mission had been accomplished. Back at the vicarage, Rosie and her mother began preparing the dinner for their expected guest. Annie simply followed her mother's instructions. She had bought the groceries her mother requested before they arrived. Timothy sat at the kitchen table and chatted with them as they worked.

"So, is this a serious relationship with this Jeremy?" he asked, eyes twinkling.

Annie turned and said obliquely. "I don't know, Dad. I wish I knew. He really wanted to get to know both of you better; I don't know if he's just being friendly or if he has further intentions."

"Well, what I'm asking is how you feel about him. Do you think he's marriage material?"

Annie laughed. "Why don't you say what you mean, Dad! I don't know. I certainly don't think I'm ready for marriage. I have far too much on my plate at the moment."

Rosie shook her head. "Remember Annie, good men don't grow on trees. You don't want to end up being one of those lonely career women who passed up opportunities when they were young and live to regret it."

Annie wasn't surprised by her mother's remarks, but her philosophy about women's role in life, never mind the church, irritated her no end. Her temper rose and she began to take it out on the vegetables she was chopping for a salad.

"Don't you think women can have a calling, just as do men?" her father asked his wife, knowing full well what her answer would be.

"Yes, I do. There have been wonderful women missionaries, working in partnership with their husbands or even alone, if they passed up a chance to marry early on, that is."

Annie was perfectly aware how strong her mother's feelings were about female clergy and it hurt Annie that her mother had never heard her preach. Somehow her mother had always engineered it so that she was never where Annie was on a Sunday. All that was about to change, because her father had invited Annie to come and preach at their church one Sunday during the coming month. She dreaded it.

Rosie O'Donnell was a woman who had had a happy marriage, due mainly to the fact that Timothy was a rare husband. He didn't cause conflict and when she caused it, he simply remained calm and waited out the storm. This was infuriating to her, but it had helped over the years to lessen her appetite for conflict. It didn't seem to accomplish anything—her husband went right on doing what he felt was right. The only good thing about that, as far as she could see, was that he also didn't interfere with her life. He let her be who she was. He never criticized her often praised her. Some of this had rubbed off on her in terms of how she treated him, but when she was around Annie, she was very much still her mother. She still felt felt that at age twenty-six and unmarried, Annie needed her advice.

Her sons were a different story. She felt very close to them. They always did what she thought they should, even before she told them what they should do. Patrick was a chartered surveyor, making his way up the ladder in Belfast quickly. He hadn't married the girl she wished he would have, but his choice was all right. And they had two wonderful little boys. The other son, James, wasn't married as yet, but that was all right for men. He should have fun as long as he could. And the fact that he dropped out of university really wasn't his fault; it was the professors who were to blame. She was certain he would settle down to a decent job soon.

What exasperated her most about Annie was that she was so completely different than herself. She was glad that Annie was such a strong Christian, but being a vicar was taking things too far. She believed she only wanted the best for her daughter and the best meant getting married and raising a proper family. She was very much looking forward to Jeremy's arrival.

When Annie greeted him at the door, Jeremy, who always seemed to know what to do in any situation, confined himself to a quick brush on her lips.

He and her father got on very well. The discussion at dinner was around the books Jeremy had published and what he was working on at the time. Timothy showed his obvious appreciation for Jeremy's intellectual grasp of deep theological issues and Jeremy charmed Mrs. O'Donnell shamelessly.

"Annie was fortunate to grow up with such an excellent chef in the house, Mrs. O'Donnell. This was the best meal I've had in a very long time and I often eat in Cambridge's finest restaurants," he purred, giving her his most charming smile..

"Oh, well, cooking is easy if you like to do it," Rosie responded.

"Jeremy is quite an accomplished cook as well, Mum," Annie said, "so that is really a compliment coming from him."

"Oh, and do you cook for Annie?" Rosie asked, and before Jeremy could answer went on to say, "You know, she's never been very interested in the kitchen."

Jeremy smiled at Annie as he responded to her mother. "Not lately, I haven't, but when we were students, lots of people gathered at my flat and I cooked for all of them. Yes, I do enjoy it. I find it a meditative occupation compared to everything else I do."

"And tell me about your church, Jeremy," Timothy inquired, "what is your role there?"

Jeremy chuckled softly as he answered, "Well, I'm afraid I do less and less. I am called on to speak at other venues, at the colleges and at meetings around town, and also I teach a class at St. Catherine's. So it looks like I'm drifting into academia and in fact, Annie, I haven't told you this because it just happened. My contract hasn't been renewed for next year."

Annie was wide-eyed. This was a huge bit of news and given the amount of time they spent talking to each other on the phone, a serious lack of communicating. "Really Jeremy, is that all right with you?"

He nodded. "Yeah, actually it is. I guess my lack of interest in the church affairs was showing through, was noticed. I think I really would like to teach and speak and write. Those are the things I'm drawn to."

Timothy leaned a bit forward toward Jeremy and seeming to change the subject, asked in a quiet voice, "Tell me Jeremy. When did you become a Christian?"

Jeremy smiled at him and at Annie. "Oh, I guess I've always been a Christian. I grew up in the church, singing in the church choir—I went to the Boys School at Exeter. I was always happy when I was in the church, so that's why I went into it. I gravitated to the place I felt happy." This last sentence was said with more seriousness.

"And now you're leaving it..." Timothy said.

"Oh, I'm not leaving the church" Jeremy protested. "I'm

just going to be employed elsewhere. Who knows, maybe I'll be more active when I don't have the responsibilities. Sometimes the inner workings of a church can cause you to almost lose your faith, it seems to me."

Annie nodded. "I sure understand that, all the problems I've had here have disillusioned me quite a bit."

Timothy reached over and placed his hand over his daughters. "I think you had a naïve experience, darlin, growing up with your father being the vicar of your church. I think a lot of the bickering that went on in our church was hidden from you. People wouldn't tell you how they really felt about their vicar, you know."

"Well, I'm sure that was true," Annie said, appreciating the support from her father whose hand still covered hers. "And I'm also sure that your church was unusual because you're unusual. Yet I never ever expected to find what I've found here in this village. As I've told Jeremy, who listens to me complain endlessly," she smiled at him, "this place is church centered rather than Christ centered. The business of running the church, of greeting and chatting with friends, whom they see almost daily anyway, take over and override growing spiritually or even worshipping on a Sunday. They come to church to take communion, which is often just a ritual, they come to greet one another and to get the service done, but I wonder, other than my women's group, if they truly come to worship."

Jeremy had barely driven off before Annie's mother said in an ecstatic tone of voice, "He is a brilliant young man, Annie. You better snatch him up quick before someone else does."

Her father, however, had reservations. "I think he certainly is intelligent and charming, but I'm worried about his personal faith. It seemed rather like an intellectual treatise to me, rather than personal experience. Not having his contract renewed is a serious thing. It doesn't happen often. Do you have any idea what is behind that?"

"No, but I can ask Jill, our mutual friend, she may know. I was totally surprised by this news, which bothers me, I have to admit. I talk to him almost every day and he hadn't mentioned it." There had been a niggle at the back of Annie's mind ever since Jeremy made his announcement and the contradicting opinions of her parents only added to Annie's confusion.

Meanwhile, there was another email from Joe and Dr. Evans phoned saying she had heard from Julie and that she was all right, but she wasn't ready to come back to Annie quite yet

And Matthew still hadn't phoned. Not that she thought of him all the time anymore, but at least once a day when she came home, she acknowledged to herself that she listened to her messages and noticed there were none from him. Well, she thought, it doesn't look like I'll have a choice between two men now, does it? I completely blew it with one and the other one hasn't mentioned anything about the future. I'll probably be alone and lonely the rest of my life. Then she admonished herself and laughed. *Come off your pity pot, girl.*

Chapter Fourteen

It was a bright, sunny afternoon as Julie made her way to Dr. Evans' office. She shivered even though it wasn't cold. It took every ounce of courage she could drum up to keep these appointments, yet she knew she must go. Something deep inside of her compelled her. Somewhere deep inside, she knew this was necessary if she was to become a real person.

She also knew she must have missed some appointments. She sometimes found an appointment time written down on a small piece of paper in her pocket, looked at the current date on the calendar Corinne hung up in the kitchen, and knew that once again, she had failed. But Dr. Evans never chided her for this. She told her she knew she was doing the best she could. She thought back to the last appointment, when Dr. Evans told her what was wrong with her.

"You see, Julie," Dr. Evans explained, "when a child undergoes extreme trauma, repeatedly, that child can, and sometimes does, dissociate, which simply means going to another place in your mind, so that you don't even know or remember what's happening to you. You become someone else; a part of you that is the strongest, takes over.

Julie stared at her, wide-eyed. "So is that why I disappear? Are you saying I have become someone else?" She looked down at her lap. In almost a whisper, she asked, "But why can't I remember where I was?"

"Part of you does remember," Dr. Evans said gently, "but in order to save you emotional pain, it is stored in another part of your memory. Dissociate means to stop associating with the person who is experiencing the pain, it's a coping mechanism. It has allowed you to survive."

"Do other people do this?"

The doctor smiled, "Yes, not many. The condition is commonly called multiple personality, but the psychological name for it is Dissociative Identity Disorder."

Julie was again quiet for a long moment. This explained so much, it explained why so many times she felt she wasn't normal, why she knew she wasn't like other people. This information frightened her, but she felt relieved at the same time. She now understood; that was why Dr. Evans didn't seem to be upset about her disappearances. She still didn't trust her completely. As Julie, she didn't trust anyone. She didn't know it, but only Rhonda trusted people. Finally, she asked, "So how many personalities do I have?"

Dr. Evans smiled gently as she responded, "I don't know yet. I know there are at least four. And that may be all. Julie, I can see you are frightened and I don't blame you. It's important, very important for you to believe that I never, ever blame you for anything. I care about you, do you believe that?"

Julie was by this time looking away at the bookcase, staring intently at the covers and unable to read the titles as there were the beginning of tears blurring her eyes. She knew she must never, ever, let anyone see her crying or she would be punished. No, she didn't believe what Dr. Evans had just said. But she wanted to; she wanted to more than anything else in the world.

She blinked back the tears, straightened her shoulders and sat up straight, looking straight at Dr. Evans. Smiling, she said, "I'm sorry I was a bit late today, I had lunch with a friend and we just got carried away with the time."

"Are you Rhonda?" Dr. Evans asked.

"Yes, Julie was too upset to continue on with the session. But that's okay. I would like for us to go back to live at Annie's. I can't do any baking where I'm living and I know the flowers I planted in the garden should be coming up by now."

Dr. Evans sat back in her chair, visibly relaxing as she said, "Annie wants you to come back. She misses you."

"Does she? Well, that's awfully nice to hear. I guess I miss her a bit, but I really miss the dogs and I know they miss me cause Annie doesn't take them for walks enough. She's so busy all the time, they don't get as much attention from her as they need."

"You're good with animals aren't you?"

Rhonda smiled. "Oh, yes. I always have been. And they respond to me. I guess I should have become a vet or something, but I couldn't stand to give them any pain, like a jab, you know."

"I know you are very kind. You wouldn't want anyone to suffer pain, would you?"

"Of course not. Well, if you're sure Annie wants me back, I guess I'll phone her and leave right away."

"Rhonda, would it be all right with you for me to tell Annie why you disappear so often? Could you come here tomorrow and meet with me as well as Annie so that way you'll know what I'm telling her?"

"Oh, and then I could go home with her from here? Sure, that's a good idea."

That evening, Annie got a call from Dr. Evans, asking her if she could come to her office, telling her Julie would be there as well. "Of course, "Annie said, "Is she all right?"

"Yes she is and she wants to come back with you, if that's all right. Could you be here by two o'clock?"

"Yes, I'll be there. I'll have to cancel some things, but I'll be there."

Annie was full of anticipation as she rode to London on the train. When she arrived at the office, however, Julie wasn't there. Dr. Evans suggested they carry on, hoping she had just been held up somewhere. What she next began to tell Annie held her spellbound.

"Julie has given me permission to tell you what's going on in her life, to tell you what her real problem is," she began. "I think you are going to be very surprised."

Annie couldn't imagine what she was going to say. Was it going to be something terrible? Was there something so bad in Julie's life that it had had to be kept secret? Some terrible crime?

All this flicked through her imagination as she waited for Dr. Evans to continue.

"I am sure you've noticed how Julie seems to change, how at times she seems to have a different personality?"

"Yes," Annie agreed, "it is rather disconcerting."

Dr. Evans nodded, "Yes, for me as well. I never know when Julie arrives who is really coming."

"What do you mean?"

"Have you heard of the condition known popularly as multiple personality?"

"Of course, is that what's wrong with Julie?"

"Yes. It's known as Dissociative Identity Disorder and it took me awhile to be sure of the diagnosis. You see, that's why Julie disappears, that's why she comes in and out of your life. Another personality takes over, packs her up and leaves."

Annie stared at the psychologist wide-eyed. "That makes sense. But how does that happen? How can another personality take over?"

"It is rather like amnesia," Dr. Evans replied. "When Julie becomes someone else, she doesn't remember it later. She was actually very relieved when I began to explain to her why she acted as she did. She thought of these periods as blackouts. She would 'wake up' in a strange place and have no idea how she got there. When she was herself again, meaning when she was Julie again, she would come back to you."

Annie nodded slowly, thinking about Julie's several disappearances. "Poor Julie! It must be terrible for her."

"Yes, it is terrible," Dr. Evans agreed. "But the good news is that it can be helped. The bad news is that it will take a very long time. The process is lengthy. All her personalities have to be integrated back into her one true self and that takes time. My main problem is keeping her coming here. As you know, she was supposed to be here today, but I suspect it was frightening for her. She may have worried that you would reject her and that fear could have made her slip into another personality."

Annie sat back in her chair. This was a lot to take in, but it all made sense. It explained so much that had happened, so much of Julie's odd behavior. Dr. Evans was silent, obviously waiting for her to assimilate this information. After a few moments, she asked, "What causes this multiple personality?"

"Usually it is a very traumatic childhood," Dr. Evans responded."We have only begun to delve into her childhood and so I don't know much myself at this point, but I want you to know that Julie cares very much what you think of her. She is very grateful for your kindness and thinks of her home with you and the dogs as the first real home she's ever had." She smiled at Annie, "I think if it hadn't been for you she would never have agreed to see me or confide in me."

Annie shook her head, "That's good to hear, but I don't think I've done much for her at all—I've often felt guilty about it. It's been frustrating for me and I've often berated myself for not being kind enough."

"Well, that's not how Julie has seen it. She very much respects you and I would even go so far as to say that in her own way, she loves you, as much as she is able to love anyone at this point."

Annie sighed and smiled, "Well, that makes me feel better and I do care about her. There was something about her that got under my skin. I have felt guilty when she disappeared. I wondered what I had done to drive her away. Where is she living?"

"She is with a friend, a girl she knew before. She sleeps on her sofa and is keeping her flat clean for her. Her friend doesn't have much money, but she shares her food with Julie and gives her the money for her tube fare to come here.

Annie thought of the emails. "And this Joe, the one I get emails from? Do you know who he is?"

"No, but I suspect he is one of her personalities."

"You mean she takes on a male personality?"

Dr. Evans nodded. "Yes, it's not as common as to take on the same gender, but it does happen. I haven't had enough time with Julie to ascertain how many personalities she evolves into, but I know of four so far."

"And Rhonda, is that one?"

Dr. Evans smiled. "Yes, Rhonda is the pleasant one, the one who is self-confident."

Annie sat in silence for a few moments, trying to assimilate all of this.

Dr. Evans went on, "I'm going to begin seeing Julie as often as she will come here. I plan to tell her when I have a free hour and I know there will be missed appointments, when she is too frightened to come, but I understand that and so we will limp along as best we can."

"What about your fee? Will the NHS pay for more than one session a week?"

"No, but I will only charge for one visit a week. I consider it a privilege to help Julie. We don't get to see those with actual dissociative identity disorders often and so she is fascinating to someone like me." Dr. Evans smiled softly, "Don't worry about my fee. Someday if Julie becomes rich, I'm sure she will pay me," she laughed. "And if not, she is enriching my life now, so don't worry about it, please."

"You are very kind," Annie said, amazed at her generosity and grateful. "I'm so glad Julie is willing to see you. Lots of things make sense now—her running away, packing up and leaving, her mood changes." She wondered if Julie had been sexually abused. "Do you know what the trauma was?"

Dr. Evans shook her head, "I can't tell you that. I only have Julie's permission to tell you her diagnosis, to explain her absences to you."

That made sense to Annie, but still, she was very curious. "Is she coming back to me?"

"She would like to, Rhonda said yesterday she would go straight home with you from here, but evidently Julie became frightened when she knew I was going to tell you about her and didn't show up."

"Oh, please tell her I want her back. And if she does

come, how am I to treat her?"

"Just like you always have, but now you'll know what to expect if she 'switches' on you."

"Well, I don't know if I will or not. What do I do?"

"You simply ask Julie who she is," Dr. Evans said. "She'll tell you. Then you deal with that person as if it is an entirely different girl. Don't worry; she isn't dangerous in any fashion. To tell you the truth, I would rather she be with you and come here on the train. She misses the dogs and your house offers more stability than where she is now. She gets frightened when her friend goes out at night."

Annie sighed and said, "Please tell her to come home right away. I really do care about her and now that you've explained her to me, I want to help her even more than I did before."

"I'll tell her. And I'm quite sure you will see her very soon."

When she arrived home, Annie phoned Matthew at once. She thought of phoning him from London, a part of her hoping he would be free to meet her, but talked herself out of it. When he didn't respond on his office number, she dialed his mobile.

"Matthew here."

"This is Annie," she began, when he interrupted and almost shouted, "Annie! I'm so glad to hear from you."

"Yes, it's me," she laughed. "How are you? I haven't heard from you in awhile."

Matthew was silent for a moment before he said quietly, "I just didn't want to bother you,"

"Oh, Matthew, you would never bother me."

"Well, evidently from your reaction when we last met, I did bother you..." his voice drifted off.

It was Annie's turn to be silent. "I know, Matthew, I was very rude that evening. It's just that—well, I can't tell you why, at least not now. Look, I'm calling about Julie."

"Has she been found?"

"Yes, but I haven't seen her. She's in contact with the psychologist and I met with her, Dr. Evans I mean, today."

"Is Julie all right?"

"Yes, I guess so, at least physically. But Matthew, I have so much to tell you, could we meet?"

"Of course, anytime, I'll even cancel a class if need be."

"No," Annie laughed. "That won't be necessary. What about tomorrow evening?"

"Sure—for dinner?"

When Annie didn't answer immediately, Matthew went on in an anxious voice, "Nothing fancy, I don't want you to avoid me because of what happened last time."

"All right, I'll meet you at the LSE in the lobby at six?"

"Six it is. Bye, Annie," Matthew said softly.

As she rode down to London on the train the next evening, Annie reflected on their phone conversation. She was proud of herself for not feeling emotional. Maybe that means I'm in love with Jeremy, rather than Matthew, she told herself. She was grateful for the cessation of confusion, as well as the misery she had suffered all the time she thought she was in love with Matthew. There was no pain in her relationship with Jeremy. It was true he had never committed to the future, had never mentioned marriage, but they had fun together. He made her laugh and she certainly did enjoy his caresses. All in all, he made her feel very special.

He also understood all her problems with the church and gave her suggestions that were pragmatic and usually worked. In many ways it was like being back at Cambridge again. He told her all the latest in gossip going around in theological circles, who was in and who was out, all the latest theological discoveries and interpretations, and he knew many people she knew. Being in a relationship with Jeremy was comfortable. And although he had never mentioned Matthew since that first lunch with him and Jill, even though he had never said they were in an exclusive relationship, Annie did not think she should be interested in Matthew; that it would be disloyal if she were anything other than a friend of his.

Those thoughts were all before she saw Matthew in the lobby of his university, however. She didn't have time to think, to remember all those rational thoughts she had been going over in her mind on the train. When Matthew walked toward her with a dazzling smile on his face, hands extended out for hers and a a light kiss on both cheeks, her emotions took over. Had she forgotten how devastatingly handsome he was? Had she forgotten his eyes, so deeply blue, like the sky on a perfect day? For a moment, time was suspended and she found it difficult to breathe. Annie,what's wrong with you, she told herself, garnering every ounce of energy to stop from making a fool of herself.

"Annie," he said, still holding her hands.

She looked down, pulled her hands away and turned toward the door, terrified he would see her reaction to him. "Let's go shall we? I'm famished," she said.

"There's a great little place just down the street, would that be okay?"

Annie nodded and walked beside him, but not too close. She concentrated on the sights across the street, which were simply ordinary shops and restaurants, yet you would have thought they were the most interesting sights in the world. By the time they arrived at the restaurant, she had recovered. Whilst she didn't gaze directly into his eyes, she did manage to look at him now and then without feeling those unbelievable feelings inside, the same ones she felt when Jeremy kissed her. Her mind was racing as well as her heart. She thought she had got this one problem sorted. She hadn't been miserable like this in a long time and now it was back. *Concentrate on Julie.*

She related her visit with the psychologist. Annie had asked her if it would be all right to share this information with Matthew and Dr. Evans said yes, that she had Julie's permission to tell Matthew. "Julie thinks of you and Matthew as a couple, did you know that?" Dr. Evans had told Annie, with a twinkle in her eye. But Annie was not about to tell Matthew this.

"Well, I've heard of multiple personalities, of course, but I don't understand how it works and I didn't know amnesia had anything to do with it," Matthew said, when she was finished.

"I don't either and I want to get on the internet and learn more. It isn't that Julie hit her head or had an accident. It isn't that sort of amnesia. It's that something happened in her childhood which was so traumatic she had to dissociate in order to handle it. Rather like becoming unconscious, except that she was conscious—does that make any sense? I don't really understand it, but when she is another person she doesn't know it. She 'wakes up' and finds herself somewhere else and she finds clothes in her suitcase that she doesn't remember wearing. Do you remember when she asked me to call her Rhonda and she looked different? She had on much less makeup and her hair was clean and she baked and gardened."

"Yes, I do remember," Matthew said. "So she was a different personality then. I'm beginning to see it now and that's why she disappears so often?"

"Yes, something happens to frighten her and she switches into another personality."

"So which is the real Julie?"

"I don't know. I don't know if Dr. Evans knows.."

"I'll talk to Donald, my psychologist friend. Maybe he can recommend a book for us to read about it. I think the more we know, well, I should say the more you know, the better, don't you?"

Annie nodded with her mouth full. She had ordered what Matthew recommended, a vegetable stir-fry dish. It was delicious and in spite of her saying earlier that she was famished, she found a constriction in her throat, making it difficult to swallow. All her energy was aimed at concentrating on Julie and not letting her emotions rise to the surface.

"So—how are things in the village? Any better?" Matthew asked when the topic of Julie seemed to be exhausted.

Annie looked out the window and at her plate rather than

directly at him. She nodded, "Um, yes, things are beginning to be better. My women's Bible study is going very well and I think is spreading to the husbands, the women are very loyal to me," she smiled. "And I'm getting out more. I go to Cambridge whenever I have the day off, to see old friends..." she hesitated, knowing she wasn't being entirely honest. Somehow, she didn't want him to know about Jeremy. She wanted to keep the two of them separate, in different compartments.

"Oh, that's nice," Matthew commented. "And do you ever come to London?"

"Um, yes, a couple of times to the theater."

He asked her what plays she'd seen and he told her about a few he'd been to. They had finished their meal and there was an awkward silence.

"And the dogs?" he asked.

Annie smiled and risked a quick look directly at him. "Oh, they're just fine. It's funny, I don't think of them as your dogs anymore. I'm afraid I've totally taken them into my possession. They're like family."

Matthew nodded, "Well, they were never my dogs anyway, you sound just like Amanda when you say things like that."

Amanda again! He couldn't seem to get through an evening without talking about Amanda. Annie was sick of her name. That was her signal to bolt. "Well, I had really better be going. Thanks for listening, Matthew."

He looked alarmed. "Well, wait, I'll take you back to the train station."

"No, that's all right. We're going in totally different directions. I'll be fine." She stood up and extended her hand to him, looking directly at him again. There it was again, the rush of warmth and confusion. She gave his hand a limp, quiet shake and left, almost running out of the restaurant and hailing a taxi before he could get out the door. She couldn't afford taxis and only did this as a defense, so she could have a quick getaway.

Hi Emily: Help!!! I'm confused again. I saw Matthew for the first time in a long time and reacted to him as I always have done – like a stupid, wimpy, silly female who doesn't have a brain in her head. When I'm with Jeremy, I feel intelligent. We talk about all sorts of intellectual and spiritual matters and we laugh and simply enjoy each other. And I've told you before how he affects me when he kisses me..... Anyway, all Matthew has ever done is hold my hand (once) for a brief period and kissed me on both cheeks as a greeting. But when I look at him, it's as if something inside of me becomes all warm and fuzzy and the only way I can describe it is as if a gas jet has gone off in my head and my brain isn't in gear. What do you think is going on? Have you ever felt this way? What does this mean about how I feel about Jeremy? Help! Love, Annie

The next day Annie went to the train station to pick up someone. She didn't know who it would be. To her relief, it was Rhonda—she could tell immediately. She was well groomed and smiling and even let Annie give her a very loose hug. "I'm so glad you've come home," Annie said, as they drove back to the village. She looked over at Rhonda. "I hope you will think of it as your home."

"Well, that's very kind of you and I would like to think of it as my home until..." she broke off.

"Until you have one of your own, is that a good way to put it?"

She didn't answer the question, but instead asked, "Have my flowers come up?"

"Yes, not in bloom yet," Annie said, wondering if she had said the wrong thing. "My, I mean our, garden will be very happy you have return...come home," she corrected herself. "And the dogs will be ecstatic—just wait and see."

Ecstatic was the word, all right—they jumped all over her with wild delight. "Goodness," she laughed, "this certainly is a good homecoming."

Later, after Rhonda had fixed a nice dinner for them,

after they had both done the washing up and moved into the living room, Annie broached the subject of her problem.

"You know that Dr. Evans has told me what is happening with you, why you disappear sometimes?" she said gently.

Rhonda nodded, looking a bit frightened.

"I just want you to know that I understand. And that if something frightens you, you don't have to pack up and leave. If you become someone else, I can deal with it. I have to learn; I realize I won't be as good as Dr. Evans is with all of this, but I can learn. The most important thing for you to know is that no matter who you are, this is your home." Annie looked at her tenderly. "You know, when you ran away this last time, I realized that I love you. And I want to help you. Is that all right—for me to love you?"

Rhonda slumped her shoulders and looked at the blank television set. Then got up and went to her room without a word.

Julie was back.

Annie looked up to heaven. *"Oh, Lord—give me the additional strength to help this girl. You obviously brought her to me. Other than the church I'm leading, she's the most important job you've given me. Help me to put my personal romantic muddles aside and concentrate on your work."*

Putting the dogs out for one last time for the night and then walking slowly up to her room, Annie was as exhausted as if she'd run a mile. There were too many things tugging on her life, she was being torn in too many different directions. Men, Julie, the church. Men only complicate your life and make you miserable, she decided, as she dropped off to sleep.

Jeremy phoned at least once a day and sent her long emails telling her in detail what he had done that day. She didn't have Julie's permission to tell him what was wrong with her and she found it hard keeping such important information from him. It now made sense that Jeremy said he had seen Julie before and that her name was different. Julie had been in Cambridge and he had probably seen her in a different personality, but Annie couldn't tell him that. At times, he was critical of Annie for complicating her life with Julie.

Meanwhile, Julie settled into a routine. She took sole responsibility for the dogs, she did the chores that Annie now explicitly told her to do, and she talked to Annie more than she had previously. Annie found herself wishing Rhonda would come back and be interested in the garden and smile, but was no longer frustrated with Julie. She understood now and was kind at all times with her, not only kind, but gentle.

It was a problem to take her to the train station mornings and pick her up later in the day. Annie had to rearrange her schedule to fit this, but she encouraged Julie to go and she was now managing to show up at Dr. Evans office four mornings a week. And the more she kept the appointments, the better she seemed to get.

The village talked about Julie. She was out and about with the dogs daily and she wasn't very friendly; it seemed she avoided people. Joy, especially, tried to befriend her, but hadn't got far. The telegraph system was still in full force in the village, as it always had been, but there was a difference, at least amongst the women who were in Annie's Bible study and prayer group. Whilst these women hadn't yet become saints, they had changed in that when there was even a hint of scandal or innuendo in the gossip, they did their best to quash it or at least, not participate in it. Annie had such a strong influence on them that if they thought Julie was strange, this was simply more credit given to Annie for helping her.

Horace had quit coming round to the Vicarage altogether. He became very disgruntled when even his wife told him to shut up about Annie and no one else would listen to his slander. He was thinking about quitting the church and starting to go to the one in the next village. Why, even in the parish council meetings, Annie now seemed to have the center stage and he found himself interrupted more and more. All his pet projects weren't getting voted in. There was a new atmosphere in the church and he didn't like it. He had been there since he was a boy. This was his church and it had been taken over. He wanted to take his marbles and go home.

Chapter Fifteen

Six months had passed since Annie arrived. There were many more young families coming to church, putting their children in the Sunday school, rather than just sending them on their own. The younger couples liked Annie; they liked her sense of humor and her intuitive understanding of them. She was from their generation. She never dropped in on anyone. She always phoned first to see if she could come over and the women had learned that she was always ready to listen to them if they had a problem.

So in terms of the village and the church, Annie was feeling much less frustrated and much more sure of herself. Analyzing it, she was sure her relationship with Jeremy helped a great deal. He provided the daily intellectual stimulation she had missed so much at first. Their only problem seemed to be time. He had time for her, but she didn't have enough time for him. He wanted her to come to Cambridge on her day off and she often did. There, they felt free from the village eyes and there were good restaurants, concerts, and the foreign film theatre, which they both enjoyed. They often met friends for dinner and when Annie was in Cambridge, in this atmosphere, the village and even Julie, seemed far away.

"I think you belong here, rather than in a village," Jeremy said one evening as they were strolling on the Backs. There was a promise of summer and the wildflowers were cheerfully coloring the meadows. What an idyllic scene, Annie thought. Jeremy was holding her hand and walking very close to her.

He still had never told her he loved her. Annie didn't know if he should have by now as she hadn't had any man tell her that. What Matthew said about thinking about her all the time was the closest anyone had come. Did Matthew mean he loved her when he said that? His actions certainly didn't show it. And Jeremy's did. He was attentive and the thrill of kissing him had not diminished one bit. So why am I thinking about Matthew, when I'm here in this idyllic spot with a man who showers me with attention?

"Annie," Jeremy prompted, stopping and holding her away from him with both hands.

"Oh, sorry, what did you say?"

He smiled ironically, "You were miles and miles away. What were you thinking about?"

"I'm sorry. I was just thinking what a beautiful scene this is, so peaceful. You know, Cambridge feels like home, more than Belfast, I guess because I spent so many formative years here."

"Well, that's what I asked you. I said I didn't think you belonged in a village. I think you belong here with me." He leaned down and teasingly brushed her lips.

Is that a proposal? "What do you mean, with you?" she asked.

Jeremy walked on, still holding her one hand. "Oh, you know, I'd like to see you a lot more often, like every night maybe, well, if I didn't have a meeting or something."

So it isn't a proposal, she told herself. *But if it had been, what would I have said?*

"Oh, gosh Jeremy, you would probably get tired of me if you saw me all the time."

"I just think long distance relationships are hard," Jeremy replied, "that's all."

So now, is he about to break up? And if he did, how would I feel about that? "What are you saying?" Annie asked, taking her hand away from his.

"Nothing, I'm just making an observation, that's all. When I'm with you, I realize how much I miss you."

"And when you're not with me….."

"Well, I miss you, of course, but we talk on the phone

nightly or morningly," he joked. "But when I see you, when I look at you with that unbelievable curly red hair—by the way, is it natural?"

Annie laughed. "Of course, you don't think I would try to make it look this way, do you?"

He ran his fingers softly through one side of her hair, "I think it is absolutely beautiful and I….." He stopped and turned away abruptly. "So, where do you want to eat? I had Chinese in mind. Is that all right?"

What was he about to say and didn't?

The moment had passed and Jeremy changed the subject as quickly as he had turned away. "So what do you think of the new Archbishop? he asked, as they walked toward the restaurant.

Dear Em: You are so blessed that you have no man in your life. I know you probably don't agree. But they do mess up your life—Jeremy will never speak his feelings, I'm beginning to realize that perhaps he's unable to, but shows his feelings in his actions. He is so tender with me and he helps me hugely with my sermons and we have such intellectual conversations. He is in on the latest 'doings' of the church, I think he may work his way up into the hierarchy – which as you know, I don't approve of. I mean, no sooner than Jesus left to return to heaven, than his followers began organizing the church, saying who was who and who should be the most important. It's true they said different people have different gifts, but the church is top heavy and I've had more than one parishioner tell me they don't like contributing to the gold robes, etc. All the paraphernalia they wear! It's like a play. In medieval times, I think people liked all that. It made them look up to the clergy. But it's outdated, way outdated. I hardly ever wear my dog collar other than Sunday— do you? Well, you know how rebellious I've always been to authority. But Jeremy isn't. He is a bit of a name dropper, I have to admit—tell me, Em—would you be honest with me? What do you think of him? Love, Annie

Hi Annie: Well, I thought you would never ask. I like Jeremy, I always did. I think everyone does; he is a charming guy. But I don't trust him. I'm glad he's in your life because he seems to have filled a void which you desperately needed. He paid attention to you, which helped in terms of your heartache over Matthew. And he is someone you can talk to—about everything except his feelings for you, evidently. But I would just warn you to be careful. I don't really know what I mean by that—if you fall in love with him or have already fallen in love with him, it does no good to tell you to be careful. But if that hasn't happened yet—then I would just be cautious, that's all. I don't think he would take advantage of you—he's not trying to push the boundaries (sex I mean!!!!) is he? Keep me posted. I will always be handy with ready advice—me who hasn't found a single man I'm interested in here so I have loads of experience....Love, Emily

"Good morning, Julie" Dr. Evans said as she came in the door.

"Hi," Julie said shyly, not looking directly at her. She was getting used to the psychologist, and was beginning to trust her a little bit, but she was still cautious. It was Monday and she hadn't been there since the previous Thursday.

After they were settled in their respective chairs, Dr. Evans asked, "So tell me what happened over the weekend."

Julie hesitated. What had happened over the weekend—she really didn't know. She couldn't remember. It was so frightening to 'wake up' and realize that time had gone by without being aware, as if she had slept since she was here last.

"Were you someone else this weekend?" Dr. Evans asked gently.

Julie nodded. "I guess I was."

"That must be a frightening feeling, but I want you to not be frightened now. Do the deep breathing I taught you and relax. You are perfectly safe here. Remember, it's just a memory problem and it's okay. It's okay, Julie."

Big tears began to roll down Julie's cheeks.

"It's fine to cry, Julie, everyone cries sometimes," Dr. Evans said, leaning forward towards Julie and handing her the box of tissues on the table between them.

Julie shook her head and blew her nose. "It's not fine to cry, you get hit if you cry. I'm sure you never cry,"

"Yes I do. When I'm sad about something, I cry." Dr. Evans was silent for a few moments. "Try to stay here, Julie. I'm telling you that you can cry all you want to here. No one is going to hurt you—it's safe. You're safe. Don't run away. Stay here, please if you can."

Julie looked up at her through her tears. No one had ever told her that it was all right to cry. She had seen girls, women, crying in movies and was always frightened, thinking someone was going to hit her in the next scene. But it didn't happen. It was always wrong to cry, she had always known that. You get hit if you cry.

"You know, Julie, the only reason we cry is because we have to. And if we have to do something, then we should just let it out. I want you to cry until you're finished, no matter how long it takes."

Julie peeked at her through the tissues she was holding wadded up in her hand. *I must be wasting her time, just sitting here crying. She can't mean it—that I can cry all I want. I don't even let myself do that alone in my room—I always stop myself.* "No, I don't want to cry. It's wrong to cry," she said, wiping her eyes furiously, smearing her blue eye shadow and mascara.

"Julie," Dr. Evans said in a gentle, quiet voice, "who hit you when you cried as a little girl?"

Julie stared at Dr. Evans with a far away look in her eyes. Then, in a much lower voice, she said, "Hello, Dr. Evans, we haven't officially met, have we? I'm Joe."

Later, as Dr. Evans was writing up her notes, she speculated that today's session may have been a turning point. Julie was told she could cry without punishment, so that concept had been planted. And the personality that Dr. Evans had suspected was there, suspected because of Annie's report of the emails, had come forth in her office. Joe, the personality that emailed Annie, was the fulfillment of a wish to be admired and wanted by a male, in an appropriate manner. He wanted to marry her, he cared about how she was, he wanted to communicate with her. He had never tried to have sex with her. And Rhonda, whom Annie had experienced, was wholesome, a hard worker, talented, fresh faced and clean. Dr. Evans suspected there was another personality, a little girl, the one who had been traumatized, but so far, she hadn't emerged in her office and she wondered today if what was needed was a change of scene.

Later that day, Annie received a phone call from Dr. Evans. "Oh, hello—is anything wrong?" Annie asked.

"No, things are going nicely," Dr. Evans reassured her, but I wanted to ask a favor of you. Could I come to your house to see Julie? I need to have an extended session with her and I thought maybe we could take a walk with the dogs and have an entire day together."

"Oh, of course, whenever you like. When were you thinking of?"

"Well, I'm free this Saturday—would that suit you? I would need for you to be out of the house, if that's all right."

Annie thought for a moment. This was the weekend she was going to preach in her father's church in Belfast. Jeremy was going with her and she had worried about leaving Julie alone. "That would work out well except for one thing." She went on to tell her the problem.

"Maybe I could stay overnight there," Dr. Evans went on.

"Oh, yes, could you?" Annie asked. "That would solve my problem as well. I could be back by dark on Sunday. But is that all right with your husband?"

Dr. Evans laughed. "Oh, he's quite independent. It will mean he has more time for golf—no, that would be lovely. I'll take a taxi from the train station—you go ahead and leave whenever you had planned."

When Dr. Evans arrived, Julie was Rhonda and had a pot of coffee made, a sparkling kitchen, and some fresh baked scones. After a quick tour of the garden and a welcome by the dogs, they sat companionably at the kitchen table.

"So what are we going to do today?" asked Rhonda, in a confident tone of voice.

Dr. Evans smiled. "What would you like to do?"

"You mean I can choose?"

"Yes, absolutely. Within reason of course," she laughed.

"Well, we could take the dogs for a walk," she suggested.

"That would be lovely," Dr. Evans replied enthusiastically. "Then I can see your village as well."

Many of the villagers saw Julie and the strange woman walking along with the dogs, chatting. They hadn't seen Julie smiling before and this gave the village lots to discuss as they went from house to house. Julie wouldn't look up and smile when they passed her, but she certainly was responding to this woman. Maybe it was her mother.

After a brisk walk, a little more brisk than Dr. Evans would have liked, they sat out in the garden in the sunshine and talked about Rhonda's flowers, which were beginning to bloom.

"Did you grow up in a village?" Rhonda asked, in a hesitant voice. Dr. Evans looked different. She was dressed casually in trousers and a matching jumper, she wore flat heeled shoes and somehow looked younger. Rhonda was curious about her. She wanted to know more about her, but didn't know if it was all right to ask. She didn't know if this was permissible, a role reversal with her asking the questions.

"Yes, I did, in Yorkshire," Dr. Evans replied, "but it was bigger than this one. It was a good place to grow up, lots of freedom to roam, and in my day, parents didn't have to worry about their children being safe."

Rhonda looked down at her lap. In a very quiet voice, she said, "Is it all right to ask you questions?"

"Of course it is. It's only natural that you would be curious about me, ask whatever you want to."

There was silence for awhile as Rhonda gathered her courage. "I notice you wear a wedding ring. Are you married?"

"Yes. Married for a very long time it seems." Dr. Evans smiled. "My husband's name is Richard and he's a chartered surveyor, working in London."

Rhonda wanted to ask if he was nice, but didn't think it was appropriate. She was glad Dr. Evans was here, glad she wasn't going to be staying alone, but didn't understand why she came. Had Annie asked her to come, to babysit her?

Dr. Evans began talking about herself. "I was never able to have children, which I regret," she said. "So I guess my clients have replaced the need in my life to nurture people. My real regret now, at my age, is that I don't have any grandchildren."

Rhonda barely heard the last of her sentence, she was wondering, as she always had, how old she was. She had grey hair and was a little plump, but her face was very smooth and her blue eyes twinkled at the slightest provocation.

After some moments of silence, Dr. Evans said in a quiet tone, "Rhonda, do you know about the others?"

There was a long silence in which Rhonda sat looking down at her lap. The warm spring sunshine highlighted the blond of her hair and she looked much younger than her eighteen years.

After a good ten minutes of Rhonda not looking up, she said, in a very little girl voice "Joe takes care of me. He's nice."

"Yes, I am sure he's nice, like a big brother?" she asked gently.

Rhonda nodded her head up and down.

"It's good to have a big brother, isn't it?"

Rhonda didn't say anything. Rhonda was no longer there.

Annie was excited about taking Jeremy to her parent's house and to her father's church. She wanted to see him in that atmosphere; she wanted to see how he would react. She hadn't spoken to Matthew since the last disastrous meal and decided to try to concentrate on one man at a time. Her mum picked them up at the airport and right on cue, began fawning over Jeremy. It's enough to make me turn against him, Annie thought.

She was nervous about her sermon. She had never preached before with Jeremy in the congregation and she was conscious that wanting to make such a good impression would work against her. She had worked hard on the sermon and hadn't, this time, asked Jeremy for help or comment.

The church was crowded on Sunday morning, but then it usually was. Despite declining church attendance in most of Britain, Annie's father's church was always full. He had such a good preaching style that word spread and people who weren't sure about religion, but were seeking, came to hear him. Annie knew this and knew she had a lot to live up to. This was one of the reasons she was insecure about her sermons—she had heard the best growing up. And whilst she knew the congregation wouldn't be expecting her to be as good as her father, she sure didn't want to bore them.

She had chosen to speak on the subject of women, even though she knew her mother wouldn't approve. When time came for the sermon, she looked down at Jeremy in the front row, at her mother sitting beside him, and then out at the sea of faces. She decided not to look at the front row until after everything was over and keep her eye on the center pillar in the back of the church. She began with a strong voice:

"We all are familiar with the story of Mary and Martha, the story of Jesus being in their home, where a small gathering was listening to his words of wisdom. And we know that Mary was sitting at his feet, taking in every word, listening intently, whilst Martha was in the kitchen, slaving away. What are your thoughts about this? Have you sided with Martha if you are a woman? Have you experienced how Martha felt—put upon, tired, wishing she was in there just as Mary was, but knowing that someone had to do it?

Let's hypothesize about these two women for a moment. Let's suppose, because the gospels do not tell us, let's suppose that Martha is the older sister. Let's say she is two years older than Mary. And let's suppose that Mary is beautiful, always has been, even from a baby. And Martha, whilst not plain, is almost invisible compared to Mary. When they were little girls, everyone stopped to admire little Mary, 'what a beautiful daughter you have' was said to their mother, thoughtlessly paying no attention to Martha. How would you feel if you were Martha? Would you have been jealous of Mary? Of course, you would. It would be only natural. Then fast forward into adulthood. The two sisters live with their brother Lazarus in the village of Bethany. Neither sister is married, which is unusual, as girls were usually married at a young age. Mary certainly had a lot of suitors, but somehow, she had been able to choose. Her brother Lazarus, who would have had authority over her, since nothing is said of their parents being alive, had not forced her into marriage. The three of them had made a home together, and since they had met Jesus, had an especially close relationship with him. Now we all know what Jesus said to Martha when she complained to him, when she, feeling exasperated, had burst into the sitting room where they were all listening with rapt attention to him. She had interrupted and said, 'Can't you see that I'm doing all the work and Mary is just sitting there?' Resentment dripped from her voice, resentment and self-pity."

Anne paused and took a deep breath before she continued: "I've often wondered what would have happened if Martha had sat there as well. Would Jesus have been just as happy if there had been no meal? What do you think? He loved to eat and drink with people, all sorts of people. And someone had to prepare those meals. But at the same time, when his disciples urged him to eat, he said, 'I have food that you know nothing about.' So would he have been upset if the meal wasn't prepared? Or if it was late? I don't think so. I think he was saying, first things first. Get your relationship with me right, listen to my words, spend time in your Bible every day, spend time with me in prayer and then go cook the meal, or sow the wheat, or sell your merchandise—whatever your job entails. Don't put those things first. Did Jesus prefer Mary to Martha? He was God, Omniscient. He knew the hurt that Martha felt. He empathized with her. I like to think his voice was gentle when he said, 'Martha, Mary has chosen the best thing.' When you stand before Jesus, when you die and go to heaven, is he going to say, 'well done, the kitchen floor was always shining, the food was always cooked, the windows were always washed.' Or is he going to say, 'when did you have time for me, for my children, for loving relationships?' He is saying, put me first, my children, whether you are male or female, whether your work is in the kitchen or in Parliament, put me first."

Her voice had remained steady and to her amazement, she felt calm the entire time. She had managed to put Jeremy and her mother out of her mind and sent up an arrow prayer of thanks as she said the last words.

Then she looked at Jeremy. He wasn't looking at her. He was looking over to his right at the blond sitting in the opposite row. He didn't even seem to know she was finished. She climbed down from the pulpit as her father stood up to finish the service, giving her a brilliant smile both with his lips and his eyes. But it wasn't enough to refill her balloon. It had lost all its air—Jeremy wasn't even listening. She didn't dare look at her mother.

As she stood in the doorway with her father, accepting kind words from the parishioners, many who had known her from the time she was a tiny little girl, her spirits were somewhat restored. Jeremy waited until everyone was gone.

He smiled at her and said, "Great sermon, Annie, well done." And with that he possessively encircled her waist with his arm and whispered in her ear "I wish I could kiss you right now."

Annie withdrew from him as tactfully as she could and went with her father to take off their robes. When they were finished, her father encircled her in his arms. "I had a hard time holding back the tears, my girl. Do you have any idea what it means to me that you are such a wonderful woman of God?" He continued to hold her. "I am so proud of you that for once I don't have any words."

Annie felt the hot warmth of tears. She laughed lightly. "I was so nervous, but God was merciful. It must have been the Holy Spirit speaking though me because I felt so calm."

"I know, I could tell." He took her hand. "Now come on. We have to go home and face your mother over Sunday lunch," he said as he winked at Annie.

Jeremy was examining the stained glass windows of the church as they came out of the vestry. He bounded over to them and began asking Rev. O'Donnell about the history of the church. And continued talking about such things over the roast beef and potatoes and cabbage. It was not until the dessert that the subject of Annie's sermon came up again, brought up by her father.

"I was so proud of Annie today. Weren't you, Mother.? He had always called her Mother, which didn't seem odd to Annie when she was growing up, but now it did seem strange.

Her mother nodded, mouth tightly closed. "Yes, it was an interesting twist to that story, all right." She smiled at Jeremy. "Tell us about the latest synod meeting. I hear you were a delegate…".

Meantime, Matthew had been struggling, not only with his emotions, but also with a profound sense of loneliness. London was an exciting place to live. There were always things to go and see—museums to wander around in, good drama in the theater, or just walks along the Thames. The plane trees were springing into life once more in the many squares and parks. Who wouldn't love living here? he asked himself. And yet, he was profoundly unhappy. He couldn't get Annie out of his mind.

After their last ill-starred meeting, he made a conscious decision to let her alone, to not contact her in any manner. It was obvious by her actions that she didn't even like him. He thought he would never forget the look on her face when he told her she sounded like Amanda. That was the highest compliment he could give to any woman. Yet she looked like a scared rabbit and left the restaurant in a rush again, just like the last time.

His friend Donald was married and his wife invited Matthew over for Sunday lunch now and then, but other than those two, he really didn't have friends. He had colleagues at work and he enjoyed his students, but it wasn't the same. He still went home alone to his flat most evenings.

However, his resolution to leave Annie alone didn't last long. He seemed unable to help himself; he just wanted to hear her voice.

The phone rang several times before Annie picked up the phone. "Reverend O'Donnell here," she said, in crisp, businesslike manner. Matthew's knees felt weak and when he finally spoke, his voice sounded queer to him. "Annie, this is...."

"Matthew! I'm so happy to hear from you. How are you?"

Her voice sounded like sweet music to him—he knew he missed her, but not until he heard her voice did he know how he felt, how he really felt.

"Matthew? Are you there?" Annie's voice sounded alarmed.

"Yes, yes—it's just that it's so good to hear......to hear your voice again, Annie."

"I've often thought of getting in touch. I never did apologize for how I acted the last time we met. You must have thought I was very rude...."

"No, no" he interrupted. "I didn't. I just didn't know why, that was all. It obviously was something I said." He paused and Annie didn't fill in the silence. "Listen, Annie, I phoned to see how Julie is doing."

There was a brief silence before Annie answered, making him assume there was bad news. Then, "Oh, Julie is doing very well, thank you. Dr. Evans has done wonders for her and she gets better all the time."

Matthew wanted to know more. He wanted to know explicit details of how well she was doing, but Annie's attitude, from what he could tell on the other end of the phone, stopped him from inquiring further. Another silence—longer this time. "Well......how are you?" he finally stammered out, feeling awkward, even foolish. He remembered how Annie used to confide in him, how she used to get tearful when they spoke, she used to say it was because he was the only person who understood what she was going through with the church. Now, she seemed cold and distant, even somewhat unfriendly. She had said she was happy to hear from him at the start of this conversation; had he once more said something wrong? Was he a complete klutz? His desire to keep her on the phone, to continue hearing her voice was stronger than his instinct to shut off the conversation, to say goodbye and hang up. "Look, Annie, I don't seem able to say the right things around you, I guess I goof up, often, but hearing your voice again makes me realize how much I've missed talking to you." Annie didn't respond, so he plunged ahead. "I....I'm really lonely down here in London and all I'm asking is for you to continue to be my friend....is that okay?"

"Oh, Matthew." That's all she said, but there was emotion in her voice, it was soft, and tender. "I'm sorry, Matthew. It's just that...." She broke off.

Matthew's imagination leapt all over the place. Maybe she was engaged, maybe she hated him, maybe she was ......he didn't know. All he knew was that he didn't want her to leave the phone. If he could just keep her talking, maybe he would find out what was bothering her about him, maybe he would find out what she wanted, maybe he would find out if she was interested in him. "What Annie....what is it? What went wrong with the friendship we had—I thought it was close, I even thought it might become something else...." These last few words were said softly, he felt his throat closing down, choking with the hope that flooded his very soul.

He heard her take in a deep breath, amplified through the

phone. "I've missed you too and yes, you were a friend I could talk to, it's just that...." Once more she stopped.

"What Annie.....what is it? I obviously have offended you in some way, but honestly, I haven't a clue. Please keep talking to me. Please, let's keep talking until you're able to tell me what I've done wrong—have I done something wrong?" The more he heard her voice, the more he wanted to keep hearing her voice. He knew he was always attracted to her, but now he wondered, was he in love with her? He must be; he felt the same as he had with Amanda. Could a man love another woman just as much? He didn't know. He only knew how he felt, which was very weak inside.

"Just a minute, Matthew. Let me go into my study, okay?" He nodded assent then laughed at himself as he realized that she couldn't see him plus, she must not have the phone to her ear. He could hear her climbing the stairs and then heard the door shut. He'd never been upstairs in her house, but he conjured an image of her sitting in a comfortable chair next to a desk.

"Okay, Matthew, I just didn't want Julie to hear me. She's in the kitchen—she bakes all the time! She makes things for bake sales at the back of the church on Sunday mornings and gives the money to the church."

"That's wonderful, Annie. Does she go to church now?" He didn't want to talk about Julie. He wanted to talk about Annie. He wanted to talk about how Annie felt about him. But this was better than nothing.

"No, I'm afraid not. And she's still shy with the village people. But the fact that she donates to these bake sales is such a wonderful improvement. And she is so talented—the things she does with flour and sugar, I'm going to get fat if I don't watch it."

Matthew was genuinely happy to hear about Julie. Settle down, he told himself sternly, enjoy talking to her—it's better than nothing. "And the dogs? How are they? he asked, although he really was not that interested in them.

"Oh, they're great! You know, Matthew, the day I moved into this house, the day I met you—this house was so big and so empty. I thought at the time that it was a wonderful house for a vicar who was married and had children and here I was, a single woman. It seemed so lonely. And now the house is always full. Julie talks to me now and the dogs are always up to something. I'm truly grateful for your gift of them. I think God put it into your mind to give them to me, don't you?"

God put that into my mind—that was how Amanda used to talk. He was about to say that when Annie went on.

"But let's get back to you, Matthew. I'm sorry you're feeling so lonely—have you not made friends there at work?"

"No, I'm afraid not. Acquaintances, yes, colleagues, but no real friends. I...I was wondering if you'd like to go to a play? There are always good ones on offer and I know you said you like the theater." He hadn't planned this. He hadn't planned to stick his neck out and be vulnerable again., but his desire to see her again was growing stronger with each minute they were talking. He thought she would never answer, the silence built up until it seemed like an insurmountable wall. "Annie....?"

"Yes, I'm here, Matthew. I would love to see a play....I just....well, why not...yes. When were you thinking of?"

Matthew laughed, "Well, I hadn't been thinking of it until just now. Why don't you tell me when you can come here and I'll get tickets."

"Well, I think I could manage it a week from today. Could we go to a Saturday matinee? So I wouldn't get home so late?"

"Yes, it's a deal. Do you want me to pick out what we see or do you want to go on line and decide, then ring me back."

"You do it. You have excellent taste, I know. And Matthew....."

"Yes?" What was she going to say? Was she going to say more about him, about their relationship, such as it was.

"I just want to say that I'm glad you called. In fact, I'm very glad you've called. I'll meet you—where?"

"I'll ring back when I know the theater and we can meet there. Matinees are usually at three o'clock. Is that all right?"

"Yes. I'll see you then, Matthew. Bye."

Matthew said goodbye and hung up the phone. He sat there with a small smile on his lips. Well, he was going to see her again. And maybe....just maybe, he could keep from offending her this time, maybe he could keep from scaring her off. But it sure would help if he knew what he was doing that made her react as she did.

Chapter Sixteen

Annie hung up the phone. She wasn't sitting in a chair by a desk, actually, she was sitting on the floor, curled up with her back against the chair. This was her favorite place to talk, this was where she talked to her father, the one here on earth. She continued to sit there on the floor for quite a long while. She didn't know what to think, but what she did know was what she felt. She felt warm inside; she felt a glow that rose to her face. She put her hands on her cheeks, expecting to feel warmth. *Well, you don't feel this way when you talk to Jeremy. He makes me laugh and he's very interesting, but warmth? Now when he kisses me, then I feel it. More than a lady vicar should.....*

As Annie rode the train to London the next Saturday, the day was crisp and clear, blossoms adorned the fruit trees all along the route. Spring had definitely arrived with promises of flowers, green leaves, and the warmth of summer. Hope—that's what spring always reminded her of. There was hope in the air. She had dressed carefully, but neatly. Annie didn't have a large wardrobe and even now with her salary, she didn't have time to shop. She wore her linen suit, its navy blue primness softened by a white ruffled blouse. Nervous wasn't the word. She was more than that about meeting Matthew once again. *Maybe this will solve my dilemma about Jeremy, she told herself. Maybe I'll realize I'm not in love with him and then I won't be so upset so often.*

Though she thoroughly enjoyed Jeremy's conversation, each time they talked, something he said bothered her. His relationship with God seemed to be from all the books he read. She had begun to think of him as a philosopher, rather than a Christian. Oh, well, God knows if he's a Christian or not. I shouldn't judge. But she did. Judge, that is.

As the rolling countryside swept past her window, she spoke to God. Not out loud, but internally. *Please, please Lord—help me with this meeting with Matthew, please tell me how to behave around him, and most of all, please let me know if he's the right man for me.*

As she approached the Apollo Theatre, Matthew was standing outside, looking up one side of the street and then the other. When she saw him her heart beat faster. And once again, she didn't know what to say. It seemed she lost all confidence around him.

"Annie" he said, smiling hugely, and kissing her on eacg cheek. "Come on, we need to get to our seats."

It was a Chekov play with Kenneth Branaugh acting the lead character. There wasn't much conversation between Annie and Matthew until the interval. As the audience all around them rose, they stayed seated and talked about the play, the acting, Chekov, anything but each other. She was enjoying the rather depressing play hugely, but it wasn't that. She often went to cultural events. It was Matthew she was enjoying sitting next to—it was the look on his face and the nearness of him. His arm was always touching hers in the closeness of the seats and she found she had trouble looking away from his eyes.

"Can you stay here for dinner?" Matthew asked. "I'd really like it if you could."

Dinner—that meant getting home late and tomorrow was Sunday. Her sermon was done, but she usually went over it on Saturday evening. Should she?

She did and Matthew chose the first restaurant they had been to together. When the waiter had taken their order, Annie said, "Matthew, I'm so sorry to hear you're lonely here. Do you think you made a mistake? Moving away from the village?"

He leaned forward with one arm across the table, and with a serious look on his face, said, "Annie, could I have your hand?"

Annie reached her hand to him and he held it tight. What was he going to say? What was going to happen next? She didn't know, but yet the touch of his hand was exciting—she didn't want to take it back.

"Annie, the last two times we met, I must have really said something that offended you. You got up and left and I've been miserable ever since. I don't want to do that again, so could you promise me you'll stay no matter what I say?" His eyes pleaded with her and there was no hint of anything other than complete seriousness in his face and voice.

Annie nodded and smiled nervously. "Of course I'll stay, Matthew. It was really rude and childish, my running off like that. It's just that I guess that's how I've always handled things, run away when I'm upset." That now familiar lump was there in the pit of her stomach. What was he going to say? What was he going to tell her? The restaurant wasn't crowded; it was early for the dinner crowd. Still, she kept her voice low and hoped Matthew would too. And most of all, she hoped she wouldn't get tears in her eyes. He was still holding her hand and she liked that.

"All right, here goes. Ever since Amanda died I've been miserable, as one might expect. And I hadn't even thought of marrying again. I hadn't thought I would want to...."

His voice trailed off and he was looking into her eyes so intently she was mesmerized. She didn't even flinch when he said the dread word Amanda.

"When you came to the village, the first day I met you....I was so strongly attracted to you that I felt guilty—do you understand? It had only been a year and I didn't think I should be attracted to anyone and every time I saw you I was so overcome with emotion that I stumbled and said stupid things. Oh, Annie, I don't even know what I said. But I do know that I made you run away." He was speaking faster and faster now, as if he was afraid she would leave once more. "And I thought maybe if I left the village, I wouldn't think about you and I would just do my job and start a new life here in London. But Annie—it's worse here—I think about you all the time, all the time."

Annie didn't know what to think. She just knew how she felt as a swarm of emotions come over her, all warm and nice and lovely. And there were the beginnings of tears in her eyes, but that was all, just the beginnings. "Matthew—I didn't know that. I thought you didn't like me at all. And I owe you an explanation of why I ran away. It's just that every time I was with you, you talked about Amanda. I knew you needed to talk about her and if it had been anyone else, I would have been happy to listen. But you see, I felt the same way about you."

"You did? You do?" Matthew's face broke into a very large smile and his voice was no longer quiet.

Annie laughed, "Yes. I felt the same way. And every time you mentioned Amanda, I felt like no woman in the world could live up to her—she sounded so perfect, so unimaginably perfect, and I'm afraid I'm not that at all. It was my temper that made me run away both times. I just didn't want to hear her name again." She smiled a tender smile to this man who had been such a puzzle to her.

"I'm sorry, I didn't realize I talked about Amanda so much. Obviously, I didn't understand how that came across, but could we start over? Could we start seeing each other? Just knowing what the problem was and knowing you felt the same way about me has made me very happy. Right in this moment, it's the first time I haven't felt miserable since I moved to London."

Start seeing each other. What did that mean? What about Jeremy? Was she in an exclusive relationship with Jeremy? She didn't know; she really didn't know.

The waiter arrived at that point with their meal. Matthew withdrew his hand and scarcely eating, chattered away like a bird let out of a cage.

Annie wrote to Emily when she got home even though it was late. And rather than going over her sermon, as she usually did on Saturday evenings, she got right into bed, snuggled deep into the covers, drawing her knees up in the fetal position, going over everything Matthew said in her mind—every look on his face, every touch of his hand. Remembering how on the train platform, just as the train came in, he leaned towards her and kissed her. It was different than Jeremy's kisses, it was short and tender, he actually barely brushed her lips with his. When Jeremy held her in his arms and kissed her long and deep, she had feelings, all right. Dangerous feelings if a vicar was to keep her virginity until marriage. But Matthew's soft kiss filled her full of wonder and she wanted to re-live every moment; she didn't want to lose the tiniest bit of the memory. And she didn't want to think about it or analyze it. She just wanted to savor it.

Julie awoke the next morning and after letting the dogs out, decided to fix breakfast for Annie. She knew Annie's routine now and she had noticed that on Sundays Annie hardly had time to eat, just a quick cup of tea whilst she went over her sermon. I'll surprise her, she determined. It made her feel good to do that. Annie was the first person who had ever been a friend to her. And now she had Dr. Evans as well.

When Annie came downstairs and into the kitchen, Julie smiled shyly at her. "I've made you some breakfast..."

"Um, I could smell the bacon from my room. Julie, how kind of you!" She looked at her watch. "But I will have to scarf it down I'm afraid, as usual I'm running late." She sat down, took a long sip of tea and then began eating hurriedly. "This is wonderful. I never have time to fix anything before church."

Julie sat down opposite her. "I know, that's why I did it. You really don't eat enough, you know."

Annie looked up from her plate and smiled with her mouth full. When she had swallowed, she said "My goodness, Julie, I think we've had a role reversal here. You taking care of me instead of me taking care of you!"

Julie didn't respond, but she was very pleased. Annie was the first person she'd ever wanted to help. Her attitude before coming to live here had always been that the world had dealt her a pretty lousy hand and why should she help anyone—

no one had ever helped her. No one had cared about how she felt, about whether she had enough to eat—no one until Annie. When she was with her dad, he took her to the pub with him and she always had her meals there. But she didn't enjoy eating, even if it was a good meal, because she knew what was going to happen later when they were alone. So she withdrew into herself and pretended she was someplace else, someone else. But lately, here, she felt safe. And she was usually Rhonda, although no one, even Annie, remembered to call her that.

Annie gulped down the rest of her tea, stood up, and came over to Julie, giving her a kiss on the top of her head. "Thank you, Julie. I really appreciated the food. I'm sorry, but I have to run!" With that, she flew into a flurry of gathering her robes, books, and Bible and left.

Julie went into the living room to look out the windows which faced the street. Several people were walking toward the church and the bells were ringing. She sat very still, listening. When they stopped, she could hear the organ begin to play. The door of the church must be open now that it was warm. She knew Easter was coming soon, Annie had mentioned it.

Why didn't Annie try to convert her? She told her she was always welcome to come to church, but she didn't urge her—she left it at that. She had read all of Annie's sermons on her computer. She was still snooping. And she thought some of them were very good. To her surprise, none of them told people they were going to hell, like she was. Surely someone who had done such vile things would go to hell. Surely holy people wouldn't want her in heaven.

Going back into the kitchen, she began clearing the table and doing the washing up. The dogs were clamoring for a walk, so when she finished, she took them out. The village seemed deserted as she walked toward the footpath along the fields. It was a most beautiful morning, she was thinking, taking in deep breaths of the clear, spring air and listening to the wealth of birdsong around her. Is this what it means to be happy? She hardly dared to think the word. She didn't think she knew what it was,but she knew others talked about happiness.

She remembered the last session with Dr. Evans. "I know you are bitter, Julie. And you have every right to be. You built up a wall around yourself in order to protect yourself from being hurt. Perfectly understandable."

"And is that.....that wall still there? Will it always be there?"

Dr. Evans had smiled. She had such a kindly face. Little wrinkles were around her mouth and eyes; she must smile at everyone all the time, Julie thought.

"No, Julie—it won't always be there. You see, that's what we're doing in therapy. We're tearing down that wall, brick by brick. And by the way, if it weren't for Annie and her kindness towards you, I think the wall would have remained for a very long time."

Julie nodded. "Yes, she's been wonderful to me. I don't know why. Do you know? Do you know why she took me in and is so nice to me?"

Dr. Evans smiled again, causing all the wrinkles to appear. "Yes, I do know. She is a Christian, that's why."

"But lots of people are Christians and they aren't like Annie." She looked into the distance towards the window in the office.

"I know, Julie. But some of them aren't really Christians and others may be, but they are still being selfish, wanting to run their lives in selfish ways. Annie is different. She is living the true Christian life, giving to others."

All these thoughts were occupying Julie's mind as they walked on and on, leaving the footpath and going into a small forest near the village. She had often been there before and had never come across anyone. Suddenly the dogs began barking. Julie turned around to see why they were barking. A man was following them. A man Julie knew—all too well.

Annie struggled through the church service this morning. Not for the first time, certainly, she wished there was a curate or someone else, anyone, who could give the sermon once in awhile. Matthew's face, his smile, and his words were in her thoughts the entire time. "Sorry, Lord" she whispered in her heart. Distraction doesn't make for good sermons...."

But if anyone noticed a difference in her, nothing was said. And when she arrived home, prior to going to the inevitable Sunday lunch with one of the church families, she found Julie sitting in the living room. But she was not alone.

Julie stood up when Annie came in the door. The look on her face was one of pure fright.

"Oh, hello," Annie began.

"Rev. O'Donnell, I'm Julie's father, Reg Sherman's the name. Come to take her for a little trip, you see, but she said we had to wait till you got home."

He was a big man, muscular, with a mustache and a ruddy complexion. Annie could smell the alcohol on his breath from the distance she kept between them. Julie once more sat down and was looking at the floor, her body slumped over. It was obvious to Annie that Julie didn't want to go with him, but she was frightened as well. She didn't know if there was anything she could do about it.

"Julie, do you want to go with your father?" she asked. Julie didn't answer. Annie went over and sat down on the sofa next to her. She could see tears running down Julie's face.

"Mr. Sherman, it doesn't seem to me that your daughter wants to go with you. And I don't think it's a good idea either. She's happy here and she's made some progress. She's of age; you can't force her."

Annie was five foot two inches tall and slight. This man was over six feet and looked as if he could pick her up with one hand and squeeze. There was fear in her heart, but her concern for Julie overcame it and she hoped he couldn't sense her fear. She had been sending up arrow prayers all along and just then, the doorbell rang. It was Horace.

Annie ran to the door and let him in. "Horace, am I glad

to see you! Come in, come in—I want you to meet Julie's father." Taking him by the arm, she steered him into the living room. "Horace, this is Mr. Sherman. Why don't you keep him company a minute whilst Julie and I go upstairs."

Even though Julie didn't appear to be listening, she must have been because she raised her eyes at that point and when Annie patted her shoulder, she obeyed and followed her upstairs. Annie quickly locked the door to her study and went to the phone. She rang Joy. "Dn't ask questions—just get five of the strongest and biggest men in the village over here as soon as you can. Tell them to come right in the door. Don't worry, Julie and I are safe."

Julie was sitting on the carpeted floor, her knees pulled up against her body. "I'm not going to let him take you. You are safe, Julie. You are going to stay here with me." But Julie didn't answer. Julie wasn't there.

The telegraph system worked for the good for once in the village. Within ten minutes, six, rather than five, of the village's biggest and strongest men had arrived in Annie's living room. Annie had left Julie in the study and come into the living room where a bewildered Horace stood. Julie's father looked angry, he sat down and started cursing, using every word he knew, evidently.

"Thank you for coming," Annie said to the men. "I'd like you to escort this man out of town and make it plain to him he should never, ever come back."

When it was all over and the men had been heartily thanked by Annie, she went upstairs to console Julie. What she found was a very little girl, sucking her thumb, and curled up on the floor. When Annie spoke, she raised her hand up to shield her head.

"Julie, I'm not going to hurt you. This is Annie....your father is gone. He won't come back."

No response. Annie didn't know what to do, but she thought Daisy might be of help, since she was Julie's favorite. She stepped outside the door and called to her. Daisy and the other two bounded up the stairs. Carefully excluding the other two dogs, she shut the door. Daisy immediately went to Julie, licking her face. Julie peeped out at her and reached out her hand to pet her. Daisy laid down beside her, wagging her tail and continuing to wet her face with her long wet tongue.

Annie quietly left the room, shutting the door after her. She phoned Dr. Evans. When Annie told her what had happened, she said, "Obviously, she has switched to the little girl, whose name we don't know. I'm very concerned about her—leaving the dog with her was a good idea, that's something she's never had before, a pet that she trusts. But I'm also very concerned about her father. We need to obtain a restriction order on him, so that he won't come near her again."

Annie sighed into the phone. "That's the trouble living in a village; there is no local constable to phone. I knew by the time someone arrived from the nearest town, he could have taken her away. But I'll see about a restraining order." She paused for a moment. "I don't know where he lives. Do you think Julie does?"

"She must. I'll try to find out when I see her. Can you bring her down today?"

"Yes, if you're willing to give up your Sunday."

"Of course I am. Julie is much more important than one day out of my life. I'm afraid if you don't bring her today she'll run away again. Maybe someone could come with you in case she tries to bolt?"

"Yes, that's a good idea. I'll phone you from the station at Kings Cross so you'll know when to expect us." Annie immediately thought of Joy as the one to accompany her. Joy's ample physique would help in this case, where strength might be needed. Joy said she would be right over.

Annie knocked lightly before opening the door to the study. Julie and Daisy lay on the floor together. Both were fast asleep.

The trip to London was uneventful in that Julie was very docile, but totally silent. She stared out the window the entire time and wouldn't respond when spoken to. Annie and Joy prayed silently the entire trip.

When Dr. Evans took Julie by the hand and took her into her office, she was extremely gentle with her. "I don't know your name, but I know you are a little girl, a very frightened little girl. " she began.

Julie didn't respond and kept her eyes on her lap.

Dr. Evans got up and from a cupboard drew out a fluffy stuffed teddy bear. "Would you like to hold this teddy? He likes little children and he's so soft."

Julie didn't say anything, but allowed Dr. Evans to put the bear into her lap. Dr. Evans was silent, but observed that Julie's fingers were slowly moving over the bear.

"I have something to tell you," she was carefully not using the name Julie. "I want you to know that the man, the man who calls himself your father.."

At that, Julie stiffened up and gasped.

"This man is never going to bother you again. The police are going to keep him from coming near you again....so you don't ever have to be afraid." Her voice was soft and low. She a knelt down on the floor in front of Julie. "Never ever, do you understand? You don't have to ever be afraid again."

"Not the police," Julie said in almost a whisper. "He'll tell them how bad I am." She was sobbing by now. "He'll tell them to come get me and lock me up—he told me. He told me."

Dr. Evans was still kneeling in front of her. "He was lying. He was telling you a lie. He is the bad one—not you. You are an innocent child and nothing, nothing ever was your fault—nothing."

She let Julie cry for quite a long time and then gently raised her out of the chair and enfolded her in her arms. "You are a child of God and He loves you," she said, in a sing-song voice. "You are a child of God and He loves you" over and over she sang the words in a low sweet voice.

Julie allowed her to cradle her in her arms, all the while

keeping hold of the teddy bear. When her sobs subsided, Dr. Evans gently sat her down again and was rewarded for the first time with a direct look from Julie.

"God couldn't love me—he knows what I've done..." she said with her head lowered and her voice so low it was difficult to hear.

"Yes he does love you and whatever you've done wasn't your fault. You were forced, but you won't ever be again. You are safe."

Dr. Evans let the silence build up as Julie buried her face in the teddy bear. Then she said, "The bear's name is Spencer and he would like to know your name."

Julie held the bear out in front of her as she looked at him. "Spencer—that's a nice name. A tiny smile appeared on her lips as she said, "My name is Teresa."

Chapter Seventeen

With the drama of Julie's father appearing and the subsequent events, Annie had not forgotten Matthew, of course, but he hadn't been uppermost in her mind. She phoned him Sunday evening after they returned from London and told him all about it. Jeremy also phoned and she told him all about it. *I feel like a juggler,* she thought, as she hung up the phone. She knew she needed to break it off with Jeremy, but didn't know how to do it.

When he phoned, he mostly spoke about himself, what he was writing, who he had seen. Of course, he asked her how she was and he did listen well, but now that she was looking at him from a different perspective, the perspective of knowing that Matthew wanted a relationship with her, she could understand her father's objection. Jeremy was a theologian, first and foremost. Whether or not he was a true Christian, she didn't know and wouldn't let herself judge. That was for God to know. But now, as if she could see him clearly for the first time, she knew their relationship wouldn't work long term. *Not that he's mentioned anything about long-term anyway.*

Along with all the troubles with Julie and with her own love life, the church work was always there and whilst she hadn't failed to call on people who needed her prayers and attention and whilst she had somehow managed to knock out a sermon a week, Annie knew her mind and time was divided. It seemed the congregation and even the village were happier with her than when she first arrived, but she wasn't happy with herself.

Joy phoned the next morning and asked her to come over for a cup of tea and a chat. Joy knew that Annie couldn't speak freely with Julie in the house, else she would have come to the vicarage. Annie settled into one of Joy's deep, comfortable chairs and relaxed, sipping her tea. "You know, Joy, I wonder if you have any idea how valuable you've been to me. I literally don't know what I would have done without you."

Joy smiled and laughed softly, or as softly as she was able. "Well, my girl, you don't know how grateful I am to you. So maybe we're even."

"What do you mean? It seems to me I've been on the receiving end of this relationship, not you."

Joy shook her head. "No, no, my girl. You don't know how many months and years I've been on my knees, asking God to send us a good vicar. And by that, I mean someone who could stir up the church, get them going, wake them up. And you certainly have done that. Why, when I phoned around asking for those men to come help you, they didn't ask any questions, they simply did it gladly. That wouldn't have happened before."

"How did you do it? How did they come so quick?" Annie asked. "It was like a miracle."

"Well, if you ask me, and you just did, I think it was a miracle. First, I rang Sam Martin and told him to call John Temple and go immediately, that you were in trouble. Then I phoned James at the shop, he dropped everything and brought along Alan, who was in the shop at the time. And last, I ran over to Thornton, next door sent him on his way, and as he was running, he shouted for Mervyn to help as well. The whole thing didn't take more than ten minutes. And it worked! They all gave me reports later, of how they 'gently' hah! escorted Julie's father to his car and threatened him. James said he told him in no uncertain terms that he was never, ever to enter anywhere near this village again, because they could form a regular vigilante group in a matter of minutes and if he knew what was good for him, he would stay away."

Annie put down her cup of tea, stood up and went over to lean down and give Joy a hug. "Thank you, Joy."

She sat back down and Joy went on. "What a difference!

You remember how you were treated at first, all the gossiping, all the resistance? And now those men love thinking they protected you. They all feel you are a part of the village and whatever you ask they'll do. How is Julie today?"

"Okay. We had a good talk this morning after breakfast. She needs time to recover from this scare, but she was talking to me, which is always a good sign. I made her promise me she wouldn't run away again, that if she's frightened, that she must talk to me about it first." Annie paused a moment, crossing her arms against her chest as if she was hugging herself. "You know Joy, her father evidently did horrible things to her—I don't know for sure, but probably sexual abuse. She needs to stay with Dr. Evans until she is healed and most of all, she needs healing from the one ultimate source, the Lord."

"I've been praying for Julie every day since she arrived, Annie, but I guess I need to spend more time on it. You're the real one, Annie. Your perseverance with her has been a topic of conversation in the village, but not in a negative way. People realize how good you are to stick with her, even though they don't know what's wrong with her."

"Have people in the village changed, Joy? Or is it my perception that has changed? You know when I first came here, I was upset at being in a village. I wanted to be back in Cambridge where there were exciting things to do, where there were intellectual conversations to be had. And I was distressed over the lack of true Christian behavior and values here. But now, I'm beginning to change my mind. Has the village changed or am I just seeing it differently?"

Joy refilled Annie's cup before she answered. "Well, my dear, I think the answer is both. You've inspired them into being Christians, rather than just church goers, so they've changed. And I think as you've come to know us a bit better, your opinion of us is higher!" She laughed as she said these last words.

"Well, whatever, I'm not so anxious to leave now, so that's good." She stood up. "I'd better get back to the vicarage. I don't want to leave Julie alone for too long just now."

When Annie left the house, Julie didn't go into her study to snoop. It was such a habit that she thought about it, but something stopped her. She didn't know what it was, but the desire to do that had lessened and she was able to resist. She played ball with the dogs in the back garden and then going into the shed to get out the gardening tools, began pulling up weeds in the flower beds. The daffodils were still blooming, surrounded by blue delphiniums, tall michalmas daisies, hollyhocks of every color, and bright pansies peeking out from underneath. It had become a beautiful garden under her care and not only was Julie proud of it, but it made her happy. This was something she had accomplished. It was beautiful and rewarded her hard work by making her feel a bit better about herself. As she dug deep into the soil, with the sun warming her back and the dogs boisterously playing around her, she felt a new sensation, something she had never felt before. She searched her mind for a word to describe it. It was lack of fear, lack of anxiety, it was calm. That was it—her heart wasn't racing, she wasn't on the alert for sudden danger. Then she found the word. Peace.

The entire ordeal surrounding Julie the past few days had interfered with seeing Annie sooner, but Matthew thought it had also brought them closer. He was seeing her tonight, as she was coming down for dinner. He couldn't wait.

But of course, he did wait, and though he was distracted all day in his lectures, he knew his subject so well that his mind could be split whilst giving them. He could stay on topic and think about Annie in one compartment of his mind. Or was it not his mind at all? Was it his emotions, emotions which had died with Amanda and were beginning to live again. Matthew whistled as he walked the short distance from his flat to the station. He didn't know for certain what would happen with his relationship with Annie, but it had begun. After such a slow, awkward start, he was enjoying his long talks with her on the phone and looked forward to seeing her. Looked forward was putting it mildly, he chuckled to himself. *Matthew, my boy, me thinkest you're in love.*

Annie was anxious to see Matthew again as well. She needed to seal her decision to break off with Jeremy. She had never been in this situation before and it was uncomfortable for her. She knew she was being untruthful with Jeremy, a double-minded woman—wasn't that something in the book of James? On the home front, everything was looking up. Julie was going to be fine, she was sure of it, and probably would leave at some point, leave to find her own way in life. The villagers seemed to be one hundred percent behind Annie and church attendance was growing every week.

When she stepped off the train at Kings Cross, she walked quickly to the area where Matthew told her he would be waiting. But he didn't wait, he came almost running toward her and before she knew it, she was in his arms and he was covering her with kisses. "My goodness," she laughed, when he pulled back. "Not very vicar-like behavior, in public and all."

Matthew was smiling broadly. "Who cares? I was so anxious to see you and then when I saw you way down on the platform, I couldn't wait. Annie..." his voice grew somber, "Annie, I can't wait till the end of the evening, I can't wait for a suitable, a proper time and place....Annie, I know now, know for certain, that I'm in love with you..."

Annie had already melted, her term for that soft rush of warm feeling throughout her entire body. The way he kissed her just now brought on the same feelings as when Jeremy kissed her, yet it was different somehow. Different because it was Matthew, whose physical attraction for her was so overwhelming, different because she trusted him. Matthew's arms were still around her and she buried her face into his chest. Did he want her to say she loved him as well? "Oh, Matthew, that's the first time anyone has ever said that to me."

Matthew stroked her hair with one hand and spoke softly into her ear. The platform was now deserted—they were as alone as one could be in a busy railway station. "Don't say anything,

Annie, I know this is sudden and I don't expect you to feel the same way yet. I just hope you will someday—no," he laughed softly, "I hope you do soon."

Annie broke away and smiled, "I....I hope I do as well, Matthew. And thank you."

"Thank me? Whatever for?"

"For saying those words. They, the words, do something to me. Deep down—do you know what I mean?"

They were by this time walking toward the stairs which lead to the Tube. Matthew was holding her hand and Annie liked the feel of his hand in hers, there was nothing sensual about it—it felt safe.

He had booked a table at a very fine restaurant, but not the same one as before. After they ordered, he once more asked for her hand across the table. Annie looked around at the myriads of waiters in their white starched jackets hovering to spring into action if needed. The table cloth matched their jackets and the china, silver, and crystal all sparkled in the reflection of the chandeliers above. "Goodness, Matthew, you can't keep on bringing me to places like this, you'll soon be broke!"

Matthew nodded. "No, I won't Annie, but this is a special evening and I wanted to give you a special treat. You know, the last time I did that, it didn't turn out so well."

"I know," Annie answered, "and I apologize again. Pretty juvenile behavior on my part." She looked around the room again. Everyone seemed to be much more smartly dressed than she was, but then she didn't have many choices in her wardrobe.

"Annie," Matthew began, "now that we've begun, now that we're having a proper relationship. Gosh, I sound like a teenager.....and actually that's how I feel, inside, you know," he gestured with his other hand to his heart. "What I'm trying to say is....do you think this can be permanent?"

What was he saying? Is he asking me to marry him? Just then one of the myriads appeared with the bottle of wine they'd ordered, went through the routine of pouring some in Matthew's glass for approval and then serving Annie. Matthew had not let go of her hand all during this. But when the waiter left, he took the glass in his other hand and held it up for a toast. "To our future," he said, smiling his devastating smile.

"To our future," Annie said, smiling back, misty-eyed.

All through the marvelous dinner of scallops en troit, they talked about Julie, about Matthew's work, about the change in the way the village was treating Annie—they spoke about everything except Jeremy. Annie didn't want to ruin the special dinner this time, so she kept silent, but in some ways it spoiled the evening for her, because she felt guilty. She told herself she must do something soon about him. She couldn't go on this way.

So it was that the next day, she sat down and wrote a long letter to Jeremy, not at the computer, but in longhand. It took her three hours. She sat there thinking and crossing out the rough draft. When she finally finished, she wasn't happy with what she'd written, but she knew she had to do it. She had prayed before she began to write and kept sending up arrow prayers during the three hours. She had assurance she was doing the right thing, but it still was difficult. As puzzled as she'd often been by their relationship, she still liked Jeremy very much as a friend. Did I stay so long because I was so hungry for the way he kissed me, she wondered? Does that mean I'm a wanton woman?! She had to admit to herself this was a large part of the reason she had looked forward to seeing Jeremy. But now that Matthew had kissed her, she knew the difference. She hadn't told Matthew she was in love with him, but deep down, she knew she was.

Telling Julie she was going to the shop to post the letter, the phone rang just as she opened the door to go out. Reluctantly, she went back in. It was Jeremy. She wished she had kept going and put the letter safely in the post box. She didn't want him to charm her into deciding not to break their relationship off.

"Annie, are you sitting down?" he asked in a softer voice than usual.

Annie laughed, "No, Jeremy, I'm not. Why?"

"Please do go and sit down. I've something important to tell you."

Now what she wondered? Is he being transferred away somewhere? She carried the phone into the living room. Julie was in the kitchen and the dogs were in there with her. "All right, Jeremy—here I am, dutifully sitting down. What is it? Is something wrong?"

"No, well, yes," he answered, "I feel like a cad telling you this on the phone, I should have come to see you, but..."

"What is it?" Annie interrupted, growing alarmed.

"It's just that...well, I might as well come out and say it quickly—it's just that I've been feeling guilty about us lately and I....well, the truth is, Annie....I've been seeing someone else."

Annie was glad she was sitting down. Her first reaction was a flood of relief. He had been feeling guilty as well; .he had been seeing someone else as well—how ironic. Her second reaction was fury at herself. Why hadn't she posted that letter sooner? Now she realized she would never post it and he would never read it. And then, finally, rolling her eyes toward heaven, she chuckled to herself. God always was one step ahead of her...wise one that he is.

"Annie? Are you there?" Jeremy asked. "I'm sorry to do this in such an impersonal way, I know you must be devastated, but there it is, Annie. You know I never seem to stick with one woman very long. I..."

Annie interrupted him. "No, no, Jeremy. It's all right. Really it is. Don't worry about me....I'll be fine. I'll be just fine."

Well, Lord, is this a sign or is this a sign. Annie sat for a long while on the sofa, thinking how events had turned out. She went into the kitchen to talk to Julie. Her hands and arms were elbow high in flour and she had the radio playing, not the kind of music Annie enjoyed, but it was music nevertheless. She turned around and smiled at Annie. "I'm trying a new bread recipe. I love kneading dough, do you?"

Annie sat down on one of the kitchen chairs and all three

dogs immediately came to her for attention. "Julie, you know I'm not a cook. I can't imagine making bread."

"Well, you ought to try it sometime. It's really fun....no, that's not the right word, it's sort of like meditating, do ya know what I mean?"

"Yes, because you get lost in it, is that what you mean?"

"Mmm, yes. But you know, before....before you and before Dr. Evans, I would have been frightened to 'get lost' as you put it. I would have been afraid that I'd switch into someone else. But now it's okay."

Switch. That's what you've done Annie. Not in the same way that Julie has, but you've switched the men in your life. She had the natural human reaction of wishing she'd done it first, of Jeremy being told before he told her, but she acknowledged in her heart that this was better. He saved his pride and she also told herself, that whilst she had found it so difficult to write the letter, he must be practiced; he must have done this many times before. She smiled to herself as she took Tibby up on her lap and tried to pet the other two at the same time. What a difference a few months makes. Here she was in her kitchen, with music playing, three dogs, and Julie seeming to be a very good companion. What a difference from the day she walked into this empty house feeling so lonely. Julie was becoming a pleasant companion and now, without Annie asking, took complete care of the house. She hoovered, polished the old furniture trying to make it shine, worked in the garden for hours, and was talkative.

By this time, Julie had put the dough to rise and washed her hands and arms and elbows. "Would you like a cup of tea?" she asked in what Annie thought was a hopeful tone.

"Yes, definitely," Annie said, with enthusiasm. "But only if you'll sit here with me so we can chat." When they were settled with their cups of tea, Annie smiled at Julie. "I'm so proud of you—the way you've changed, Julie. You are such a help to me now, cleaning the house, cooking all these wonderful meals. You know I'm not much of a cook and I'm sure I'm healthier now."

Julie was silent, staring down into her cup.

Oh, dear, I hope I'm not frightening her away Annie thought. She just sat quietly, hoping Julie would respond.

Finally, she looked up at Annie, all the while petting Daisy, who had her head on Julie's lap. "I didn't know people lived like this...." she began, in a very quiet voice. "I saw films where people were quiet and not violent, where they seemed to enjoy each other, where they didn't yell or hit or.........or anything." She took a deep breath and then sighed. "But I thought that was make-believe. I didn't know that it could be real."

Annie's eyes never left Julie's face, but she reigned in her impulse to speak. This was the most intimate thing Julie had ever said to her, the most she had ever revealed.

"And I didn't trust you. I didn't think you were real—I thought you were just pretending, you know? And I was sure you would kick me out in no time, like everyone else." She wasn't looking at Annie, her gaze was out the window, to the back garden now resplendent with spring flowers. "But you didn't. No matter what I did, you just kept trying, you just kept on being nice. And then Dr. Evans was so clever. She knew way before, before I wasn't scared anymore to tell her; she knew what had happened to me. And she told me over and over, every time I went there, she told me that it wasn't my fault. Over and over she said it. And no one else had ever told me that. I always thought everything was my fault, you know?"

Julie finally looked at Annie. Then she shook her head, first you helped me by letting me stay here where I felt safe, then Dr. Evans, and now—I don't know what's going to happen. I mean, you don't want me to stay forever, I know."

Annie put her hand on Julie's arm, a gesture she wouldn't have dared attempt before. "Oh, is that what you're worried about? Julie, you can stay here as long as you like. In fact, if you left, I would miss you terribly." She saw a big tear beginning to roll down Julie's cheek. "Oh, Julie, you have blessed me—don't you see that? My father always told me that the only reason we're here on earth is to help other people. And he was so right. I'm not in any hurry at all for you to leave. Please, please believe me."

Dear Em: I know I haven't been writing much lately. Great friend I am, I only write when I'm unhappy—sort of like poetry. Anyway, you know about all the excitement around here concerning Julie. We had a good talk today and I reassured her that I want her to stay. Would you believe it? After all my complaining? And you were absolutely right about Jeremy. I spent literally hours writing him a Dear John letter and before I could post it, he phoned, telling me he was seeing someone else!!! So that ends that dilemma and Julie seems to be fine with the status quo. And dear Matthew—Em I definitely am in love! I wish you could meet him By the way—how are you? Love, Annie

Matthew, however, hadn't forgotten what Annie did, hadn't forgotten she was a vicar, and as much as he was certain he was in love with her, as much as he was revelling in knowing they were now starting on a relationship in earnest—he was worried. How would he fit into her life? Would he have to move back to the village? Well, that would be all right, he guessed. He could once more commute. But more than that worried him. He knew he wasn't nearly as good a Christian as Annie. He certainly thought he was a Christian, however, in spite of his talk with Joy that evening, when together, they drained the sherry decanter. Yet, he knew Annie had something he didn't have. She seemed to have an unerring faith, with no doubts whatsoever. She seemed to live her faith, not just talk about it or represent it. He didn't want to broach the subject now though; he didn't want to do anything that might drive Annie away. He had been miserable too long and wanted to relish every moment he was with her. It was no time to be honest about his doubts.

It was a long week until Annie was able to come down to London again. It was Saturday and they took in a matinee performance at the Globe Theatre. "I never tire of seeing

Shakespeare and especially in this setting," Annie enthused, as she looked around the playhouse which was built close to the exact spot where the original Globe stood. The audience was in a semicircle on three levels and for £5 those who couldn't afford the better seats stood surrounding the stage. Groundlings, they were called, and just as in the days of Shakespeare, they were encouraged to boo or shout out their opinions.

"I agree," Matthew said, putting his arm around her. "I can't imagine living anywhere but London—there is so much to do and see here." As soon as he said it, he realized it was a dangerous opening. Just then the actors came onto the stage and the play had begun.

Afterwards, they went for Chinese food in Chinatown. Matthew knew just the right place to go as he'd been there often by himself. He tried to keep the conversation light, talking about the play, about what he knew about Shakespeare, about Julie. Anything except about their relationship and more importantly, about his relationship to Annie's boss—God.

After dinner, as they were walking along the Strand, he said, "Why don't you come see my flat? It's nothing to brag about, but at least we'll be alone."

Annie stopped walking and faced him, her hand still in his. "I would like to see where you live, but you know......I can't......" She didn't finish the sentence, but looked concerned.

"Oh, Annie, I'm not going to try to seduce you," he said earnestly. "I just want to be alone with you. We never are, you know." He took her in his arms for a few seconds and spoke into her ear softly. "I do love you, but you're safe. I won't take advantage of you."

"I'm sorry," Annie said, pulling away from him. "Maybe it's me I don't trust, anyway, yes, let's go see your flat. Can you make coffee?" she laughed, lightening the mood.

As she rode home on the train, late, Annie went over the entire evening in her thoughts. She was certain, absolutely certain that Matthew was the one for her, absolutely certain in every way, except one. Never once during the entire evening, was God mentioned. She realized it was just as much due to her reticence as Matthew's. She realized she was loath to ruin their evening—would it have ruined it? She also realized for the first time, that not only was she not talking to Matthew about God, but she wasn't talking to God about Matthew.

Chapter Eighteen

The next morning, Julie had a hot breakfast ready when Annie came downstairs before church. "You are spoiling me, Julie, but I sure do enjoy it," she said in between hurried mouthfuls.

"Annie," Julie began, in a soft voice, "could....would it be all right if I came to church this morning?"

Annie swallowed quickly, looking up at Julie, who was standing by the sink. "Oh, Julie, yes. In fact, that would make me very happy." When Julie didn't say more, she went on, "why don't you come on over with me and help me set things up? I would like that very much."

Julie looked down and gestured toward her jeans. "Oh, I can't go like this."

"Well, yes you could. Lots of the young people wear jeans, but if you'd feel more comfortable, go change and then come on over."

As she walked the short distance to the church, Annie hummed a little tune. And looked up to the sky. *"Thank you, Lord."* She smiled up at him.

However, when the service began, Julie wasn't there. Annie just hoped she hadn't switched and disappeared again.
She had become more and more confident with her sermons and usually had it finished by Tuesday of the previous week. So the service went well and just before the last hymn, she spotted Julie slipping in quietly and sitting alone on the last pew. She left before any of the congregation turned around to leave.

Afterward, when Annie returned home, she apologized. "I'm sorry, Annie. I really wanted to go and I changed my clothes and did my hair and all, but I just kept thinking I didn't look good enough....so I was late. Really late." She was sitting on one of the sofas and didn't look directly at Annie.

Annie went over to sit beside her. "you look just fine. And even if you didn't, people wouldn't care. Don't you know that the village has accepted you? Ever since those men came to help you out, they feel protective toward you."

"Do all those men go to church?" she asked, looking down at the floor.

"No, not all of them. Not everyone in the village goes to church. I wish they did, but there probably isn't a village in the world where that's true."

"Are people who don't go to church bad?" she asked.

Annie sighed, "No, Julie, of course not. Whether you go to church or not doesn't make you good or bad. It's what's inside of you." She put her arm around Julie, who flinched just slightly, but didn't move away.

"Well, then," she asked in a tone barely above a whisper, "why do people go to church?"

Good question, Annie thought. Sometimes she had wondered the same thing, especially when she first arrived. And she knew the question couldn't be answered in a blanket fashion; she knew there were many reasons for church attendance and not all of them pure. She also knew Julie wasn't sophisticated enough yet to understand all the nuances. But she knew this was a rare moment, a moment when Julie was opening up a tiny bit of herself which would be enough to let God in. So she prayed silently and quickly for the Holy Spirit to help her. "Julie, when you come into a relationship with God, a real relationship, one in which you know God loves you and you in return love Him, then there is a desire to go to church to worship him. It's like being hungry—you go there to satisfy that hunger."

Julie was silent, but she looked up, she wasn't staring into her lap anymore. "Well, what about Horace? He goes to church and I don't think he's a good person."

I don't think so either Out loud, Annie simply said, "There are people who have always gone to church, out of habit, out of a way to socialize with others, and who believe they are Christians. And there are some who are Christians, but have never grown in their faith." She paused for a moment, not knowing how deep she should go.

Julie spoke before she had decided, "So will Horace be in heaven? With you?"

Annie laughed. "I don't know. I'm not the one who has to decide that, thank goodness. God only knows who will go to heaven and who won't. My job, which I often fail miserably at, is to try to get people like Horace to change, to get them to realize he needs to change." She took in a deep breath. "If you want to come to church, I'd be thrilled. But I want you to know that your home is here, whether you go to church or not. And I also want you to know that I will always be your friend, whether you go to church or not. Okay?"

Julie looked directly at her and smiled a very small smile, lips compressed. She shook her head in the affirmative a few times and Annie thought she saw a glisten of tears in her eyes.

Annie stood up. "We're invited to Joy's for Sunday lunch. You're coming, aren't you?"

"Yes," she responded, standing up as well. "I like Joy. She's a good person."

Annie smiled at her. "Yes, she is. And she goes to church."

The lunch reminded Annie of her first Sunday in the village. Joy had invited the widows again and since they all had a wicked sense of humor, the meal was anything but dull. Julie was very quiet and kept her head down most of the time, but Annie caught the flicker of a smile now and then. Joy didn't try to bring Julie into the conversation, she appeared to sense she just needed to be an observer and she had thoroughly warned the ladies beforehand that they were not to ask Julie any questions about herself.

As they walked back to the vicarage, Julie said, "I didn't know church people had such a good time together."

Annie laughed. "Well, I'm afraid not all of them do, but these women are a special bunch. I think they're delightful."

The next day Annie determined she needed to begin to

talk to God about Matthew. She walked over to the church, where she would have solitude. She knelt at the altar and looked up to the face of Jesus, smiling down at her. *Oh, Lord, remember the first time I knelt here? So alone, so lonely, so apprehensive? Of course you do—you remember everything. And now so many of my problems have been sorted—obviously by you. I'm very grateful. You knew all along it would work out, didn't you? But now, I don't know about Matthew and his relationship to you. I know you know, but I don't. Please give me guidance. He is a good man and he does love me and I know we will be happy together.*

There was no answer from the Lord right away. So Annie postponed the wedding by a few months, much to Matthew's regret. However, the more time they spent together, the more he was willing to talk about faith and ask questions.

One night as they were having dinner in his flat in London, he was the one who brought up the subject. "Annie, I know why you have postponed our wedding and I want you to know that I'm not saying this just to get you to move it up sooner."

The look on his face was so grave that Annie reflected his mood and took his hand in both of hers, holding them tight.

"I know you have a strong faith, else you wouldn't have wanted to be a minister. And I know that you have something I don't have—never have had. You seem to know God is real and you talk to him."

Annie smiled tenderly at him. "Yes, that's right and what's more, he talks to me!"

"Well, how do you get that? How did you get that? I know there are people in the church who aren't like you, but some of them are. Is it because this God that you know loves them and loves you more than the others?"

Annie sat back on the sofa, still holding Matthew's hand and sending up a prayer of thanksgiving. "Oh, Matthew, I thought you would never ask! Of course, God doesn't love those who know him more than others. It's just that he has a relationship with us. We know him and he knows us. We pay attention to him; we talk to him, and as you just said, he talks to us."

Matthew withdrew his hand from hers and stood up, looking down at her. "So how do I get this? What do I have to do?"

"Would you be asking these questions if you weren't anxious to marry me?" Annie asked in a soft voice, looking up at him.

"I don't know, Annie. I only know that since I've known you so intimately, I'm drawn to the kind of faith you have." He paused and once more sat down next to her, brushing the top of her head with his hand. "Help me, Annie. Help me to come to know your God."